Forcing a measure of boldness into her limbs, and hopefully into her voice, Sarah looked up at him.

He smiled down at her with an expression that held no trace of humor. Instead, she saw a promise that chilled her blood and drew a gasp from her.

"Let me go, William."

"No. I am not one of your court swains you can order about on a whim. You married a battle-hardened warrior, Sarah. Perhaps it is time you realize what that means."

***

Bedded by the Warrior
Harlequin® Historical #950—June 2009

Author Note

William and Sarah. I've lost count of the number of letters asking about Sarah's story. I'm pleased to tell you that here she is, in all her glory.

Sarah's had a rough life; so has William. It's about time they found what they've been looking for, and what they both need: romance, love and their own happily-ever-after.

Come, join me in the 12th century for a little while. Discover if William and Sarah's rock-strewn road leads them to what they so desire.

BEDDED BY THE WARRIOR

DENISE LYNN

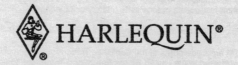

HARLEQUIN®

TORONTO • NEW YORK • LONDON
AMSTERDAM • PARIS • SYDNEY • HAMBURG
STOCKHOLM • ATHENS • TOKYO • MILAN • MADRID
PRAGUE • WARSAW • BUDAPEST • AUCKLAND

Recycling programs
for this product may
not exist in your area.

ISBN-13: 978-0-373-29550-0

BEDDED BY THE WARRIOR

Copyright © 2009 by Denise L. Koch

This edition published by arrangement with Harlequin Books S.A.

® and TM are trademarks of the publisher. Trademarks indicated with ® are registered in the United States Patent and Trademark Office, the Canadian Trade Marks Office and in other countries.

www.eHarlequin.com

Printed in U.S.A.

*To the Readers.
Wishing you all a little romance to lighten your day.*

And to Tom who unknowingly lightens my days.

Chapter One

Queen Eleanor's Court at Poitiers—May 1171

'You should be grateful for your freedom.' The hard edge of warning beneath Queen Eleanor's words was unmistakable.

Lady Sarah of Remy felt the Queen's glare against her back as she walked toward the chamber door. Icy fingers of dread clutched her spine at Eleanor's implied threat.

Unmindful of the voice inside her head urging her to leave the chamber without comment, Sarah turned to face the Queen. Eleanor's relentless stare prompted Sarah to temper her response. 'Marriage to a brutal stranger is not worth more than my freedom.'

'I know you well, Sarah. A temporary marriage to Bronwyn will prove less of a trial than rotting in a cell.'

Sarah trembled at the mere mention of his name. William of Bronwyn was too large and frightening, his shoulders too broad, his manners too coarse. She closed her eyes against the memory of being found naked in bed with him.

The task assigned to her had seemed so simple. Yet, like a bad dream spinning out of control, it had all gone so horribly wrong.

Bronwyn and his friend Earl Hugh of Wynnedom were somehow involved with King Henry. Ever since Archbishop Becket's death last year, the Queen had become suspicious of anything her husband the King did. Especially when she hadn't been consulted. Even more so when his secret dealings took place on her lands.

King Henry had been seen with Bronwyn and Wynnedom near the castle. The three men had met with a foreigner unknown to Queen Eleanor and she wanted to know why.

Unfortunately, her questioning of the Earl had produced no suitable answer. In fact, the man's arrogance had angered her more than his unwillingness to provide the information she wanted. Determined to serve him a taste of his own insolence, the Queen had devised a plan that would place him firmly under her control.

He would be caught compromising one of her favoured ladies—Sarah. Eleanor knew that the Earl's honour would convince him to wed Sarah, making him a member of her court. She'd been certain that he would then be more willing to share his secrets with her. The Earl of Wynnedom would prove an excellent informant once he realised the benefits of bending to the Queen's will.

Something Sarah knew well. As the Queen's spy, she had successfully completed every assigned task—thus far. This task should have been no different.

'You failed me, Sarah, and left me no choice.'

Sometimes she wondered if Eleanor could read her

mind. 'I didn't know the Earl was married to Adrienna until it was too late.'

'Then you should have discovered it sooner.'

And how was she to have done that? While Adrienna was also one of Eleanor's ladies-in-waiting, it wasn't as if they'd been fast friends.

'Instead, you let yourself be found in bed with his friend.' The Queen rose and walked toward her. 'Sarah, we have been through this already. Even had Bronwyn forced you to do so, he offered marriage.'

'Offered?' He hadn't *offered* marriage. After the Queen had ordered the four of them—her, Bronwyn, Wynnedom and Adrienna—to leave her court, he'd nearly commanded that they wed.

Waving off her question as if it were nothing more than a flea, Eleanor countered, 'While the delivery might not have been to your liking, the end result will be the same. You will wed Bronwyn.'

Sarah had been with the court long enough to know that once Eleanor's anger at being foiled lessened, the Queen could be convinced to see reason. That was why she'd slipped away from Bronwyn in the first place—to hopefully change the Queen's mind. However, were she to leave the court, how would she ever gain another audience in which to plead her case?

'My Queen—'

'No!' Eleanor's shout dissolved Sarah's complaint before it left her mouth. 'Wed him. Get me the information I seek and then you will have your freedom.'

The Queen paused in front of her and asked, 'Do you understand me?'

Unable to speak past the lump thickening in her throat, Sarah nodded.

'Now go. See that you, your new husband and his friends are gone from my court before morning.'

'What more could one expect from Eleanor's whore? She is getting no less than what she deserves.'

Sarah held her tongue as she walked quickly past the darkened alcove on her way to the chapel. She heard the snide remarks of the other ladies, just as they'd intended. But she knew any response would be foolish—it would only add strength to the vipers' tongues.

It wasn't as if she'd not heard the same spittle repeated numerous times during her prolonged stay with the Queen's court. So, why now did it sting as much as her father's hand slapping her face? Sarah held her head high. She'd give no one the satisfaction of witnessing her pain.

Once beyond the alcoves and away from the biting words, Sarah dragged her feet, seeking to delay her arrival at the Queen's private chapel. She wondered if this was how a condemned man felt as he walked to his death.

Did a sick dread churn in his stomach as he approached the executioner? Did the blood flowing through his veins slow as if thickening from the icy touch of fear?

Regardless of her failure, it wasn't supposed to happen like this. She'd been promised more—so much more. For countless months, Sarah had held fast to the sworn promise of a grand marriage.

And now her treasured dreams had turned into a nightmare of doom. Sarah choked back a threatening cry.

It wasn't that she didn't want to wed—she did. As a young girl, she had come to Queen Eleanor's court, hoping for many things. Like the other girls and young women sent to court, she had grown up hoping to eventually find a husband.

Not *just* a husband, but a knighted lord. An honourable man who would care for her, protect her, give her children, a place to call home and a life worth living.

But most of all, she wanted to hold tight to the things she'd gained at court—respite from her father's sharp tongue and easy rage. And freedom from the harshness of life in a poor keep occupied only by men-at-arms. She couldn't return to living a life of fear.

Sarah fisted her hands at her sides. She wanted to rail at the unfairness. She'd willingly ruined her reputation by posing as the Queen's whore—for what? A worthless vow?

Her arrangement with the Queen had seemed simple—if Sarah wished to leave the court under better circumstances than which she'd arrived, she only had to use her appearance of fair-haired innocence, and her wiles, to convince specific lords and ladies to speak freely. Any information gleaned was then relayed to the Queen, who would use the knowledge to her benefit.

In return, Sarah had been promised a wealthy, titled lord as husband. One who could provide the security and safety she'd never had.

Instead, Queen Eleanor was forcing her to wed Bronwyn.

The tears choking her throat were as much from fear of William of Bronwyn as they were at the thought of leaving the court.

Even though she had little reason to believe the Queen's latest promise, Sarah clung desperately to the slender thread of hope that this time Eleanor would keep her word.

Since the plan had gone so awry, Sarah needed only to marry this man, find out all she could about him and the Earl, and then discover their dealings with King Henry. Once Eleanor had the information, the Queen swore she would ensure Sarah quickly became an eligible widow, with enough gold to entice any man of her choosing.

Sarah's steps faltered as Bronwyn stepped away from the shadows darkening the corridor and into the light gleaming out from the chapel's entrance. It was one thing to dupe a man she did not know and would not see on the morrow. But she would see this man every day—and every night.

She held his stare, in a show of bravado, as she resumed her walk down the long corridor. But the thought of being his wife, even for a brief period of time, made her insides tremble.

William of Bronwyn was not just large—the top of her head barely reached his shoulders—he was built of solid rock beneath his flesh. He could easily maim, or kill her, with one blow.

Sarah wanted to faint into oblivion. But fate would not be that kind.

Every fear she'd ever experienced, every memory of harsh cruelness she had ever faced, raced back to grip her chest in a crushing hold. She struggled to breathe, then wondered why she bothered. Would it not be easier if her breath simply ceased for ever?

'Lady Sarah.'

She stopped just out of his reach, ignoring his extended hand. 'My lord.' She couldn't help the coolness of her tone. At the moment, coolness was the best she could muster.

'I was not certain you would come.'

'What choice had I?' At his frown, she wondered

if perhaps he regretted his demand for this marriage. Hope flared anew. She stepped closer. 'There is no need for us to wed.' If the Queen would not see reason, perhaps William of Bronwyn could be convinced to do so.

To her dismay, he disagreed. 'I will not take you from here without the benefit of marriage.'

'Why not?' She sought desperately to correct his flawed reasoning. 'There is no need to concern yourself with my reputation. You can do nothing to ruin it further. That was accomplished long before you arrived at this court.'

William shook his head before directing her towards the chapel's door. 'Belittling yourself will not change my mind.'

He made light of her reputation? Did he believe she degraded herself to him out of hand? The questions racing through her mind gave her pause. No man of self-worth would willingly take a harlot to wife.

She knew nothing of this Bronwyn except for the fact he was at court. And while he possessed no title, he was on friendly terms with the Earl of Wynnedom. From what the Queen had claimed, both men were involved in something with King Henry.

Without making it obvious, Sarah studied him. The man was clean. Even though his hair was overlong, light from the wall sconces reflected off the recently washed strands.

The two of them were close enough for her to smell sandalwood—a beguiling scent that called to her senses. Ignoring the effect that scent had on her, she took in his court clothing and well-heeled boots.

The leather wrapping on the scabbard hanging from

his side was new. And the hilt of the sword was far too ornate to belong to a lowly man-at-arms.

Oh, yes, this man was drenched in self-worth from the top of his head to the bottom of his feet.

Sarah drew her gaze to his face. From the intensity of his piecing stare, she knew he'd been studying her as well. She needed to be careful and make certain he would discover nothing she didn't wish him to see.

This could be her last chance to convince him to change his mind. She lowered her head and looked up at him from beneath her eyelashes. 'My lord, I seek not to belittle myself.' She softened her voice to a whisper, beckoning him to lean closer. 'I wish only to warn you of the truth.'

Sarah peered up, making certain she'd captured his attention, then continued, 'You are the Earl's man. As such, marrying the Queen's whore can do little to help your status.'

'Status? I care nothing for what others may think.'

In all her years at court she'd yet to meet one person, man or woman, who cared naught about the opinions of others. She tried again. 'You may not care at this moment. But some day you will.'

Sarah placed a hand on her chest and glanced into the chapel before appealing to his common sense. 'Would you have your children know their mother was rumoured to be nothing more than a harlot?'

He stood upright and answered her question by rolling his eyes briefly to the ceiling, before saying, 'If all rumours were true, I would be a monster from Hades.'

The sudden look of terror distorting her features at his comment surprised him. Surely she didn't believe such nonsense? 'Lady Sarah, fear not, for I *am* human born.'

She remained silent and he wondered for a moment if perhaps he had made a mistake in demanding this marriage. He cared little if his wife-to-be held any regard for him—it would be easier if she didn't.

While she might consider this entire episode a failure, for him it had provided an opportunity he couldn't let pass. He wanted someone to help run his household, and bear his children.

His blood warmed at the thought of this woman in his bed. He would gain more than a wife for his keep. He would also have a woman who was not only pleasing to his eyes, but one rumoured to be well versed in bed.

The one thing he didn't want was a wife who feared him. He could live with her disdain, and cared not if they never found any tender feelings for each other. But he'd had enough of fear.

When he'd left Sidatha's Palace with Hugh and the others, he'd vowed to put that life behind him. No more would he suffer the taste of the lash. No more would he kill to put food in his belly. And no more would he intentionally seek to make another fear him. Especially not his wife.

One of the women already inside the chapel to witness this union raised her voice. *'It is only fitting that the whore be given to such a lowly brute.'*

Another woman snickered, then added, *'His rough treatment of her will not be harsh enough in my opinion.'*

The urge to give these women the tongue lashing they deserved was wiped away by the look of resignation settling on Sarah's face. She'd heard the spiteful words and had chosen to ignore them. How many times had she been forced into this same situation?

From the lack of surprise, or outrage, on her part,

William could only assume the answer to his unasked question would be—many times.

But something…the paleness of her face, the odd brightness shimmering in her eyes…told him she was not immune to the barbs directed her way. The women's comments bothered Sarah a great deal.

His resolve to see this marriage through strengthened. No, he hadn't made a mistake. Even if she feared him now, Lady Sarah was alone in this court. She was without a champion, without a friend.

He'd been a captive all of his adult life. He knew what it was like to be alone in the world. Taken captive before he'd had a chance to be anything other than an overgrown youth, he'd soon learned to keep to himself. He'd quickly been taught to trust no one.

William turned to stand at her side and offered his arm. 'Come, Lady Sarah. We were ordered to be gone from court by sunrise. But before we join Lady Adrienna and Hugh, we have a marriage to make.'

She stared at his arm without moving. 'I wish not to wed you.'

'I know.'

'Sir William, we are not suited. Would you not rather have someone of your choosing?'

Not suited? They were well suited from his perspective. She'd been given the choice of a cell, or leaving the court. Lady Sarah needed someone to protect her. A woman alone would not fare well outside these walls. Regardless of its appearance, this court was little more than a jewel-encrusted prison, where one did what they were told to do.

'We are suited for each other more than you realise, Lady Sarah. And if you remember correctly, I did choose you.'

'That was nothing more than a whim of the moment. Futures are not built on whims.'

'Many decisions are based on the whim of a moment.' How many times had he escaped death by making a snap judgement based solely on the man he fought at that moment? But he wasn't going to explain that to a woman who already showed signs of fearing him. 'Our marriage will not have been arranged by strangers. Does that not count for something?'

'No.' Her answer was a mere whisper.

William harshly reminded her of the choices Queen Eleanor offered, 'It is this, or a cell.' He could not imagine Lady Sarah in a dark, damp, airless cell. Rats, the cries of the other prisoners, hunger and bone-chilling cold would quickly take their toll on a court lady.

Her luxurious, pale hair would soon hang in grimed snarls. The fine gown would rot on her body from the constant dampness. As she lost weight from the lack of proper food, the garment would hang in tatters. Her sparkling eyes would lose their shimmer, her lips would soon forget how to smile.

'You would not fare well.'

Sarah stared up him. The clear blueness of her eyes, large against her pale flesh, took his breath away.

'You think I would fare better with you?'

The vision of his lovely and desirable wife-to-be wasting away lent a harshness to his voice as he responded, 'At least you will live.'

She hesitated a few seconds more, making him uncertain if she would bolt from his side again or not. But finally, she sighed in what sounded like defeat, and then tentatively placed her trembling hand on his forearm.

William led her down the aisle, stopping before the

waiting clergy. Why the Queen had insisted their vows be witnessed by the Church baffled him.

Legally, they needed to do nothing more than exchange their vows and live as husband and wife. At the most, had the ceremony been left to him, he would have been more than satisfied with the Church's blessing afterwards.

But William knew he was in no position to argue with Queen Eleanor.

Sarah's heart pounded so loudly in her ears, she could barely hear the clergy's words. Instead, two things tossed about in her mind—the woman's comment about Bronwyn's rough treatment not being harsh enough, and the way he'd nearly snarled when he'd told her that at least she would live.

Would she? An unstoppable shiver snaked down her spine. Her father had often used his hands—and fists—to demand obedience from all in his care, including at times her mother. Sarah had lost count of the times she'd witnessed some men at court using physical force to control their wives and children.

To most, the aggressive acts were normal...nearly expected. But since coming to the Queen's court she'd been spared that treatment, so it no longer appeared normal to her. In those years, no one had once raised a hand in anger towards her.

She didn't know the man standing next to her. She'd met him less than a few hours past. And now, in a matter of mere moments, he would be her husband. He would own her as surely as he owned the clothing upon his back.

Her throat tightened, as another tremor of fear shook her. Bronwyn squeezed her hand. Had he sensed, or felt, her traitorous shivers? Sarah forced the building terror aside.

The ceremony passed in a blur. She paused when the clergy asked if she willingly took this man as husband. Only the memory of the Queen's thinly veiled threat of a cell, or worse, prompted her to answer, 'Aye.'

Finally, it was over and she stared up at the man beside her. The man who had just become her husband. Light from the torches ensconced into the wall flickered across his face. Flecks of gold glittered menacingly against his brown eyes.

His hand engulfed hers and she willed herself to remain still. It was one thing for him to know she hadn't wed him willingly. But letting him sense her fear would give him too much power. She knew well the danger that lay in appearing weak.

The women gathered in the Queen's private chapel to witness the Church's blessing twittered. Their hushed voices, and half-giggles, seemed to echo in the well of silence that had fallen over the holy room at the conclusion of the blessing.

Sarah flinched under the spitefulness of their tongues. This was one thing she would not miss. These women knew her not, yet they'd formed an opinion of her based on things they had heard, and thought they had seen. Apart from Adrienna, not one had taken the time to seek out the truth.

Most of them had come to Eleanor's court for the same reason as she—to find a husband. The only difference was the land and gold they would bring into a marriage.

The father cleared his throat, discreetly reminding them that the blessing was over. They had but to kiss, and then depart from the chapel.

'I am sorry,' William apologised, leaving Sarah to wonder if it'd been directed towards her, or the churchman.

All she knew for certain was that he was suddenly leaning closer, looming over her before he brushed his lips against hers.

The chapel again buzzed with whispers and smothered laughter. Sarah knew the women made fun of her, and the man who now owned her. But she refused to cower under their snickers. She wanted to prove their assumptions wrong.

In deference to the Church, she tempered her response, but she still placed her hand against William's chest, rose up on her toes and returned his kiss.

His lips were warm, and surprisingly gentle. Unlike other kisses she'd encountered, he did not seek to devour her mouth. William barely moved his mouth against hers, and a flash of liquid heat trailed down her spine.

What had been offered as nothing more than a chaste touch of their lips to seal their vows turned to an unspoken promise of shared desire to come.

The snide whispers faded away as she realised that the notion of shared desire did not overly frighten her. Nor did it repulse her.

Confused, Sarah pulled away slowly. To hide her uncertainty, she graced him with a dazzling smile before turning towards the women. One by one they looked away, giving her an odd sense of satisfaction. For the first time, she'd not been the one to avert her face in shame.

Chapter Two

'Sarah.' William's deep voice floated across her ear. 'It is time to leave.'

As she turned with him toward the double doors, he grasped her hand, asking, 'Is there any you wish to bid farewell?'

A curt response at the tip of her tongue, she stared up at him. But the twitch at the corner of his lips, and an amused glint in his eyes, stopped her from speaking. He was teasing her. Had he heard the women's whispers and laughter? Had he somehow understood how much the venom behind their spiteful mocking hurt her?

She leaned forwards, intentionally craning her neck to look around him at the women, and answered, 'No. I think not.'

William paused to slip his arm across her tense shoulders and pull her closer before turning his focus towards the surprised women. 'I fault you not for having sense enough to recognise those unworthy of your time or attention.'

He'd raised his voice enough to be heard, and darkened

his tone enough to be understood. Sarah couldn't be certain of what astonished, or befuddled, her more—his open defence of her, or the looks of shock and shame written on the women's faces.

After once again starting towards the doors, William looked down at her, and she had the sudden sensation of drowning in his golden-flecked soft brown eyes. Her breath caught in her throat, making it difficult to swallow.

Worse was the way her heart raced, and her chest swelled with an emotion she feared to name.

She didn't know this man, didn't trust him. She didn't want to be his wife. She couldn't possibly feel anything for him. Nothing at all.

When they left the chapel, Sarah eased out from beneath his arm. She needed to keep her distance from him. And needed to remind herself that he was nothing more than a way to complete this last task for the Queen.

William couldn't help but notice his wife's sudden withdrawal once they were away from the women's sight. He'd wondered why she had responded so ardently to his kiss, and now he knew it had been for the women's benefit—not his.

Why did that knowledge cause a twinge of regret? It wasn't as if the act of exchanging vows had changed anything between them. Except that one taste of her lips served to make him want more.

'Sarah, wait.' He laced his fingers through hers. William knew better than to let her get away from him, since he had the feeling she would once again bolt at the first opportunity.

After Queen Eleanor agreed to his demand, Sarah had run away from him. He couldn't be certain, but he suspected she'd run after Eleanor to convince the

Queen to change her mind. Obviously her attempt had been unsuccessful.

Sarah tried to free her hand, but before she could say anything, a woman William recognised as another of the Queen's ladies approached.

'Lady Sarah, this is from the Queen.' The woman gave Sarah a small pouch.

His wife opened the jewel-adorned bag to glance inside. Her eyes widened before she reached into the pouch to retrieve what appeared to be enough gold to see them well on their way.

When Sarah tried to hand the pouch back, the woman shook her head and refused to take bag. 'No, it is yours. Queen Eleanor wishes you a safe journey.' She glanced shyly from William to Sarah. 'As do I and I wish you well.'

His wife's expressive eyes widened for less than a heartbeat, but she smiled and said, 'Thank you.' Sarah paused, as if uncertain, and then added, 'I wish you well also, Lady Elise. May your stay here be enjoyable and brief.'

Elise laughed. As she turned to leave, she advised, 'Daylight will arrive within the hour. You need to be on your way quickly.'

William nodded his acknowledgement of the warning and started for the chamber he shared with the Earl. But Sarah tugged his arm in the other direction. 'This way is quicker.'

She knew the castle far better, and since her freedom was also at stake, he would trust her judgement in this. 'Lead on.'

Sarah took them quickly down a semi-lit corridor, which ended at a landing that ran the length of the Great Hall.

William glanced over the railing into the nearly deserted hall below. His breath caught in his throat.

Richard of Langsford and Stefan of Arnyll were deep in conversation as they approached the stairs leading up to the landing.

Without thought, William grabbed Sarah. He ignored her gasp and dragged her into a small, unlit alcove.

The sight of Langsford didn't bother him. That man was nothing more than a bully and a drunken fool—a useless pawn of the Queen's in her ceaseless attempts to thwart the Earl.

But Arnyll was another matter. What was that soulless son of the devil doing here?

Like William, Arnyll had also been captured and sold into slavery. When Hugh had won his freedom and the lives of three others, he had requested that Arnyll be included only because the man was a fellow countryman.

William had felt sorry for the smaller man's plight, when Arnyll had first been tossed into Sidatha's dungeon. William had taught Arnyll how to use speed and agility to conquer his opponents. The two of them had often been paired together, literally fighting back to back, as one.

However, Arnyll had soon shown his true character. The man had proven to be as bad as, if not worse than, the slave master Aryseeth.

The memory of a scrawny dog that William and some of the others had saved from the cook's pot flooded his mind. He fought not to tremble like a spineless fool at the memory. They'd hidden the starving mongrel for months—until Arnyll, in a fit of spite over an extra portion of bitter wine given to another, had told Aryseeth of the animal. The very next morning they had all learned how futile their attempts to preserve the dog's life had been.

The men's footsteps drew nearer. They were so deep in conversation neither man had noticed William and Sarah on the landing.

William dropped on to a stone bench in the dark corner of the alcove, and pulled Sarah down on his lap. Most times it was near impossible to hide his size. With any luck the appearance of lovers in a private tryst might work. It might also provide the perfect opportunity to eavesdrop on the men's conversation.

When she pushed against his chest in a futile attempt to escape, he wrapped one arm around her to hold her close. Certain she'd not remain silent for much longer, William wove his fingers through her hair and lowered his mouth to hers.

She gasped against his lips, and he whispered, 'Be still. I will not harm you, but Arnyll would.'

Sarah frowned. *Arnyll?* It only took her a few moments to realise that he spoke of Stefan. She'd seen the cur Richard with Stefan in the hall, and had witnessed William's reaction in confusion.

If these men caused a brute like him to act in such haste, perhaps she'd be wise to follow his lead.

Keeping her voice soft and low, she warned him, 'This is only for appearances, it is not real.' She felt him smile against her lips as she raised her arms and clasped her hands behind his head.

She narrowed her eyes, wishing she could see his face in the dark. For a reason she could not name, Sarah had the feeling that his smile would be smug, and that his eyes would sparkle with mischief.

Unfortunately it was becoming apparent that she'd

not married a man lacking in wits. That could prove a detriment to her task—and perhaps a danger to her.

Above all else, she needed to make certain William didn't learn she was still under the Queen's orders. He would never understand. No man would take kindly to know that, regardless of their vows, *their* wife still answered to another.

Richard and Stefan's conversation grew louder as they approached the alcove. Sarah could almost make out some of their words, and what little she heard set her mind spinning. There was disjointed talk of a task being successful.

Only someone involved with court intrigue would be able to make sense of the snatches of overheard conversation. They spoke of the Queen and her, but it was doubtful if William would be able to piece the snatches together.

She hoped his hearing was not as attuned to the hushed voices used at court as hers. Because the task the two men discussed was the one she'd recently failed completing.

They'd done their part—the two of them had kidnapped Adrienna, preventing her from seeking out Wynnedom. Even though none had known about their marriage at the time, all had been aware that the pair were always together. So, the kidnapping had been deemed necessary to enable Sarah to be found in the Earl's bed.

But some niggling thought had urged Sarah to see to Adrienna's release. That was when she'd learned about their marriage.

Sarah wasn't certain if either Richard or Stefan knew she'd been the one to release Adrienna. Nor was she certain they knew of her marriage to Bronwyn. She wasn't eager to discover what they did or didn't know.

She moaned softly, so only her husband could hear, and pressed harder against his chest. It was all she could do not to sigh with relief when William relaxed his arm and stroked gentle circles on her back.

Perhaps Queen Eleanor had been right. After all, William *was* just a man. And maybe like the other men at court he could be easily swayed.

She'd learned early on that a soft smile, a teasing look, or a brief touch against his chest, or arm, went a long way towards convincing a man to see things her way. Seldom had she been forced to resort to making promises that would never be kept.

When Richard and Stefan walked in front of the alcove, her heart beat so hard she thought it would burst. Silently she prayed they would say nothing to give her away. She feared William finding out that she still spied for the Queen more than she feared discovery by these men.

William tightened his fingers against the back of her head and covered her mouth with his lips. Sarah's pulse raced even faster. There was nothing gentle about the way he held her close, or teased her lips until they parted as if under their own will.

He kissed her thoroughly, wiping away any thought of the men, or the Queen, from her mind. She could think of nothing except the heat rushing through her veins, melting her resolve to keep herself distant from this man she'd wed.

The only thing that filled her mind, the only thing she could concentrate on, was the sure and certain magic of his mouth moving against hers. And on the heady warmth he traced along her lips.

When he ceased his kisses, Sarah quickly realised that he no longer held her close. Instead, she clung to him, her breasts pressed against his chest, her hands gripping his shoulders.

She quickly pulled away. Folding her hands in her lap, she drew in a deep breath, seeking a measure of calm against the storm still raging in her chest. Never had a man's kiss affected her so.

She corrected her earlier assumption about how easily he could be swayed. The Queen had been wrong—William of Bronwyn was *not* just another man.

'I think they are gone.' His breath raced hot against her ear. He leaned closer, to ask in a heated whisper, 'Are you sure nothing about that kiss was real?'

Sarah nearly lunged from his lap, suddenly wondering if she'd wed a rogue.

He rose from the bench and brushed by her, taking her hand in his as he passed. 'Come, we need to join Hugh and Lady Adrienna, then leave this court.'

Still uncertain how he had so easily stolen her wits, Sarah wordlessly led him to the chamber.

Chapter Three

Daylight barely filtered through the denseness of the trees when William's senses alerted him to danger. A quick, but thorough, study of the woods and bramble surrounding them gave no clue to the unease pricking at him. He'd long ago learned to depend on his gut reactions, and while he saw nothing, he was certain they were being followed.

After visually checking on Hugh and Adrienna riding a short distance ahead of them, he glanced across the path at his wife. Her features were as strained as they'd been when leaving Eleanor's castle. William doubted if her unease was caused by anything more than outrage at being forced to marry him, and her unwitting response to his kisses.

A response that promised him more than words ever could.

He'd heard the rumours about Sarah being the Queen's whore. How could he not? They were bandied about the court so often that it would have been impossible to miss them.

He hadn't demanded this marriage out of any feelings he had for the woman. He'd done so to offer her protection and to gain a wife for his keep.

It seemed a good choice for all concerned. She would be spared the horrors of a cell, or the danger of life alone outside the court. And he would have the benefit of a wife without any emotional attachment. In addition he'd gain an experienced woman in his bed, not a simpering, frightened virgin.

Perhaps the appearance of Langsford and Arnyll had been a blessing. It had given him the opportunity to witness Sarah at work firsthand, instead of watching from afar.

He'd heard the men's voices as they had neared the alcove. Although he had been unable to hear their words, Sarah's reaction made him aware that she *had* heard them. At first, her response to his closeness had been tentative.

But the nearer the men had come to the alcove, the louder their voices had become, the more passionate she had acted. For some reason, Sarah had felt it necessary to make certain he hadn't heard what the men had been saying.

He wasn't some court dandy that she could ply with her wiles in an attempt to distract him. While knowing that Sarah had secrets so dire she needed to keep them from him did not please him in the least, it had been interesting—near amusing—to discover that turning the tables served to fluster her.

'What is wrong?'

Sarah's question startled him out of his musings. 'Nothing.'

'Ah, so not only are you thick-headed, you lie, too.'

Certain he couldn't have heard her correctly, he looked at her, asking, 'What are you talking about?'

'I did not live this long without learning to read a person's expressions.' She studied him intently, as if looking for something, and then explained, 'Your frown, the stiffening of your body, and your sudden interest in our surroundings—all tell me that something is wrong.'

'It's nothing that concerns you.'

Sarah reached up and flicked a braid over her shoulder. 'No, of course not.' She paused to smile and flutter her eyelashes before adding, 'I am but a simple woman with not a care in the world, nor a useful thought in my head.'

They weren't in the castle; they were no longer at court. There was no need for her to put on such airs, or take such a snappish tone with him.

William was certain there were two ways to get her to drop her play acting—seduction or an insult. At the moment, seduction would be rather difficult. He stared hard at her and said, '*Simple* woman? No. I am guessing you have all the makings of a shrew.'

Instead of flinching away in shame, or becoming angry, as he had hoped, Sarah's laughter rang loud, chasing the birds from their perches overhead. 'Perhaps you might have discovered that before insisting I become your wife.'

Not quite the response he'd expected, but she was right. 'I imagine there are a great many things I might have discovered about you beforehand…had I the time.'

'Do not place that blame on me. It wasn't my idea to wed.'

'No, but you didn't argue too much about being discovered in bed with me.'

A faint tinge of red covered her cheeks, but Sarah didn't turn away. 'You know that I had a task to perform for the Queen. What other choice did I have?'

She might not have had a choice then, but she had choices now. 'I find it all rather odd.'

She curled her fingers tighter around the reins, but calmly asked, 'How so?'

'Even after Eleanor ordered you from her sight, you ran away from me. I can only assume you went to seek refuge from the Queen. Why is that?'

'I wanted her to stop this marriage.' Sarah reached over and briefly touched his arm. 'It was nothing personal, William. I simply did not wish to be forced into a marriage so quickly.'

He looked down at her hand just as she jerked her arm away. 'Becoming someone's wife is very personal.'

'It need not be.'

'Some marriages, perhaps. But this one will be.'

'How so?'

William folded his hands atop the pommel of his saddle. 'I knew what was said about you when I requested this marriage.'

'Requested?' She leaned slightly away and stared up at him. 'You never *requested* that I wed you.'

He shrugged. 'Regardless, I took you as wife, knowing you were the Queen's whore.'

'I tried to talk you out of wedding such a woman as I.'

Ignoring her, he continued, 'In return, I expect little from you.'

'Then that is what you will get.'

William tightened his fingers around the top of the pommel, holding his temper in check. For whatever reason, Sarah was itching for an argument. If she wasn't a little more careful, she might get more than what she wanted.

'You are alone in this world, Sarah. There is no one

to take care of you, or to protect you, except me. If you desire that security, you need to learn to trust me. You have no other choice.'

He lifted his gaze to capture hers. 'Tell me again, how can two people sharing a life, a home, a name and a marriage bed not be personal?'

'We have shared no marriage bed.' She held his stare, while adding, 'Nor will we.'

'Oh?' Her direct challenge surprised him. Didn't she realise he'd not ignore her dare? He wanted to tell her that one day she would be more than willing to come to his bed. But he fought to hold his comment back. Finally, he asked, 'What makes you think we won't share a marriage bed?'

All colour left her face at the mere suggestion that she couldn't stop him. Sarah turned away, stiffened her back and stared out over her horse's head. 'You would not force me.'

He didn't believe he'd have to force her. But why did the idea frighten her so? And she was afraid. He knew what fear looked like from experience. He could see her fear in the stiffness of her bearing, in the paleness of her face and heard it in the hesitant, less certain, tone of her voice.

The need to ease her worries prompted him to move closer, to uncurl her fingers from the reins and take her hand in his. William lifted her hand to his lips and dropped a chaste kiss on her knuckles. 'I doubt if force would prove necessary, my lady.'

Sarah jerked her hand free. 'You have a high opinion of yourself, my lord.'

'Perhaps. But there is not a man alive who would dismiss your challenge.'

'I issued no challenge.'

'No? Do you truly think me that naïve?' At her bewildered look, he explained, 'Your ruse is as ancient as time. An experienced woman boldly tells a man that she will not share his bed, knowing full well that it will be a challenge he cannot refuse. You have no secrets in that regard. Every man knows she does it intentionally, Sarah, in expectation of eventually losing the chase.'

She parted her lips, then clamped them tightly together without saying a word.

Her reaction baffled him. He expected more of an argument from her. William moved away. His wife was a ball of mass confusion wrapped in beautiful finery.

He glanced sidelong at Sarah again riding silently beside him. A man in his position would never imagine himself wed to one as lovely as Lady Sarah.

She turned briefly to glare at him and he hid a smile of amusement. No battle to the death had made his stomach knot, or sweat bead on his forehead in such a manner. Yet, this little bit of a woman sent his body, and mind, reeling with nothing more than a glance his way.

And when she once again turned away, a cold wind swept over his body, leaving him strangely bereft of warmth. He sighed at this unfamiliar womanly nonsense teasing at him.

After once again surveying the area for someone following them, and finding nothing, William wondered if he'd imagined the feeling of danger.

Maybe their hasty exit from Eleanor's court, combined with his even hastier marriage, had made his senses overwrought. His weapons were at hand, and Hugh was also well armed. So, for now, William would set aside his worry.

For a more pleasurable distraction, he concentrated

once again on his wife. The women in the church were justified in their jealousy. Despite a crooked nose and a thin scar cutting across one eyebrow, Sarah was a vision of beauty.

Besides her blonde hair, the first thing one noticed when looking at her was the vivid blueness of her eyes against the unblemished paleness of her face.

He briefly wondered how many men had wished to drown in those eyes. As his attention retraced her nose and the scar, he realised that at least one man had not wished to lose himself in her gaze. Had that been the reason for her sudden fear of him?

'What are you looking at now?'

'You.'

'Why?' She swiped a hand across her cheek. 'Is something amiss?'

'No, everything is in place. I was just admiring your beauty.'

Sarah's eyes widened before she schooled her features into a mask of contempt, then turned her face away. The forced look didn't bother him. He'd witnessed her doing the same thing to others at Eleanor's court. While they may have been put off by her contemptuous expression and left her alone, he knew exactly what she was doing and wouldn't be intimidated quite so easily.

'I cannot believe that none have commented on the fairness of your features.'

'Aye, they have. When they either wanted something, or were so far gone in their wine that they knew not what they were saying.'

'I know exactly what I am saying, and I already possess all I desire.'

'And what is that?'

'You.'

At his answer Sarah swung around to face him. 'Me?' Shock fired her cheeks before she shook her head in disbelief. 'We just wed, and yet already you count me as one of your possessions?'

William cringed at the idea. He knew what being a possession entailed. 'That is not what I meant.'

'But isn't that what a wife is?' Her voice rose, and she paused to swallow hard before adding, 'Just another item to add to your assets?'

'My assets?' He shook his head at the absurd statement. His possessions amounted to his weapons, the armour on his back, the horse beneath him, and the promise of gold coin and a keep from King Henry. The weapons and armour he could always count on. The promise, however, was nothing more than words and counted for little. He'd not yet seen the gold, or the keep.

He kept a tight rein on his voice as he answered, 'Oh, aye, Lady Sarah, that is all a wife is to me. Simply another possession. One to use when, and how, I see fit.'

A red haze clouded her vision. Sarah parted her lips to spew curses at him. Just then she caught sight of a glint of humour in his eyes, and she knew instantly that he'd baited her. She closed her mouth, giving him her fiercest scowl and watched in disbelief as he burst into laughter.

When his mirth calmed, she said, 'You did that on purpose.'

He cocked an eyebrow at her, and asked, 'Me?'

'Yes, you, William of Bronwyn.'

'Perhaps I did. But teasing you is a far cry from keeping secrets from your husband.' He reached over and caught her chin before she could turn away. 'Would you not agree, Sarah of Bronwyn?'

She wanted desperately to close her eyes. To shield herself from the accusation and distrust in his unwavering stare. But to do so would give proof to her guilt. She couldn't do that. Not yet.

The pouch Lady Elise had delivered from the Queen contained more than a measure of gold. A brief missive had been included. One that only reconfirmed the importance of gaining the information Queen Eleanor wanted.

Sarah willed her eyes to stay open and her breathing to remain calm. It would not be the first time she'd been forced to lie; she could only pray it would be the last time.

For the moment, instead of lying, she thought it best to feign dull-wits. 'Do I not agree with what?' She pulled free of his hold. 'Are you accusing me of something?'

'You were so afraid I might have overheard Langsford and Arnyll that you thought to distract me with your charms. A dangerous distraction considering you don't know me well enough to feel that safe in my arms. You can't deny it.'

The man was far too quick-witted. Sarah realised that staying one step ahead of him was going to prove difficult at best. Eventually, if she did not keep her wits about her, he would discover her guise of whore was nothing more than a fabrication.

She didn't fear that overmuch, because she doubted if William would be offended to discover his wife was not a harlot. But instinct warned her his reaction would be far from accepting if he learned she continued working for the Queen. Forcing an affronted tone to her voice, she asked, 'Deny what?'

'That you are keeping secrets from me.'

'I can, and do, deny it. What could I possibly gain from doing so?'

'I know not. I'm waiting for you to tell me.' He leaned back in his saddle as if content to wait all day for her answer.

He'd wait longer than that. Sarah wasn't about to tell him anything. She stared directly between her horse's ears and set her jaw.

William chuckled softly. 'You can ignore me now, Sarah. But some night in the future, when it's dark...' he stroked her cheek with the back of his fingers '...after the fire has burned low...' he deepened his voice to a spine-tingling timbre '...and we're wrapped in nothing but each other...' William leaned across the distance separating them to promise '...you will tell me.'

Chapter Four

The campfire crackled, providing light and warmth in the small clearing where they'd settled for the night. After their weeks at court, William and the Earl had decided to spend the night some place quiet, and less confining. So, they'd made camp just off the side of the road instead of seeking shelter in the next town.

Stiff from hours on the back of a horse, Sarah would have preferred the softness of a bed. But she'd no wish to argue something so minor. Instead, a blanket on the hard ground would have to do.

Seated on a log facing the fire, she stretched her legs and savoured the warmth. Without appearing too interested, Sarah returned her attention to the men's conversation about Arnyll.

Earl Hugh snapped a dead tree limb, and then tossed it on to the flames. 'I am surprised you did not slay him in his tracks.'

William shrugged. 'I didn't think that would much please the Queen.'

'True.' Hugh laughed softly.

Adrienna, seated on the log next to her, leaned over to ask, 'Remember Lady Waltrop's reaction upon discovering that old man's body in the Great Hall?'

Even though the man's unexpected demise had been far from humorous, Sarah laughed at the memory. 'Queen Eleanor thought Lady Waltrop would perish of shock.'

Adrienna's burst of laughter sent Sarah into another bout of giggles. When she caught her breath, she admitted, 'I fear I would have been more than surprised myself had I been the one to find the man slumped in the corner staring at me over my morning repast.'

Hugh asked, 'How did he die?'

'No one knows.' Sarah explained further. 'He was far beyond his prime and there were no signs of any injury.'

'I could not help but feel sorry for him,' Adrienna mused, then she asked, 'Did anyone ever discover his identity?'

'I can't remember his name, but he had been one of the Queen's guards in his younger years. Since he was so ancient and had no place else to go, she had kept him in her service doing small details for his...food... and...' Realising the other three were staring at her, she let her explanation trail off, and instead asked, 'What is wrong?'

'Nobody else seemed to know who he was.' Adrienna asked, 'So, how did *you* know?'

William's stare pierced her through the fire. 'It is a little odd that you would know those details.'

'Odd? How so?'

Earl Hugh said, 'A man's position, his wealth, or lack of wealth, isn't something the Queen, or any lady of the keep, would openly discuss with one of her ladies-in-waiting.'

'Oh.' Sarah swallowed a curse. How could she have been so careless? She quickly sought an explanation. 'I told you that I had been acting as a spy for the Queen. She must have mentioned it to one of her men when I was present.'

Adrienna relaxed at the admission, but said, 'It must be a relief not to have to perform such vile tasks any more.'

Without taking her gaze from Adrienna, Sarah knew William was watching her closely. She could feel his attention burn across the distance. She was well aware that he had sensed something was wrong—he hadn't figured out what that something was, just yet. He was waiting for her to make a mistake that would give him the hint, the clue he needed to put it all together.

Sarah let her shoulders slump as she sighed. 'Oh, yes, it is a huge relief.'

'I don't know which would have been worse—spying for the Queen, or having the reputation of being a… whore.'

Before Sarah could answer, William said, 'Reputations physically harm no one. But spying for one's master can harm many and end in death.'

Sarah's stomach clenched. The Queen had hinted at William's death being the way for Sarah to remarry. While she had no wish to remain wed to him, neither did she desire his death. She turned to look at him. 'I have harmed no one. And I can assure you that nobody has died because of some crumb of information I may have passed on to the Queen.'

'How can you know that for certain?'

In all honesty, she couldn't be certain. But with the pained expression furrowing William's brow, and the tightness of his mouth, she wasn't about to admit that to him. 'It wasn't as if I had gathered information of any great importance.'

'Even a tiny scrap of information in the wrong hands becomes important.'

'William, cease.' Earl Hugh placed a hand on William's arm.

While Sarah wondered at William's emotional response, Lady Adrienna brought the conversation back to the Queen. 'You said the Queen permitted her elderly guard to remain in her court?' She shook her head, admitting, 'I didn't know Queen Eleanor could be that soft-hearted.'

Sarah assured her, 'She often treated her subjects with more kindness than many could imagine.'

'Oh, yes.' William stared at her. 'The Queen's compassion is apparent to all of us.'

'I said *often*, not *always*.' Sarah shrugged. 'Other than this instance, she'd always treated me…justly.'

William noted Sarah's hesitation. Had 'justly' been the correct word?

'Justly?' To his surprise, Lady Adrienna badgered Sarah, asking, 'How can you say that? If using you to do her underhanded bidding was just, then I am truly thankful she never saw fit to treat me thusly.'

His wife's eyebrows rose as she turned to answer Adrienna. 'Ah, but you came to the court as a woman fully grown, with gold in hand and prospects of a grand marriage. I came as an unwanted child, with nothing more than the ill-fitting clothes on my back. Queen Eleanor gave me a safe place to sleep, enough food to eat, and permitted me the opportunity to learn how to read and write.'

Sarah plucked at the skirt of her gown, a golden-hued

garment fitted more to the court than for travelling. 'I am indebted to the Queen for everything. The clothing I now wear.' She raised a hand to the jewelled clips decorating the ends of her braids. 'And even for the little trinkets that you would take for granted.'

'I am sorry.' Adrienna touched Sarah's arm. 'I—'

'No.' Sarah leaned away from Adrienna's touch. 'I am not seeking your pity. I have no complaints with my lot in life. I sought only to explain why I am beholden to the Queen.'

William tossed Sarah's words around in his head. He rose from his seat next to Hugh. 'You are wrong, Sarah.' After assisting Adrienna to her feet, William took her place on the log. 'Those days are over. You are not beholden to her. Queen Eleanor is no longer your master.'

'Master?' Sarah frowned. 'What a strange way to refer to the Queen. It was not as if she owned me.'

'Then how would you describe it?' Hugh asked from across the fire. 'You depended on her for food, shelter and clothing. In return she used you any way she saw fit. Is that not the relationship between a servant and a master?'

'No. It was more that I performed services in exchange for her generosity through the years.'

'Since she had accepted you into her court, I can only assume that she had made a promise to your father to care for you.'

'I suppose.' Sarah shrugged. 'I have not spoken to my father since he left me with the Queen.'

William asked, 'How long have you been with the court?'

'About twelve years. I was not yet seven years old when my father brought me to court. He did so only because he had not the gold to foist me off on the Church.'

Sarah didn't know it, but they had more in common than she realised. She had been under the Queen's rule nearly as long as he'd been a captive. William sidled a little closer to her. 'And your mother?'

Sarah stared into the fire for a few moments before she finally answered in a whisper, 'I barely remember her.'

'Did she die?'

'Not exactly.' Sarah picked up a twig and snapped it into little pieces.

William glanced towards Hugh and Adrienna. They sat forehead to forehead, talking softly to each other. He drew his attention back to his wife. Covering her shaking hands with one of his own, he asked, 'What happened?'

She turned her face away and tugged to free her hands. He moved closer; putting an arm across her shoulders, he forced her to lean against him. 'What happened, Sarah?'

'I killed her.' Her trembling voice was barely above a whisper.

'At six years old? I doubt that, Sarah.' *Who in their right mind would convince a child of such vile nonsense?* 'How did she die?'

For a few moments he didn't think she'd answer him, but finally, she said, 'I had been playing with my baby, on the stairs, when the nursemaid called me to get ready for bed.' Sarah paused for a heartbeat as if trying to remember the incident. 'Later that night, I was awakened by my mother's scream. She tripped over the doll I'd left behind and fell down the stairs.'

William tightened his embrace. He lowered his head and whispered against her ear, 'That was not your fault.'

'Yes, it was. My father carried her and the doll up to the bedchamber. After she'd taken her last ragged breath, he threw the doll at me, shouting that I'd killed his wife and unborn child. He then ordered me to take my cursed toy and leave his sight for good.'

William's heart ached for the child. He could only imagine her fear and confusion. 'Ah, Sarah, he didn't mean that. His angry words came from grief.'

She struggled against his chest, gasping, 'I can't breathe, let me go.'

He relaxed his hold, but didn't release her. When her breathing calmed, she said, 'My father had meant exactly what he said. I hid in a tower chamber, and ate only when someone remembered to bring me food.' She touched her crooked nose. 'And I quickly learned to stay out of my father's sight.'

Speechless that a father could treat a child so, William kept his mouth shut. The man's responsibility had been to protect her—to care for her, not place her in danger. Above the sound of blood rushing through his head, his mind shouted, *She was but a babe herself. How could you?*

The feel of Sarah's fingers against his cheek drew him from the sudden, evil urge to kill the man with his bare hands. 'William, do not.'

He shook his head, trying to clear away the vicious thoughts of revenge. 'Do not what?'

'Do not fret for the child. She survived.'

Survived? He knew exactly what it was to simply survive. He'd done so by using his wits and size. As a child, she'd had neither. She'd deserved more than simple survival. He covered her hand with his own. Rubbing his cheek across her palm, he kissed it, then asked, 'How did you come to be with the Queen's court?'

'My father's men convinced him to take me to the

nearby abbey. But when he discovered that he would have to pay for my keep, he refused to do so. After that, they had to bully him into bringing me to the King and Queen. The men thought perhaps Henry or Eleanor might be better able to find me a family in which to foster.'

'Yet, the Queen kept you at court instead of finding you another place. Why?'

'I don't know.' Sarah shrugged. 'By then it did not matter to me. I'd learned not to care. If I simply did as I was told, I would have food and shelter. What else was there?'

Food and shelter. He was amazed that at six years old she'd managed to think and survive as an animal would.

'What of your father?'

'I've neither seen nor spoken to him since the day he left me at court.' She sent him an uneven half-smile. 'It is probably better that way.'

There was little wonder that she'd done whatever the Queen had asked. He now understood why Sarah felt the Queen had treated her *justly*. His wife would have felt indebted to any who had shown her anything other than anger.

He reached out and cupped her cheek, drawing her closer. Uncertain what to say, or do, William only wanted to offer her a measure of comfort.

Sarah closed her eyes as his breath rushed warm across her cheek. In her hope to make him understand the things she'd done, she had said too much, revealed more than she'd ever intended. Worse—she'd given him the impression that she needed his compassion, his pity, when she wanted neither.

Before he could kiss her, she placed a hand against his chest and held him away. 'William, don't.'

He leaned back. Confusion furrowing his brows. 'I—'

'No. Do not feel sorry for me. I am no longer that child. What happened to her has no bearing on my life today. I do not need, or want, your pity.'

'No bearing?' He lowered his arms from around her. 'It has impacted your every action.'

'Do you at least understand why I do not see Queen Eleanor, or her requests, in the same light as others may?'

While it was true that Sarah did not know the chafe of ankle irons, or the weight of chains, she had been as much a slave as he. 'I may see it, Sarah, but I do not agree she was right in making those decisions. She used your circumstances against you.'

Now Sarah shared William's confusion. 'Isn't using another person simply the way of things? Aren't most marriage contracts formed on the basis of what each party brings to the union? Are not keeps fortified with men suited to their position? I do not understand what you think Queen Eleanor did wrong.'

William traced the outline of her jaw. 'I have not the words to argue with you. But, Sarah, now that you are out from beneath the Queen's control, you will find that your life can be different than the one you've known.'

Except she wasn't out from beneath the Queen's control. Her life would always be the same. She couldn't very well tell William that, though. Instead, she glanced at a spot just beyond his shoulder and said, 'We shall see.'

He leaned slightly to the side, coming directly into her line of vision. He'd let her know, without words, that he'd seen her ruse. Most people never realised that while her face was pointed in their direction, she wasn't actually looking at them.

It only confirmed her belief that this husband of hers was too clever by far.

William rose. 'I will see to the horses.' He leaned over and kissed her forehead. 'Then we can retire for the night.'

She said nothing. But after he'd left, Sarah glanced nervously at the darkened sky. Normally she welcomed darkness and the solitude it brought.

Regardless of the season, she would wander the castle walls at night. The twinkling stars were the only company she'd required. Night was a quiet time when the world slept, and she was left alone with her dreams and wishes. So alone, that at times, it nearly felt as if she lost herself to physically mingle with the celestial bodies.

But tonight…tonight she dreaded the rising of the moon and the unanswerable questions it would bring.

Guilt nagged at her. Every thought in her head urged her to withhold the truth from him. Since she would not remain with him for long, logic dictated that she protect herself with silence.

Sarah's stomach clenched at the thought. Even though she would not be wed to him for ever, he'd been kind. And in one very long day he'd made her weak with desire using nothing more than a kiss. He'd teased her. Not in a cruel way, but in a manner that made her heart secretly laugh, even when she was scowling.

More than those things, he'd urged her to talk, and then he had listened. Even when the listening seemed to have horrified him, he had not stopped her.

Somehow, before it was too late, she had to convince her heart not to be foolish. These simple acts of kindness were nothing on which to build a life. These misplaced images of her and William together, running rampant through her mind, were nothing more than pity for the child she'd once been.

Sarah gasped at the sharp pain of regret for that child that laced through her. If she kept this up, she'd soon drown in self-pity. Before that happened, she needed a few minutes alone to compose herself. She jumped up from her seat on the log and headed toward the nearby stream.

From across the small clearing, William's intent stare nearly singed her back, but he said nothing. Instead, the Earl called out, 'Lady Sarah, do not wander off alone.'

Before she got too far away, William was at her side. He looked down at her, an unspoken question etched on his face. But he remained silent as he escorted her to a secluded spot in the woods. He let her slip off alone and stood guard until she rejoined him at the edge of the stream.

She immersed her hands in the frigid water, hoping the chill would ease the trembling a few moments alone had not. When that failed, she splashed the water on her face. If nothing else, maybe it would calm the worry heating her cheeks.

'Sarah, come.'

She bit back a tart comment about following him like a loyal dog and fell silently in step behind him. When they returned to the camp, Hugh and Adrienna were curled together beneath a cover on the far side of the fire.

Suddenly terrified of what lay ahead, she stood rooted to the ground, watching William. He cleared sticks and stones from the earth, before unrolling covers for their makeshift bed.

He sat on the log to unlace, then remove his boots before he moved to the bed and stretched out on his side.

He stared up at her and extended his arm, inviting her to willingly come to him, giving her the choice.

Sarah wanted to run away from William's outstretched hand. She wanted to fall into his arms. She wanted to hide—not just from him, but also from herself and everything she'd become...and everything she'd never be.

In that one heartbeat of indecision, it all crashed in on her. She was a liar, a spy, the Queen's whore...over and over every rumour that had ever been bandied about reverberated loud in her ears. Never would she be able to escape who, or what, she was.

Unshed tears blurred her vision. A cry lodged in her throat, nearly choking her as she turned away. William cursed softly. Before she could move, he sat up and took away her opportunity to choose by pulling her down next to him.

She rolled on to her side, facing away from him. With one arm wrapped firmly about her waist, he held her fast. 'This day has been too long. I will bedevil you no further, Sarah. Go to sleep.'

Thankful that this would not be the night for more questions, she closed her eyes. But sleep would not come. It was held at bay by the solid length of his body behind hers, and by the strong beat of his heart against her back.

Every passing heartbeat fed her guilt. And each moment that he held her close, offering protection instead of ravishment, made her worry that she'd not be able to see this plan of Eleanor's through to the end.

Dear Lord above, what would she do if that proved true? If she betrayed Queen Eleanor, she could likely lose her life. Yet, if she betrayed William, he would lose his. Unless she could somehow talk the Queen out of seeing him dead. Thus far, she'd never been able to change the Queen's mind on anything, so Sarah held little hope for doing so in the future.

The pounding inside her head was nearly unbearable. And the tightness in her throat, from holding back tears, threatened to strangle her.

William loosened his hold from around her waist, reached up and brushed a thumb across her cheek, wiping away a tear she hadn't realised had fallen. 'Rest easy, Sarah, I am not going to hurt you.'

She sniffed, then said, 'I know that.' The second the words were out of her mouth she wanted to quickly push them back inside.

He raised up on his elbow and leaned over her. 'Then what are you crying about?'

'Crying? What are you talking about? I am not crying. What would I have to cry about? There's no reason for me to cry. Everything is fine. Go to sleep.' She spoke so fast that she knew he'd realise she was lying—a witless fool would know.

With his lips against her ear, he whispered, 'Surely you know that blithering only exposes your lie.'

Since he hadn't posed a direct question, she said nothing.

William feathered kisses on the sensitive flesh of her neck. His gentle touch sent her heart racing anew, and her mind spinning.

Before she had a chance to calm her flitting senses, he moved back to her ear. 'I would have thought... that you...would be much better...at fabricating the truth.'

Between words, his lips against her neck, then her ear, chased thrills the length of her spine. Without thought, she answered, 'So did I.'

At his chuckle, Sarah's groan of dismay changed quickly to a gasp. The lout had done that on purpose. She pushed at his forearm, hoping he would release her from his embrace.

But instead of releasing her, he tugged her on to her back. 'Ah, Sarah, how were you ever successful spying for the Queen?'

That was a question she'd like to know the answer to herself. The few men who managed to get her alone long enough to play these games of seduction had never made her mind go numb. Her heart hadn't pounded like it did now.

In the dim light of the fire she could see only the outline of his form. Still propped up on his elbow, William leaned down towards her. 'You are such a fraud.'

He brushed her hair from her face, before tracing a finger down the side of her cheek and then across her lips. His touch left a fiery trail on her skin.

William leaned closer and kissed the corner of her mouth. 'I wonder how much truth there is to the rumours about you.'

Thankfully, he didn't pursue the issue further, but when she went to move away from him, William draped a leg across hers, effectively preventing any escape. She tensed her muscles and held herself stiff as she waited for him to say, or do…something.

Finally, she reminded him, 'You said you would not hurt me.'

'Hurt you?' He drew a fingertip along her lower lip, repeating the motion when she shivered. 'Did that hurt?'

Sarah turned her head away. 'Please, I just want to sleep.'

His sigh echoed into the clearing before he cupped

her cheek and brought her back to face him. 'One kiss, then you can sleep.'

She pursed her lips, then raised her head to quickly touch her mouth to his. 'There, you've had your kiss.'

'Oh, is that what that was?' His question wisped across her lips.

'Ye—'

He quickly covered her mouth with his, cutting off her reply. And for the first time since she had been a child, Sarah felt the icy touch of terror as it weighed heavy and cold within her chest.

Her pulse raced so fast it left her dizzy. This was dangerous. She had to stop him. Had to find some way to make him see reason.

William moved his lips more firmly against hers. Sarah lifted her arms to push him away, to break this maelstrom stealing over her, setting her afire.

But her arms refused to obey, and instead, she encircled him in an embrace, clinging to him for a steady purchase against the shifting ground.

William broke their kiss on a ragged groan and touched his forehead to hers. '*That* was a kiss.' He rolled on to his back, gathering her against him. 'Go to sleep.'

Sarah stared across his chest at the fire, wondering if her heart would ever slow down enough so she could sleep.

Chapter Five

Sarah leaned over the rail of the ship in fear she would once again disgrace herself. She had never travelled well across water and hated crossing the channel.

But at least she wasn't alone in this as Adrienna appeared to be having the same difficulty. The only difference was that the Earl was at Adrienna's side.

'Are you always this ill aboard a ship?'

She jumped at William's question. He'd come from behind, startling her.

'Yes. And I swear if I never again have to cross another body of water it will still be too soon.'

William rubbed her back and Sarah rested her forehead on the rail, accepting his offer of comfort.

'Stand up and open your eyes.' He leaned next to her on the railing, drawing her closer to his side. 'If you don't look at the water, it isn't as bad.'

She peered at the rolling waves and swallowed hard. 'But that's all there is to look at.'

'Look at the sky instead.'

Sarah closed her eyes. 'I would rather look at nothing.'

'Don't you think that just makes it worse?'

Her stomach rolled. How could it be any worse? 'How so?'

He moved behind her. 'If you look at the water, you see only the rolling of the waves.'

She couldn't argue with that assessment.

William pulled her against his chest, forcing her to stand upright. 'And if you keep your eyes closed, your mind still sees the rolling.'

Sarah groaned. 'Let me go.'

He only held her tighter. 'No. Look up at the sky. It remains still.'

Too weak to argue with him, or fight his embrace, she tipped her head back, resting it against his shoulder and looked up at the cloudless sky.

When the ship swayed with another swell, William spread his legs, planting his feet further apart. To her amazement, he held her steady against him. And to her relief, the rolling of her stomach lessened.

'Why are you being so kind?'

'Because you are ill.'

She pressed harder into the warmth at her back. 'And if I wasn't?'

Against her ear, he whispered, 'I wouldn't be holding you in my arms.'

His answer gave Sarah reason to pause. He wasn't being kind because he cared, but because he felt obligated. Not that it mattered, she didn't want him to care for her. But for a reason she couldn't name, the knowledge made her uneasy.

'Since I'm no longer ill, you can let me go.'

Without a word, the arms holding her close fell away and the warmth at her back disappeared.

* * *

William cast a sidelong glance at his wife and toyed with the urge to reach across the distance separating them to draw her forcibly to his side. But her near total silence since leaving the ship had made him realise that it would eventually prove useless. As soon as he left her alone, she would retreat back into this cave of silence she'd erected around herself.

She spoke only when addressed directly, and never offered anything of a personal nature. She had seemed content to sleep next to him last night and to accept his assistance while crossing the Channel. So why now did she ride silently at his side?

Since he had given her no reason to act in this manner, William knew he'd be a fool to think this was a normal reaction.

His years in captivity might not have given him much chance to figure out how to deal with women, but he'd had plenty of time, and opportunity, to study people in general. Sometimes his life had depended on his ability to read an opponent's body language, or even the slightest shift of a gaze.

After a while he'd come to understand that sudden kindness, or attentiveness, would soon spell disaster—if not death. When a jailer doled out extra food, permitted a man to slack in his training, or feigned interest in one particular person, that person had been chosen to die in the arena.

Unfortunately, it also worked in the other direction. When the guards intentionally singled out a prisoner to withhold food and human contact, that person was slated for death, too.

In either case, the death was never in a quick, or easy manner.

Out of self-preservation, the prisoners manipulated each other as much as the guards did. If a man started to pay closer attention, or suddenly decided he wanted to befriend you, he was looking to discover your weaknesses. Once a weakness was detected, it would be used against you in battle.

But sometimes the intentions were even more devious. Stefan of Arnyll found great amusement in breaking a man's spirit. He thought nothing of befriending others only to pass on information to the jailors. Information that would be used by the jailers, or the slave master, to mentally beat a strong man down until he could easily be defeated and killed.

Due to Arnyll and his vileness, William had learned that his own spirits could be slashed. However, he'd also discovered that sometimes beating a man down did not weaken him…it only made him stronger.

He glanced again at his wife. She'd been so intent on making certain that he understood why she'd so readily spied for the Queen. Too intent. At the same time, she'd never voiced any believable relief that those days were over. Which led him to wonder if perhaps they weren't.

Eleanor had accepted his offer to wed Sarah far too easily. He was penniless and untitled. Had he made a formal offer for her hand, he would have been laughed out of the court.

The Queen was experienced with playing court politics. Especially since it was *her* court. She was not a simple participant in the intrigue—she was the manipulator in charge.

So, what had been behind her easy acceptance of

Sarah's marriage to one who could advance nothing? He had never come under the Queen's direct focus. But Hugh had.

Was it possible that Sarah was keeping an eye on the Earl through him? If so, why? She needed to understand that he'd not let anything happen to Hugh.

More than friends, William, Hugh and Guy of Hartford had shared more than a cell. In a place where friendship often spelled death, they'd shared their loyalty to each other. More than once they'd gone hungry for each other and borne the bite of the lash together.

William cursed. He'd had enough of this. He grabbed the reins to her horse, jerking them through her hands. Before she could say anything, he shouted ahead to Hugh, 'I will rejoin you shortly.'

Sarah reached for the reins. 'William, what are you doing?'

He ignored her, and turned their horses around to head back the way they'd just come. The Earl's men were nearby. They'd been following, guarding their lord, since the ship carrying them across the channel had docked.

The men were familiar with William, so he didn't worry about them distracting him. While they might be curious, they'd stay close to the Earl, leaving William alone with Sarah.

Once William had led them a short distance away, he dismounted, and looped the horses' reins around the stout branch of a bush. Sarah was halfway off her horse when he pulled her hard against him.

'What are you doing?' She pushed against his chest. 'Let me go.'

He might not know much about dealing with women in general, but he had learned a thing or two about his wife.

With one hand twisted into her hair, and the other holding her firmly to him, he tugged her head back and cut off her shout with his lips.

William knew she'd be angry, but at the moment, he didn't care. He was done being nice. It had got him nowhere thus far.

And if he knew nothing else about her, he knew for a certainty that she could be kissed senseless. Right now, it seemed the perfect weapon. In truth, it seemed the *only* weapon.

She leaned against him, her hands on his shoulders as she returned his kiss, and William feared this weapon was two-edged. He'd meant to set her senses afire, to take her off guard.

Yet *his* pulse pounded in his ears. *His* blood rushed hot through his veins. And *his* senses flamed. A kiss would not be enough. The mere touching of their lips, the feel of her soft body pressed against his chest and the meeting of their tongues did nothing to squelch the growing desire.

He wanted her. And while he was man enough to admit that he wanted her to feel the same, William also recognised the anger flaring beneath his desire.

They were wed. As much as Sarah would detest his logic, she was his. He tore his lips from hers and hoarsely berated, 'You have no right, no cause for this, Sarah.'

She stared up at him, her eyes luminous and large against her flushed face. 'What? I have no cause for what?'

'No right to withhold yourself from me.' Even as he said it, William knew his allegation sounded like an insignificant complaint. But he couldn't help how it sounded. No more than he could help how he felt.

She blinked twice before asking, 'This is because I will not share your bed?'

'No.' That was a lie. 'Yes.' And that was not quite the full truth. 'Partially. You withhold yourself in all ways. Do you think I do not notice your coldness, or your complete lack of attention? You speak to me only when you have to do so.'

Sarah could hardly believe what she was hearing. But his firm hold on her braid, the suppressed rage simmering beneath the pain in his tone, and the intensity in his hard stare made her aware of the deadly seriousness of his accusation.

Ignoring him with hopes he'd leave her alone in disgust had worked against her. William was not disgusted. He was angry—and his rage was beyond simple anger.

Why had she not seen this coming? How had she been so blind?

Sarah closed her eyes against the all-too-familiar tightening in her chest. She'd not seen this coming because she'd been too absorbed in her own misery.

While staring into the fire last night, she'd decided to protect herself by not letting this man get too close. Then again this morning aboard ship his actions had only confirmed her decision. It was the only way she could think of to save herself the pain of guilt when her task was completed.

Unfortunately, it seemed that her tactic to ignore and avoid him had gone horribly wrong. She'd seen his sidelong looks and had felt his increasingly intense stares. She should have known that William was not the type of man to fade quietly into the background. She should have stopped this before it'd gone too far.

Her ploy had been selfish and childish. And where had it got her? She looked up at him and nearly gasped at the blatant hunger on his face.

Sarah swallowed hard before she whispered, 'William, I—'

Again he cut her words off with his lips. And all she could do was hang on to his shoulders for support, otherwise she feared falling to the ground.

A part of her briefly wondered what manner of spell he wove around her so easily. How could just a kiss steal her will, her strength and leave her near swooning?

And how was it possible that, while she feared his brand of sorcery, she hungered for more of the same?

Sarah knew without a doubt that if William so desired he could easily lay her down upon the ground and make her his wife in more than name. She also knew that she would not lift a hand, or speak a word, to stop him.

'Why have you acted so?'

To her surprise his breath rasped hot against her ear. She hadn't even been aware that his lips had left hers.

Not sure how to answer him, she said, 'I don't know, William. I don't know.'

When he dragged his teeth lightly along the side of her neck, before following the trail with his lips, Sarah felt the ripple of shivers clear to her toes. She tilted her head as if offering him more of her flesh to torment.

'Ah, Sarah, I will have no more of your half-truths and lies.'

How did he know? What did he mean he would have no more of them? What did he intend to do? The questions flitted about her mind. But before she could make sense of them, he again kissed her.

This time there was no mistaking his intent. He seemed determined to steal her ability to think, or to form any rational thought, from her mind.

Sarah leaned closer against him and wound her arms about his neck. He stroked her side, then cupped her breast, his touch barely grazing the sensitive tip. She moaned softly as her senses fled.

When he held her so tightly, caressed her so deftly, and kissed her so thoroughly, what need had she for rational thoughts?

'Ah, Sarah.' He breathed her name against her ear. The heated warmth only fuelled her desire to a fevered pitch. 'What game do you play with me?'

Unable to form a coherent sentence, she shook her head and leaned into his still-teasing touch.

'Are you still spying for the Queen?'

Before she could answer, he traced the seam of her parted lips with his tongue. William smiled briefly against her mouth when she shivered. He repeated the movement, then asked, 'Are you, Sarah?'

'Yes. I—' At her own breathless whisper, she froze, leaving her sentence unfinished. The desire flowing through her limbs vanished, leaving behind an icy-cold chill.

William released her and stepped away.

Unwilling to look at what she knew would be smug-laced anger on his face, she turned away. He hadn't wanted her. He hadn't cared that she'd been ignoring him. He'd only wanted answers, so he'd tricked her.

And she'd fallen for his tactics like some gullible, foolish girl.

Sarah wrapped her arms round her stomach, trying to hold the twisting and churning at bay. Had she followed the Queen's sage advice and held him at arm's length, this would not have taken place.

She had only herself to blame.

'Explain yourself.' His voice cut through her self-pity as easily as a sword would slice through warm beeswax.

'Explain myself?' Without turning around, she shrugged. 'What can I tell you? That I will most likely die of old age still in the Queen's service? That there is no escape for me?'

'Your escape was at hand when you left the court as a married woman. You no longer had to serve Queen Eleanor. So, why? Just tell me why, Sarah.'

'I—'

'At least have the decency to look at me.'

Sarah tugged at her lower lip. She didn't want to look at him. Didn't want to see the disgust in his eyes— even though his disgust was what she'd been trying so hard to find. But more than that, she had no desire for him to witness her shame.

He pulled her around to face him, giving her no choice in the matter. 'I said look at me.'

Even as he released her, she kept her eyes tightly closed against the harsh tone of his voice. Her mind chided her relentlessly, *It is your own fault.*

After taking a deep breath, she opened her eyes and looked up at him. What she saw nearly took her breath away as she stumbled backwards.

Instead of the smug rage or disgust that she'd expected, she was almost certain what she saw was the tightly concealed look of pain and confusion. The confusion was understandable, but the pain? Surely she'd only imagined it.

She gritted her teeth, hoping the act would lend her

strength against the guilt that seemed to be growing each hour. Certain she could now speak without dissolving into a bout of self-loathing, she said, 'I—'

The shouts of men and the pounding of hooves cut off her explanation.

William grabbed her and the horses' reins at the same time. He quickly tossed her up on the saddle, turned the horse in the direction the Earl and Adrienna had gone, and ordered, 'Go.'

Fear that the men charging toward them could be from the Queen kept her from questioning William. Sarah had no information for Queen Eleanor and she wished not to lose her life, or his, for that lack. So, she leaned as low over her horse's neck as the saddle would permit and rode for her life.

Over the deafening beating of her heart, she heard the deadly hiss of a sword scraping out of its wooden scabbard. When she lifted her head to look behind her, William shouted, 'No. Just ride.'

Not in a position to argue, Sarah rode. She flew past trees and bushes so quickly that her stomach lodged in her throat. Yet she hung on, insanely trusting that this man she'd plotted to betray would keep her safe.

She glanced ahead and saw the Earl and Adrienna also riding like the wind. When the Earl turned his head and spotted them, he took the lead, putting the women in the middle, with William to bring up the rear.

Hugh careened to a halt at a small clearing and quickly dismounted, as he ordered, 'Into the woods.'

On foot they led their horses off the path and into the more protective cover of the woods. Sarah pushed another small tree branch out of her way. "I no longer hear anyone. Why are we leaving the road?"

'Simply because you do not hear, or see, them does not mean they are not there.' William explained.

'So we are hiding from someone we can neither see nor hear?'

William walked alongside her and said, 'If you would rather wait for them here, you can do so alone.'

The brisk tone of his voice let her know that he was not jesting. She shook her head. 'No. I'll stay with you.'

He raised an eyebrow, but said nothing. Which was fine as far as Sarah was concerned. She'd had enough of his attention for this day.

They plodded along in silence behind the Earl and Adrienna for what seemed hours, or perhaps years. Tired and hungry, she wasn't certain any longer.

William grasped her elbow and slowed their steps, putting a little more distance between them and the other couple. After a few moments, he stopped.

Sarah held her breath. Surely he wasn't going to continue their discussion now?

'We need to talk.'

She glanced toward Hugh and Adrienna before dragging her gaze back to stare up at William. 'Now?'

He reached out and wiped something from her cheek, hesitating for a heartbeat before removing his touch. 'No. It is apparent to me what it's going to take to get you to tell me everything. So, obviously we're going to need more privacy than these woods can provide.'

From the glimmer in his eyes and the tilt of his lips, she knew exactly what he was planning. The knowledge made her want to scream. Instead, she swallowed, then asked, 'You intend to what? Turn my body against me to get the answers you want?'

William stroked the tip of his finger lightly along her

lower lip. At her involuntary shiver, he shrugged. 'It seems to work.'

'Why, you—you—' She was so livid at his dispassionate attitude that she couldn't find words vile enough to spew at him. She took a deep breath and narrowed her eyes. 'And how will you know if I lie or not?'

He cupped the side of her head. When she tried to jerk away from his touch, he simply curled his fingers into the hair covering the back of her head, and held her in place. 'Because I will ask you over…' he leaned closer '…and over…' he lowered his head to whisper against her lips '…and over again.'

She hated what he did to her. Hated it. Hated him. Hated herself and her weakness more. Yet she let her eyelids flutter closed in expectation of his kiss.

When it did not come, Sarah opened her eyes and stared into his steely stare. He thought he was going to toy freely with her? She raised her leg, and with all her might trounced soundly on his foot.

While she gained a slight measure of satisfaction from his flinch, she hadn't expected him to jerk her forwards and cover her mouth with his. The moment she relaxed, he released her and pushed her away.

Sarah swiped the back of her hand across her mouth. 'Do you plan on doing that every time you need to coerce or punish me?'

Not for a moment did William think her question unfair. He deserved the query and her dismissive action. But he wasn't about to back down now by begging her forgiveness. He didn't want her forgiveness. He wanted her honesty. Was that too much to ask for in a marriage?

Instead of apologising, he pinned her with a glare and

answered, 'If that's what it takes to get an answer from you, then yes.'

Without waiting for her to respond, he waved a hand toward Hugh and Adrienna. 'Let's go.'

'Go?' With her fists braced against her hips, Sarah drew herself up to her full height, putting her face just about level with his chest, and then stared up at him. 'Just like you're ordering about a dog, is that it?'

If she had the slightest hint of how her flashing blue eyes and flushed cheeks made his blood rush, she'd close her mouth and chase after the other couple as quickly as possible.

Thankfully, she didn't have the slightest hint. She was convinced that the only reason he touched her, or kissed her was as she'd said—for coercion or…punishment. William swallowed a groan at the thought of punishing her. He'd sooner cut off his sword arm than lay a hand, or mouth, on her in a fit of rage.

Once she calmed down, she'd likely figure that out for herself. In the meantime, what harm was there in taking advantage of her misplaced thoughts?

'Just like a dog?' He winged one eyebrow higher. 'No. A dog would listen.'

The curses rushing out of her mouth surprised him. He didn't think lips that kissable knew such words. But he kept that thought to himself as she retrieved the reins to her horse and stomped off toward the other couple.

William shook his head and started after her. Hugh would think he'd lost what little common sense God gave him. And maybe he'd be right. But at the moment, doing anything he had to do to get Sarah to confide in him seemed reasonable.

No matter the cost. Whether it be her anger, or his own.

His will was much stronger than hers. Eventually, he would win this battle. Her little slip-ups when her mind was fixated on desire, and lust, had let him know that she wasn't as determined to keep her secrets as he was to ferret them out.

He also knew that once this battle was waged and won, he'd have to work just as hard, if not harder, to win her trust.

This marriage may have been quick, and may have been forced on her. But it would last until death parted them. And he had no intention of spending the rest of their years together being at odds.

The sound of twigs snapping in the woods to his right caught his attention. Silently sliding his weapons free, William held his sword and dagger at the ready.

Chapter Six

When the first man came into view, William sheathed his weapons, breathing a sigh of relief. He had known the Earl's men were nearby. He'd assumed they'd engaged in combat with the group that had charged them on the road.

He picked up his pace and joined them just as Hugh was telling Adrienna about the men.

'We have twelve guards travelling with us.'

'Eleven, my lord.' Alain, the man currently in charge of the guards, corrected Hugh.

Quickly scanning the others as they joined the group, William asked, 'Who is missing?'

Alain turned to face him. 'Osbert took a fatal arrow.'

Without thinking, William said, 'At least he was not taken alive.' The lad was far too young to be able to withstand the rigors of captivity.

He checked the backs of the horses. 'We need to return his body to his family.'

'Sir.' Another man leading a horse stepped forwards. 'We have him.'

William heard Sarah's slight intake of air and moved closer to her. He didn't want her causing a scene, nor did he want her frightened. To his amazement, she sidled nearer to him.

He gave the body draped over the saddle a cursory look before he nodded and said, 'Good. His mother will thank you.'

At that moment, William suddenly realised he'd overstepped the bonds of friendship and authority. He turned his attention to Hugh. 'My lord, I—'

'No.' Hugh waved a hand toward the men. 'Please, continue.'

William shifted his focus back to the men. 'What about the group following us? Was it Arnyll and his men?'

'Aye. But he now has three men instead of fifteen.' Alain near swaggered in triumph while the others shouted their own victories. 'Using bows, as you'd suggested, instead of swords, worked well.'

William had suspected that Arnyll had been the one following them. Thankfully, Alain had taken his advice in regards to the choice of weapons. Of course the bows would prove successful. In close quarters the men didn't need to be expert archers, enabling Hugh's force to take out most of Arnyll's party without getting within the reach of a blade.

William raised a hand, signalling silence. 'What of Arnyll?'

'He kept to the north road. We didn't follow for long. I thought it best we return to the Earl.'

'Well done.' Hugh stepped in. 'Perhaps after a good night's sleep we'll make decent progress tomorrow.'

Alain pointed toward the west. 'There is an empty hut and a stream straight on, my lord. Some of the men can help prepare camp, while the rest of us hunt for some food.'

William went ahead, taking Sarah with him. Just as Alain had stated, there was an empty hut…of sorts. To call it a dwelling would have been an exaggeration.

The single window faced the east. There would be light in the morning, but now the hut was drenched in darkness. William pushed the door to open it, but instead it fell to the dirt floor inside the hut. Layers of fine dust billowed from beneath it.

Sarah jumped back as a long slinky animal scurried through the window and disappeared into the woods so fast William couldn't be certain if it'd been a stoat or a weasel. She motioned toward the building. 'You first.'

After propping the door against a wall, William peered into the darkness. He didn't see or hear anything, but until they had a fire going so he could have some light, he didn't relish accidentally cornering anything with claws and teeth.

He backed out of the hut and cleared an area for a campfire. Adrienna joined Sarah sitting on a boulder at the edge of the clearing.

After he and the Earl had the fire going, they gathered enough dead wood to keep it flaming through the night. As they set off for another armload, Hugh said, 'The men seem to take direction from you.'

William grimaced. He had been out of line when questioning Hugh's men. 'I didn't mean to overstep your authority. Sometimes I forget that you're now an Earl and I'm—'

'My friend.' Hugh cuffed his arm. 'That wasn't why I brought up the topic.' He glanced briefly at the women.

'I need a captain for my guard. Someone capable of training them to fight.'

'You've suddenly forgotten how?' William kicked a broken branch on to the pile of gathered wood.

'I can still best you.'

'Since you never could before.' William stood upright and looked down at Hugh. 'That's something I might like to see.'

'Name the weapon.'

William frowned as if contemplating the absurd idea. Finally, he suggested, 'Mace.'

Hugh shook his head. 'Your reach is too long. Name another one.'

'Pike.'

'No. Another one.'

'Axe.'

'No.' Hugh sighed. 'How about something that would give us a more even match.'

Since Hugh was so obviously trying to keep the mood light, William snapped his fingers. 'Bocce.' He looked around the clearing. 'There is enough room. We just need find something to use for balls.'

'A game?' Hugh crossed his arms against his chest. 'That's all you can come up with?'

'If that's too strenuous for you, I may have some dice in my saddle bag.'

'I surrender.' Hugh raised his hands. 'I can't even win a battle of words with you, I'm certainly not going to risk getting beat in a game of chance.'

William picked up a pile of the wood, asking, 'So, what did you really want to discuss?'

'That obvious?'

'Slightly.' He smiled. 'You tend to jest right before getting to the crux of the matter at hand.'

'Pity you know me so well.' Hugh loaded his arms with wood. 'I need a captain. And I would be grateful if you would take the position.'

'Why me?'

'Because I trust you.'

'I have no experience leading men.'

Hugh dropped his armload atop the pile near the fire. He waited for William to do the same. As they headed back for more, he admitted, 'Neither do I.'

'Then would it not be better if you found someone with that experience?'

'My men already know how to follow orders. I need them to know how to fight. They will listen to you. And if they don't, a few cracked skulls will get their attention.'

William had oversight of what King Henry referred to as a God-forsaken tower near the Welsh border that needed to be put in order. But the King had suggested he wait until he had enough men willing to make the arduous journey with him.

From the way King Henry described the area and its inhabitants, William had the sinking feeling that it wouldn't be just the journey that proved arduous. He glanced toward Sarah.

It had been a long time since she'd lived in a warrior's keep. Even then she'd been nothing more than a child. The adjustment from court life to crude outpost would be hard.

He'd vowed to keep her safe, to protect her. Could he do so in a tower keep built for war, not comfort? More importantly, could he do so while rebuilding the keep and training the men?

William wasn't at all certain it would be possible.

However, he was certain that it wouldn't be fair to drag her into what could prove to be endless battles for months…or years…to come.

Perhaps having her settled in at Hugh's keep wouldn't be a bad thing. It wasn't as if it would be for ever—only until he could see to the training of the Earl's men, and then see to the safety and training of his own. 'If I accepted your offer, it would have to be on a temporary basis.'

'Yes.' Hugh nodded. 'I realise that. I would ask only for a year of your time at most.'

William hoped that training the men wouldn't take a full year. He still had another qualm. 'And, if I accepted this offer, you would be…my lord?'

Hugh adopted the most innocent look on his face possible, before asking, 'You don't think Lord Hugh has a nice sound to it?'

'It depends.'

'On?'

William quickly swung out his foot and swept Hugh's legs from beneath him. Reaching down to assist his now-cursing friend to his feet, he answered, 'On whether you deign to train with the men or not. You are getting rather…slow.'

Hugh grasped his hand. Glowering at William, he challenged, 'And at the end of a year our positions will be reversed, my friend.'

With a laugh, William accepted the challenge and the offer. 'Good. I will see to it that you focus on your speed.'

'Then you'll accept the position?'

William huffed out a hearty sigh. 'It seems I must. You certainly aren't in shape to train the men.' He glanced sidelong at Adrienna. 'Must have something to do with being married.'

'Speaking of being married…'

'No.' William held up one hand. 'Let us not.'

'If you have not yet bedded the woman, you could set her aside easily enough.'

Hugh's suggestion sparked an unexpected flash of rage. Taken aback by his sudden desire to rearrange the Earl's face, William stepped back. 'I have no wish to set her aside.'

'You only wed her out of your need to protect those smaller and weaker than yourself. There was no need for such a sacrifice on your part. I give you leave to set her aside. I can see that she is safely delivered wherever she wishes.'

'You give me leave?' The urge to crush something—anything—grew by leaps and bounds. William curled his fingers into tight fists. 'How chivalrous of you.'

Hugh's eyes widened at William's curt tone. 'I only thought to rid you of a wife you did not plan on having.'

'You speak of her as if she is a malady I need to toss out of my life.'

'Isn't she?'

'No.' William looked across the clearing toward Sarah. 'She is far from that.'

'Ah. That's the way of it, then.' Hugh leaned closer. 'Why do you not just bed her and put that devil to rest?'

'Like you have?' He turned his attention back to Hugh. 'I've noticed that bedding your wife has made your life much more pleasant.'

Hugh shrugged at the pointed jab. '*Touché.* Marriage to obstinate women is a cross we each must bear.'

Obstinate wasn't exactly how William would describe his wife, but he wasn't about to argue. Instead he asked, 'Do we head for Wynnedom?'

'You and the men do. I am taking Adrienna to see her father.'

William knew that Hugh was going to Hallison to wreak revenge on her father. Not that he blamed him. Hallison owed much for selling Hugh into captivity. However, William knew the journey could be fraught with danger. 'Not alone you aren't.'

'Oh? Now you think to tell me what I will or won't do? I asked you to be the captain of my guard, not my wet nurse.'

'Seems a fair trade for your attempt to get me to set aside my wife.'

'Enough. What do you suggest, then?'

William wanted Hugh to take all of the men, but he knew that idea would never be acceptable. 'I'll take three of the men with me to Wynnedom.'

'I have a shorter distance to travel. You take seven of the men.'

'No.'

Hugh glared at him. 'Six. I will not let you travel on to Wynnedom with less than six.'

That would leave only five men to accompany Hugh. William smiled. Alain had enough experience to count as two men. He nodded. 'Agreed, but Alain goes with you.'

'We could stand here all night and argue.'

'That would be fine with me.' William nodded toward the clearing. 'But your wife just walked off into the woods—alone.'

Hugh whipped around just in time to see Adrienna disappear between the trees. He cursed, then quickly agreed to take Alain and four others with him. 'I'll talk to Alain and then the two of you can decide who goes in which direction.'

William watched the Earl leave, then turned his attention to Sarah. She held his gaze as he walked towards her. Taking a seat next to her on the log, he asked, 'Are you hungry?'

'Yes.' She motioned to the men now entering the clearing. 'But that'll soon be remedied.' She turned to look up at him. 'What were you and the Earl arguing about?'

'Arguing?'

'You knocked him to the ground. And at one point your hands were fisted. That was not arguing?'

'No, not really. That is just the way we talk.'

She turned her head away. 'Then you need do so in private.'

'Why?'

'For the love of…' She took a breath and started again. 'He is an Earl, William. An Earl. You showed great disrespect when you acted the way you did.'

First Hugh was going to tell him what to do with his wife. And now his wife was going to tell him what to do with Hugh? He choked back a laugh of disbelief. 'He has not always been an Earl, Sarah.'

'But he is now.'

'Since it bothers you so much, I vow that while we are at Wynnedom I will temper my actions in public.'

'We are going to Wynnedom?'

Her tone was suddenly too bright. The attention she'd turned on him was too…attentive. William frowned. 'I have agreed to train his men for a time. So, we are taking some of them to Wynnedom with us, while Hugh and Adrienna take the others to Hallison to see her father.'

'No.' Sarah jumped up from the log. Pacing before him, she shook her head. 'You can't do that.'

William leaned back, asking, 'And why is that?'

In her haste, she missed a step and stumbled. Quickly finding her footing, she answered, 'Because it isn't safe. We should all stick together.'

Her voice had risen and some of the men turned to stare at her. William lunged from his seat and pulled her across the clearing to the hut.

The men had cleaned out some of the debris and placed pallets on the floor for sleeping. A small fire blazed in the pit. William pushed Sarah down on to one of the pallets and went to prop the door across the opening. When she made a move to rise, he ordered, 'Stay there.'

'What are you doing?'

'I am going to have an uninterrupted discussion with my wife.'

'I'll scream.'

'If you must.' He unbuckled his sword belt and dropped it on to the floor. His tunic quickly followed.

Sarah's eyes grew large, shimmering in the flickering fire light. 'You wouldn't.'

He dropped down beside her on the pallet and unbuckled her girdle. She batted at his hands, causing him about as much distraction as a springtime breeze.

William flung the girdle on to the floor, then grasped the hem of her gown. She clung to his wrists, but it didn't prevent him from pulling the garment out from beneath her and then over her head, although he did have to free his wrists to tug the sleeves of her gown from her arms.

It would be rather difficult for her to leave the hut,

since he'd left her in nothing but her stockings, shoes and chemise. As he lofted her gown aside, he asked, 'I wouldn't what?'

She grabbed a blanket and held it up before her. 'You said you would not—'

William tore the cover from her clenched hands and laughed at her high-pitched squeak. He loomed over her, forcing her on to her back. 'I swear to you, Sarah, if you say that one more time I may change my mind about hurting you.'

'You are frightening me.' She tried to roll out of his reach. 'Just leave me alone, William.'

'And you are driving me to madness.' He easily pulled her back beneath him. 'I will never leave you alone.'

She trembled and turned her face away, whispering, 'What do you want?'

He traced the line of her jaw with a fingertip. Her skin was soft beneath his touch. 'You know what I want.'

Yes, she knew what he wanted. He wanted her to betray her vow to the Queen. And while a part of her urged she do just that, another part, the side of her that feared death, kept her quiet, when in truth what she should be fearing was this man pinning her to the ground, with nothing but the thin fabric of her chemise separating them. Yet, no matter what she'd said, his feathery touches, his warm breath and the weight of his hard thigh resting between her legs didn't frighten her in the least.

The heat washing over her wasn't from fear. She recognised the warmth, and knew that once again her body was striving to betray her.

Mustering all the bravado she could summon, she pushed at his chest. 'Get off me.'

He laughed softly, seductively against her ear. 'Not this time.'

'I despise you.' She silently cursed the lack of conviction in her voice.

He nuzzled the side of her neck until shivers raced down her body. 'That'll be a fine thing to tell our children.'

'Children?' Sarah laughed, hoping to anger him enough to make him stop this sweet torture. 'We will never sire children together.'

'Oh, and why is that?' William reached down and one agonising inch at a time, bunched the skirt of her chemise in his hand.

'Because I say so.' Sarah gasped as the night's cooler air raced along her legs.

He stroked her thigh with the back of his fingers. Once again she tried to roll away from his touch. But this time not only was she unsuccessful, the movement freed her last remaining garment from beneath her.

Before she could rectify that, William quickly removed even that small amount of protection from her.

He rose up on his knees, one leg still between hers and stared down at her. The unsteady light from the fire seemed to glow with an unearthly promise from his eyes.

Sarah crossed her arms over her naked breasts. 'William, please.'

'Please, what, Sarah?' He easily tugged her arms free and pinned them to the pallet with his hands. Leaning over her, he asked, 'Did you not tell me that a wife was nothing more than another possession?'

'Yes.' She closed her eyes and willed her frantically beating heart to slow. But it ignored her, racing fast and hard in her chest with expectation, waiting for his touch.

And when that touch came, it wasn't at all what she'd

expected. His calloused palm traced a swath of fire across her belly and up her ribcage before trailing down to stroke against her hip.

'What's to stop me from treating you as nothing more than another thing I own?'

Sarah opened her mouth to answer, but he placed a finger against her lips. 'Think before you speak, Sarah.'

She looked up at him. The hunger in his eyes was not that of a greedy man looking to claim another possession. Aye, it was still hunger. But it was a lingering type of hunger that sought more than a moment of pleasure.

Sarah was well familiar with that type of hunger. It was the kind that longed for human contact and friendship. The kind of hunger that wanted a touch to linger, to mean so much more than a hurried grope in the dark.

His hunger mirrored her own. When he cupped her face and traced his thumb over her cheek, she leaned into his touch and whispered, 'You will stop yourself, William.'

He nodded. 'People assume, because of my size, that I lack control and wits. I am capable of more control than anyone you have known, or will ever know. And do not mistake me for an oaf, Sarah. I am far from witless or uneducated.'

She felt her cheeks flush hot at his words. She had mistakenly thought those very things.

'You are naked beneath me. There is nothing you could do to prevent me from losing control should I wish to do so. Nothing. Not one man outside of this hut would answer your screams. No one would come to your aid, Sarah, no one.'

And she knew that was her own fault. She understood that her reputation had put her in this position.

What she didn't understand was why he warned her of all he could do.

She placed a hand on his arm and asked, 'Why are you doing this?'

'Trust me.' He leaned closer. 'Trust me, Sarah. I have stripped you naked and defenceless, but I have not harmed you. I have not given you cause to truly fear me. Nor will I. No matter what, you are safe with me.'

Trust. It was such a small word. Yet it meant so much. Could she trust him? And if she did, would he ever trust her? She took a deep breath. Finally, when her stomach stopped clenching and her heart slowed enough for her to speak, she admitted, 'Yes, yes, I still spy for the Queen. I was ordered to find out all I could about you and the Earl.'

She'd expected him to shout. To yell at her in anger and rage. Instead, he gritted his teeth, rose and then tugged his tunic over his head.

As he strapped on his sword belt, he pointed at her clothing without looking at her. 'Get dressed and come eat.'

Before she could shake away enough of her shock to say anything, he was gone.

Chapter Seven

William crossed the campsite and headed for the thick stand of trees opposite the hut. With each purposeful stride his chest tightened. And his stomach knotted as he tried to ignore the wildly growing havoc that used to be his self-control.

He dragged his fingers through his hair, surprised that his hand didn't shake harder. What had he been thinking?

'Sir William?'

Barely glancing at the guard who'd hailed him, William held up his hand and shook his head. He hoped the man understood his silent request for solitude.

The last thing he wanted at this moment was to be forced into thinking rationally. Outside of the memory of Sarah's lush, naked body, he possessed very few thoughts—none of them rational in the least.

He knew that he should be focused on the coming journey to Wynnedom. Arnyll was still out there, free to attack again. He'd failed once, so it was doubtful he'd repeat that mistake.

William needed to ensure the safety of the Earl's

men and Sarah. Ah, Sarah…soft, pale flesh, flat stomach, full hips…the visions spun through his mind until he thought he'd go mad with need.

He should be angry with her and he was…to a point. She'd finally confessed to what he'd already assumed—that, yes, she was still under Queen Eleanor's command. The thought sickened him.

And of course the Queen had commanded that Sarah discover all she could about him and the Earl. Why else would she have been so willing to accept this marriage and order Sarah from her court?

If they were still close enough to Poitiers, he might be tempted to send her back to the court—whether the Queen wanted her or not. But, as fate would have it, they weren't.

And there weren't enough men to spare as an escort. He'd not send her off on her own. It wasn't in him to be that cruel. A woman alone on the roads would face dangers worse than death. He'd not have that stain on his soul.

Besides, like it or not, she *was* his wife. And in truth, she bewitched him. He was honest enough to admit that this fascination with her was purely physical. He couldn't deny the lust he felt for this woman. Nor did he want to—not permanently. But for now, he had to find a way to concentrate on the task at hand.

Hugh's men had acquitted themselves well against Arnyll. They'd been outnumbered, inexperienced and still had come out of the skirmish the victors. But Arnyll hadn't expected an attack. The guards from Wynnedom hadn't been in Normandy with their lord, so Arnyll most likely had not been aware of their existence.

He was now. And he'd not make the mistake of being caught off guard again. That meant, of course, that Arnyll would be watching them.

Once the group broke into two, on which set of men would he focus his attention? Who was he more intent on killing? Him, or the Earl? William narrowed his eyes and stared toward the clearing. Who might have the answer to that question?

Sarah.

Whether she'd be willing to share that information or not was something else altogether. Especially since he'd so abused her sensibilities.

He rubbed his knuckles against the stubble on his cheek, wondering if he'd dare try anything that high-handed again. It was doubtful she'd be so easily seduced a second time. The look of outraged horror on her face when he'd left the hut had been murderous. In his mind's eye he could envision Sarah using his own dagger against him if he were foolish enough to try something so bold again.

A smile crossed his mouth at the thought of such a tempting challenge. Though it was unfair to use such a ploy against her, it did break up the monotony of the journey.

As the memory of her body, her sigh of surrender and her obvious sensuality flooded his mind and body, he frowned. On the other hand, using such a ploy didn't necessarily work only against *her*.

Why was it so difficult to remember that he'd had to use such extreme measures to force, or rather, to trick the truth from her? What was it about this woman that bewitched him so and caused him to act with such single-minded determination?

He'd wed Sarah for many reasons—none of them related to tender feelings. Since King Henry had given him a keep—ramshackle as it might be—William knew he needed to be thinking about sons. Once the keep was in order, it would need a lady. Most of all, he had thought, and still did, that she needed someone to care for her, to offer her protection and safety.

Protection? He'd used her own passion against her in a cold, calculating manner. Perhaps she needed more protection against him rather than from him.

Trust him? Sarah jerked her gown over her head with a curse. When had he given her reason to trust him? She scooped her girdle from the floor, tied it around her waist, and then straightened the skirt of her gown.

With a heavy sigh, Sarah sank down on to the pallet. This was the very reason she had avoided emotional and physical involvement with others. Even as a child she had been able to identify the hunger, the need deep inside that so desperately wanted someone, anyone, to care for her. She'd learned time and time again that taking the risk was not worth the price one paid.

Had her father not cast her aside? When, at an early age, she'd begun to look more like a woman than a child, had not the other girls tormented and shunned her?

Had not the young men showered her with affection only to turn away when she would not share their bed? Even the Queen, who had treated her fairly as a child, demanded payment for that treatment once Sarah had grown into a young woman.

No, the risk of trusting William was not worth the price. Why had she forgotten the pain that came with the price? How could she trust him when she could not even trust herself?

She knew her weaknesses. It wasn't so much that she was unable to control the desire racing through her veins at his touch, it was more that his touch awakened the hunger.

Once awakened, the need seemed to claw at her. It cried out so strongly for fulfilment, that for a reason she could not name, she'd been willing to attempt the risk. What had it gained her?

Sarah angrily swiped at her watering eyes. It'd gained her this tightness in her chest, and this nearly unbearable heaviness that had settled around her heart.

She didn't blame William. He was only the instrument that caused her hurt. *She* had allowed herself to willingly open the door and invite the pain inside. Now, somehow, she had to work out how to close and lock that door.

'Sarah, I thought you were asleep.'

Asleep? Shaking her head to rid herself of the fog clouding her mind, Sarah looked up at Adrienna. 'No.'

'Have you eaten?'

'I'm not hungry.' Actually, she feared that putting food into her churning stomach would only upset it more.

Adrienna stretched out on the opposite pallet. Rolling on to her side, she asked, 'Is something wrong?'

'No. Nothing at all.'

'Are you sure? You appear overwrought.'

Sarah forced herself not to laugh. 'What reason would I have to be overwrought?'

'Has William talked to you yet?'

Oh, he'd done more than *talked* to her, but she wasn't admitting her foolishness to Adrienna. 'About Wynnedom and the guards? Yes, he told me.'

'What do you think of their idea?'

It was obvious by Adrienna's lacklustre tone of voice that she wasn't at all pleased with the idea.

At the moment, Sarah had no opinion of their plans. It would make fulfilling her task for the Queen impossible—for now. She would not be able to complete her task until the Earl and Adrienna joined them at Wynnedom.

While it would be a mere delay, she knew the Queen would be enraged. And while that should upset her, or even frighten her, Sarah simply didn't care.

After all, what was the worst Queen Eleanor would do to her? Kill her? The realisation that it suddenly didn't matter to her was rather intriguing…frightening in a way…but what did she have to look forward to?

'Sarah?'

She shook her head, trying to clear the darkening thoughts teasing at her. 'They will do what they wish, Adrienna. What difference does it make if I like their plans or not?'

A few moments passed before Adrienna broke the silence. 'I can see that something is wrong. Is there anything I can do to help?'

'Why would you want to help me?'

'Because you helped me escape from Richard. I can see that you are unhappy.'

'Unhappy? Why would I be unhappy? Nothing has gone as planned.'

Adrienna sat up. 'I know you were supposed to marry Hugh.'

Sarah blinked. To her surprise, she'd nearly forgotten that little detail. 'The man himself didn't matter. But I was supposed to be wed to someone with a title, someone with wealth. Instead I received neither.'

'William is a good man.' Adrienna reached across the distance and touched Sarah's arm. 'Perhaps in time you will come to care for each other.'

'In time?' Sarah moved away from Adrienna's touch. 'He is my husband, nothing more.' She ignored the sharp stabbing in her stomach and added, 'It matters not what we feel for each other.'

'Matters not? Wouldn't it be better if you…' Adrienna hesitated a moment before finishing her question '…cared for each other?'

'Are you talking about caring, or love?' Sarah resisted the urge to roll her eyes. 'You do realise that love only exists in the troubadours' tales? It is an ideal, not something on which to base a marriage.'

'Can't marriages be for something other than what two people bring to the union?'

'For people who possess nothing—perhaps.' Sarah shrugged. She doubted the veracity of her statement. Everyone possessed something. Whether that something be tangible or not. 'But for those with title, gold or land, no.'

On a sigh, Adrienna said, 'I feel sorry for you, Sarah.'

Not wanting anyone's pity, Sarah rose. 'There is no need. I am not afraid to see what I have, or will not have. You, on the other hand, would do yourself a great favour if you ceased your foolish notions. Do not waste your time, or your tender heart, looking for something you will never find.'

Before Adrienna could respond, Sarah left the hut. She had no idea where she was going. With luck she would be able to find someplace quiet where she could be left alone.

Unfortunately, her husband saw her exit the hut and immediately approached her. With a curse, Sarah quickly turned on her heels and headed toward the stream. She was in no mood to defend herself against William.

'Sarah, stop.' He stepped in front of her, preventing her escape. 'We must talk.'

'No. We have *talked* enough, thank you.'

'No? If you are waiting for an apology for earlier—'

She looked up at him, cutting off his words. 'What new game is this?' What tactic was he employing now?

'Game? This is no game.'

She couldn't have stopped the short, brittle laugh from escaping had she tried. While his comment, and this entire situation, was far from humorous, if she didn't laugh, Sarah knew she'd cry from pure frustration. 'Fine. I accept your apology.' She tugged her wrist free. 'Now, leave me alone.'

'Since I did nothing wrong, I did *not* apologise.' He let her pass, then followed her along the path that circled the perimeter of the clearing. 'And I won't leave you alone. I can't do that.'

'Of course you can.' Without stopping, or looking at him, she said, 'It is very easy, William. You turn around and go back to the fire with the other men.'

'You don't understand.'

'I understand enough.' She stumbled over a root and shook off his assistance. 'I understand that you are but using another tactic to garner more information, or—' Sarah stopped and turned to face him. 'You wish to torment me further. Would you like me to remove my gown myself this time?'

When he didn't respond, she pointed deeper into the woods. 'Should we retire to some place more private?' She grasped the skirt of her gown. 'Or would here do just as well for you?'

Something in his stance, the tightening of his muscles, the squaring of his shoulders, warned her that she had gone too far. She took a step backwards and released her gown, letting it fall into place.

Instinct urged her to run. But the twin reflections of the raging fire glittering in his eyes held her spellbound. Intent on coaxing her suddenly wobbly legs to move, to take her away from the danger she'd incited, Sarah took another step backwards.

Just as she started to turn, to make good her escape, William grabbed her arms and pulled her roughly against his chest. Any hope for escape evaporated, but she knew better than to let him sense her building fear.

Forcing a measure of boldness into her limbs, and hopefully into her voice, she looked up at him. 'Yes, you are much larger, and stronger, than I. Didn't we already know that?'

He smiled down at her with an expression that held no trace of humour. Instead, she saw a promise that chilled her blood and drew a gasp from her. 'Let me go, William.'

'No. I am not one of your court swains you can order about on a whim. You married a battle-hardened warrior, Sarah. Perhaps it is time you realise what that means.'

Unwilling to back down, even when she knew this skirmish was doomed, she held his stare and asked, 'So what do you intend to do, *warrior*? Use brute force to teach me my place?'

Without releasing her, he started moving, forcing her to walk backwards. 'The idea has much merit.'

'You wouldn't dare.'

'For someone who knows me so little, you say that quite often. I wonder what you will do once you discover your mistake.'

Sarah paused. Until this moment she'd not thought

there was truly a reason to fear him. Had she been mistaken?

'You said that no matter what, I would be safe with you,' she reminded him of his earlier vow. 'Did you lie?'

'Safe doesn't mean you can say, or do, whatever you please. You are my wife, Sarah, and it is past time you acted as such.'

She knew exactly what he implied and chose to misunderstand him on purpose. 'Acted as such? Meaning what, William? That I should be meek and obedient? That I should obey your every command, jump to satisfy your every whim?'

'That would be a place to start.'

'What?' Her question split through the night about two octaves higher than she'd intended. Sarah swallowed hard, then asked in a less strident tone of voice, 'Surely you are not serious?'

He stopped walking and released her. 'We will find out soon. Go inside.'

Inside what? Confused, she turned around and stared in shock at the makeshift lean-to tent situated just off the edge of the clearing. A lit torch nearby let her see that this structure, devised of ropes and covers, would provide far too much privacy, while at the same time keep them close to the guards.

'No.' She shook her head. 'There is a perfectly sound hut to sleep in tonight.'

'The Earl and his wife are sharing that hut.' William held the end flap open. 'Besides, I didn't ask you. Go inside, Sarah.'

She tried stalling. 'Would we not be safer with the others?'

'They are but a few feet away. Inside.'

She eyed him warily. 'We aren't going to…you won't…we—'

He pulled her towards the tent. 'We won't what? Validate this marriage? It is about time, don't you agree?'

She tried to back away from the tent, but he blocked her retreat. 'You can get inside of your own free will, or I will drag you in. The choice is yours.'

Choice? What choice was there in that? Sarah fought the tremors setting her legs shaking. Knowing he'd make good his threat, she crawled into the tent and knelt on the pallet.

William entered and then dropped the flap, dousing them in a semi-darkness illuminated only by the wavering torchlight. He removed his boots and tunic before he stretched out on his side next to her. Propped up on one arm, he held the other one out to her, beckoning, 'Come here.'

She wrapped her arms round her stomach and shook her head. But he ignored her obvious refusal, and easily pulled her down next to him, suggesting, 'Let's try something different this time.'

Sarah didn't want to try anything—different or not. But she was fairly certain he'd leave her no choice in that either. With her arms crossed tightly against her chest, she held herself as stiffly as possible, and leaned away from the warmth of his body.

William stroked her neck before resting his hand on her shoulder. His touch had been gentle, almost soothing. 'See if you can pretend that being married to me isn't the worst thing that ever happened in your life.'

Is that what he thought? 'I never said that.'

'You didn't have to say it, you've made it plain without words.'

'What difference does it make to you? You forced me to accept this marriage. It is not as if we shared any feelings for each other.'

He laughed softly. His breath lifted the stray strands of her hair before rushing warm against her cheek. 'After tonight it won't make any difference.'

After tonight? 'Why is that?' No sooner had she asked the question when the answer slammed against her temples.

He trailed a fingertip up and down her arm, chasing the shivers from shoulder to elbow. 'I am done being your husband in name only.'

Sarah tightly closed her eyes against the thoughts crowding her mind. It would take little more than the feel of his calloused hands against her flesh, the touch of his lips against hers to coax her into agreeing.

As if seeing into her thoughts, William nudged her on to her back and pulled her arms apart, holding them loosely over her head. 'You have no comment, no argument?'

Silently cursing the languid warmth coming to life in her body as he settled himself atop her, she asked, 'What would you have me say?'

His lips singed the tender flesh of her neck. 'I would have you decide yes, or no.' He traced the line of her jaw to her mouth. 'Tell me to go…' her lips tingled under his teasing touch '…or…tell me to stay.'

Chapter Eight

Once again William was giving her a choice. Truly become his wife, or keep believing that somehow the Queen would set her free from him. Sarah didn't know which choice to make.

She gritted her teeth. Queen Eleanor would not set her free. Not now. Not once she discovered that the men had separated, delaying Sarah in discovering the information the Queen wanted. But if she turned William away now, would he ever give her the chance to do so again?

Uncertain, she blurted out, 'I don't know.'

He released her wrists. 'Then let me help you decide.'

His voice was gravelly against her ear. The deep tone rippled through her, chasing away any anger, any fear that he was but using her, employing yet another tactic to gain something he wanted. And when he cupped her breast, brushing his thumb across the sensitive tip, she no longer cared.

Sarah arched into his touch. She would hate herself tomorrow.

He inched up the skirts of her gown and chemise. The

cool night air rushed against her legs, but William chased away the gooseflesh with his calloused palms. She would fret and worry…tomorrow.

Slowly, deliberately he slid his hands up her legs, over her hips and stomach, pushing her garments higher with each passing inch until he finally tugged them from beneath her and over her head. Tonight…tonight Sarah knew she would foolishly risk assuaging the need that clawed at her.

William leaned forwards and captured her trembling sigh of surrender with his lips. What began as a soft, gentle kiss quickly deepened, leaving her dizzy and wanting something more.

She slipped her hands beneath his shirt and stroked his back. His skin was hot beneath her touch. Her fingers traced the myriad of scars marring the flesh that covered hard muscles. Briefly she wondered what had caused such long, thin marks, but he distracted her from her unspoken questions by caressing the fullness of her hip.

To her amazement, he suffered her exploration of his body without comment. She marvelled at the play of his flesh over the bunching muscles of his hips as he moved. And when she grew more bold, sliding her hands up his chest, pausing to circle his flat nipples, he buried his face in her neck.

Concerned she'd done something wrong, she pulled her hands from beneath his shirt.

William rose up on his knees and nearly ripped his shirt off before placing her hand on his chest as he came back over her. 'Don't stop.'

The deep husky tone of his voice wiped away her concerns and she eagerly resumed her exploration.

Where she was soft, he was hard. Where her body curved into roundness, his was hard planes of muscle.

Yet his flesh trembled beneath her fingertips the same as hers did beneath his touch. His heart pounded in his chest as fast, and as hard, as hers did. And his ragged breaths mingled with hers.

Did her touch feed his hunger in the same manner? Did it grow stronger, more ferocious with each seeking stroke? Did he still yearn for something more, something that would stop the ceaseless throbbing at her core?

Sarah arched her back, curling her fingers into the flesh of his back and moaned in frustration. His shoulders shook briefly beneath her hands, before he rose up on his knees between her legs.

'You know full well what I want, Sarah. Yes, or no?'

A few heartbeats passed before she could form a logical thought. The man believed her to be a whore, to have enough experience to know exactly what he wanted.

While she knew what the physical act consisted of, Sarah hadn't the slightest clue of how she was to act. What was she to say, or do? How was she to respond?

'Sarah?'

She looked up at him. He held her stare as he trailed one hand the length of her torso, coming to rest low on her belly.

Had someone placed a lit torch against her skin she doubted if it would have burned as hotly as his touch. Until he trailed lower. Then she knew what would burn hotter and what would satisfy the hunger clawing at her.

'Yes,' Sarah answered, surprised at the rasp of her own voice.

She closed her eyes, expecting him to remove the rest of his clothes and take her with no further teasing.

She jumped when his lips followed the path his hand had just taken.

Her senses swirled impossibly faster as his feathery touch skimmed down her body, chasing the flames gathering at her core. His hands encompassed her hips, fingers pressing into the soft flesh, holding her steady.

Suddenly, for some reason she couldn't fathom, the urge to stop him, to protect herself by not taking such a large risk, washed over her. Afraid, she tensed, prepared to cry out for him to stop. But the urge vanished beneath William's seductive touch.

The heat built, sending the hunger and need raging out of control. Unable to bear the sensations racking her, she did cry out.

Before her next breath escaped, he loomed over her. 'Kiss me.'

Nervous about what was to come, she tentatively met his lips. He swore softly at her gentle kiss, then moved his mouth more firmly over hers, stealing her thoughts and worries.

Her breath caught in her throat. She wrapped her arms around him, pressing up against his chest, seeking to somehow get closer.

William gathered her tightly against his chest. Something wasn't right. She was too hesitant, too wide-eyed surprised, far too…inexperienced.

He'd told her once that if all rumours were true he'd be a monster from Hades. Did the rumours about her contain any truth whatsoever? Somehow he suddenly doubted it.

If his wife was a virgin, then everything he'd been led to believe about her had been nothing more than artfully contrived lies. An odd feeling growing in the pit of his stomach persuaded him not to discover that answer this night.

His raging desire rebelled at that decision. William gritted his teeth against the building frustration, telling himself that nobody ever truly died from not satisfying lust.

He loosened his embrace from around Sarah and rolled on to his back.

'William?' Confusion rang loud and clear in her voice.

'What?'

'Did I do something wrong?'

It was all he could do not to laugh at the question. How ironic that his *harlot* wife worried that she'd done something wrong.

When he didn't answer, she sat up beside him and slid her hand down his chest. 'Is there something that I need to—?'

'No.' He caught her hand, stopping her from stroking his heated flesh. 'There is nothing you need do. Just be still.'

After she settled alongside him, William pulled the covers up and turned on to his side, facing her. He brushed his fingers across her face, and asked, 'Sarah, if I ask you something, will you answer me honestly?'

She remained silent for a few moments, but finally nodded.

'Who is Arnyll chasing?'

When she began to move away, he held her fast. 'Sarah, I need to know.'

She drew in a slow breath, then answered, 'I don't know. I met him only once and the Queen never spoke of him.'

William rolled on to his back. This time he kept her

in his embrace. He stared up at the ceiling of tent. The torch flickered out, leaving them in darkness.

Had she told him the truth? Unfortunately, if she had, that meant Arnyll was chasing him and the Earl.

Why? Who had sent him? What evil did the man plan?

His questions drifted off at the feel of tears soaking his chest. He didn't like the tears. And while he had no reason to feel guilty for them, he did. Tears were useless and guilt always proved a weakness.

He pulled Sarah closer to his side, hoping to stem her tears. But the tightening of his embrace only startled her. She'd been crying in her sleep.

William sighed. He'd cast himself into a fine net. He was wed to the most beautiful, sensual, desirable woman he'd ever met. And he didn't trust her in the least.

How could he, when she'd admitted that she was spying on him and Hugh for the Queen? And to make matters worse, he suspected that she wasn't who, or what, she'd pretended to be.

Certain by her easy breathing that she once again slept, he gently stroked the back of her head. 'Ah, Sarah, what am I to do with you?'

Sarah stared at a spot between her horse's ears. Her back and shoulders ached from holding herself so stiffly for most of the last two long, agonising days.

Yesterday, she had awakened to a heavy pall of regret that had still not lifted. Despite her vow not to shed any tears, she knew she'd fallen into a fitful sleep crying— for no apparent reason. To make matters worse, some time during that night, between dreaming and waking, she'd felt William gently stroking her hair. His voice had been soft, almost…tender.

Obviously it had been in a dream—or in one of the nightmares that chased her from sleep. Because from the way he had ignored her yesterday, then left her to sleep on the pallet alone last night, only to avoid her today also, he'd made it painfully aware that he wanted nothing to do with her.

Why? More to the point, why did his avoidance leave her emotionally exhausted? Instead of brooding about being left alone, she should be happy and relieved. But she felt far from relieved.

He had been the one who had changed his mind about sealing this marriage. Sarah lowered her head to hide her face as her cheeks and body flushed with warmth at the memory. He needn't have changed his mind, for she wouldn't have lifted a hand to stop him.

Had the thought of bedding a whore been too much to bear? Or had she done something to make him realise she wasn't as experienced as her reputation led some to believe?

Unfortunately, she didn't know. How could she? Never had she found herself naked in a man's bed before. Her pitiful experience at being the Queen's whore had been limited to stolen kisses and laughing promises that were never fulfilled.

Nor could she understand why William would be bothered to know his wife might possibly be a virgin. And she most certainly wasn't going to ask. Doing so would be admitting that once again she'd lied to him.

Could her life get any worse? It wasn't enough that obtaining the information Queen Eleanor wanted would be delayed. Or that her husband was apparently angry with her.

But Sarah also had the impression that William

hadn't believed her about Arnyll. She'd told him the truth though. The one, and only, time she'd met Stefan of Arnyll had been in the Queen's chambers. Shivers racked her at the memory. She'd been in his presence mere moments and that had been too long.

He'd been polite enough, but something cold and evil had lurked behind his piercing stare. That single meeting had told her all she needed to know—he was vile and held little, or no, regard for human life. After that, she'd gone out of her way to avoid him.

Whether William believed her or not, she had no idea why Arnyll followed them—or who he was after.

Eleanor would be angry. William was already angry. And she simply loathed herself.

'We'll stop here for the day.'

William's voice startled her out of her morose thoughts. She'd not heard him ride alongside of her. She turned to respond, but her tongue stuck to the roof of her suddenly dry mouth.

He'd dressed in a fashion she'd never seen at court. Breeches covered his lower half. The snug-fitting garment did little to conceal the bulging muscles of his thighs.

But those muscles, while well defined, were still covered by something, unlike the ones of his bared arms. Instead of a tunic, William wore a sleeveless shirt that did nothing to hide over-developed biceps.

His only form of protection was a short, mailed habergeon. The short, sleeveless piece fell just to the top of the wide leather belt cinching his waist. The belt only served to accent the flare of his chest.

But the final touch, the one that made him look like a warrior of old, were the crossed swords strapped to his back. He obviously gave little thought to his own protection. The absence of not only a full-length hauberk to cover his body, but also of a shield and helm, proved that.

Her husband gave more thought to the attack than to defence. Ah, but with his weapons, clothing and fierce scowl, who would notice he was essentially unprotected?

Not that she was complaining at the vision, but it did little to keep her mind focused on her hurt feelings.

Sarah tore her gaze away to glance at the sky. It was harder to tear her tongue free. Finally regaining the ability to speak, she said, 'But there are still hours of daylight left.'

'I can see that.'

'So, we should keep going.'

His eyebrows disappeared beneath the hair that had fallen across his forehead. 'I said we stop.'

She resisted the odd urge to brush the brown strands of hair from his face. Sarah closed her eyes, certain she was losing her mind. What was wrong with her? After not speaking to her for nearly two days, he was now brusquely ordering her about and she found herself utterly fascinated with his body and hair.

She jerked her horse to a dead halt in the middle of the road. 'Fine, my lord, we stop.'

William just shook his head and moved his beast around her to the clearing ahead. Five of the six guards travelling with them followed William. The last stopped beside her. 'My lady?'

She stared at him, trying to remember his name. Finally, her fog-shrouded mind found it. 'I am fine, Matthew, join the others. I will be along in a moment.'

'No.' The young man glanced toward William. 'I think it wiser if you are not left alone.'

Her husband didn't seem to care, why should this

guard? 'It isn't as if they are leagues away from us.' She nodded towards the clearing a few yards ahead, asking, 'What can happen between here and there?'

'I suppose nothing, my lady.'

Lady. She hadn't been called that since leaving the Queen's court. This man had addressed her as such twice already and she realised she liked it.

Sarah glanced toward her husband. She knew she could soon be treading extremely hot water. She didn't know William well enough to determine if another man's attention, no matter how innocent, would anger him even further. It wouldn't be fair to pit this slightly built youth against her husband.

'Please, Sir Matthew, I wish a few moments alone.'

The young man frowned as he looked at the clearing, then back at her. 'I like it not, but if you are certain…'

'I am.'

Thankfully, he didn't argue any further and left her alone. In no hurry to join William and the other men, Sarah relaxed on the saddle.

The streaming sunshine that broke through the canopy of tree branches overhead was warm. She closed her eyes and lifted her face to the sun. A slight breeze brushed gently against her cheeks. Sarah inhaled deeply, taking in the scent of spring. This was nice. She would be content to sit here the rest of the day.

A strong arm wrapped around her waist. She screamed, 'Let me go!' and lashed out with her hand, catching the intruder across his temple, before she could determine who had grabbed her.

'Cease!'

At William's roar, Sarah froze. She stared down at him. 'What were you thinking to come up on me like that?'

He lifted her from the horse. 'Me? What were you thinking to sit here alone and unguarded?'

When he lowered her to her feet, she pulled away from his hold. 'I could have hurt you.'

'With what? Your scream?'

His arrogant tone pricked her anger to life. 'Don't you make fun of me.' She reached out and poked a finger against his chest. 'If I'd had a dagger at hand, I could have done you serious harm.'

'Don't.'

She narrowed her eyes. Poking at his chest again, she asked, 'Don't what?'

'That.' William grabbed her hand. 'Don't do that.'

She shoved her hand forwards, poking his chest yet again.

'Sarah, I am warning you.'

His tone wasn't one of anger, it sounded more irritated, more frustrated, than irate. She got the impression he was as open to an argument as she was. It was time to clear the air between them, and perhaps this would be the way to do so.

This time when she made a move to poke him, William took a step forwards, bringing him against her. Instead of stopping, he kept walking, forcing her to step backwards until the trunk of a tree halted their progress.

Pinned between the hard tree behind her and the hard chest before her, she took a deep breath. Then she looked up at him, asking, 'Are you trying to frighten me?'

'No. If I were trying to do so, you would be trembling with fear.'

'You think you could make me that afraid?'

He released her hand and tilted her chin up with the

side of a finger. 'My dear wife, I have killed armed men with my bare hands in order to eat. I am certain you would prove an easy mark were I set on terrifying you.'

Killed armed men with his bare hands in order to eat? His statement ran round and round inside her mind. What sort of life required something that horrendous? None that she could think of.

Certain he was making it up, she jerked her head away from his touch. 'Yes, I'm sure you could frighten me. But then you'd have to pay attention to me and it is doubtful that is going to happen.'

'What's wrong, Sarah? Are you angry that I've ignored you and left you to yourself?'

There was no reason to lie about it. 'Of course I am.'

'Now you know how it feels.'

'You were just repaying me in kind? I ignored you for good reason.'

'And what *good* reason would that be?'

'I was not pleased to have been forced into this marriage.'

'And neither am I.'

Shocked at his admission, she reminded him, 'You are the one who demanded we wed.'

'I demanded to wed the Queen's whore. I have to wonder if even that had been fabricated.'

This arguing was a mistake. She should have been meek instead of combatant. It was just as she had feared. He'd guessed at her inexperience. Now what was she going to do?

Before she could think of a response, he pressed tighter against her. 'Is everything a lie, Sarah? Is there anything honest or true about you? The Queen readily accepted this marriage so you could still play her spy.'

When she remained silent, he asked, 'Do you now deny that?'

She shook her head. 'No. I don't. But I told you that.'

'Of course you did. Long after we'd left the Queen's court and only after I coerced you into admitting it.'

'William, I—'

'What about your family? Your father, your mother. The reason you were brought to court. Was any of that truthful?'

'Yes.' She nearly choked, but managed to shake her head and add, 'Yes. That was all true.'

He lowered his head and threatened softly against her ear, 'Don't start crying.'

She swallowed the lump building in her throat. 'I did kill my mother and for that my father set me aside.'

'No, Sarah.' William's lips brushed across her temple. 'You did not kill your mother.'

She wasn't going to argue with him. He hadn't been there. She had and knew full well that her mother's accident had been her fault.

'What about Arnyll? Did you tell me all you know?'

Sarah nodded. 'Yes. Yes, I did. I swear I did.'

He straightened, but didn't move away. 'Did I wed the Queen's whore?'

She looked up at him. His eyes blazed, giving lie to the gentle tone he'd use a moment past. Oh, he was good and angry. And his rage refuelled her own.

'Is that what you want? To be wed to a harlot?'

'It is no less than what I expected.'

Far be it for her to deny him. Set on convincing him she was everything her reputation claimed, Sarah stiffened her spine and laced her fingers behind the wide belt at his waist. 'Then rest assured, a whore for a wife is what you have.'

When he said nothing, she knew she'd have to brazen this out on her own. Sarah smiled and tugged at his belt. 'Does that frighten you?'

His speed was breathtaking. Sarah gasped as he held her against tree. She refused to flinch from the bite of the mail pressing into her breasts, or the ire radiating from him like hot coals in a brazier.

'That's it, William. Show me how much you desire a whore.'

'Do not tempt me, Sarah.'

The deep tone of his voice, and the raw lust shimmering in his eyes, awakened her own desire, making her feel reckless.

'Why not? Isn't this what you wanted? Or does it make you despise me even more?'

'That isn't possible.'

With her body held against his, it was impossible not to feel the hardness of his so-called *hate* pushing against her belly. Yet, he'd made no attempt to seek privacy, leaving them in full view of his men. Sarah realised this was nothing more than a test of wills. One she wasn't about to lose.

'But I don't hate you, William.' She slid her hands up the solid hardness of his biceps, grazing his flesh with her nails, then across his shoulders to brush her fingertips along his neck. 'And I don't think you hate me either.'

Before he could say anything in response, she threaded her fingers through his hair and then jerked his head forwards. Sarah whispered against his lips, 'Kiss me, William.'

To her relief he did as she bid. His kiss wasn't gentle,

but she didn't expect it to be—didn't want it to be. She had no wish for soft, feathery touches.

She was angry. He was angrier. She wanted to merge their rage into passion, and then let it burn hot enough to extinguish itself. If that was wrong, and he found it revolting, so be it.

Far from acting revolted, William branded her with his lips, laying claim to her, and yet she still wanted more. This testing of wills seduced her as much as it did him. Sarah wrapped her legs around his waist, moaning when he slid his hands beneath her to pull her tightly against him.

Too soon he broke their kiss on a ragged groan and buried his face against her neck. 'Sarah, what are you doing?'

She tightened her legs about him, not wanting him to stop. 'Only what you wanted.'

'Ah, Sarah, you lack the experience to play with fire in such a manner. You could get burned.'

'Then burn me, William. Do you forget? I am the Queen's whore.'

'I forget nothing.' He released her.

The air rushing between them did little to cool the heat of her body. She reached for him, wanting to be back in his embrace. But he stepped away. 'There is work to be done.'

Sarah caught his hand and tried tugging him towards her. 'There is work waiting for you here.'

He easily shook off her hold. 'Sarah, this is neither the time, nor the place, to give lust free rein.'

Aye, he'd been testing her. Through gritted teeth, she said, 'Then go.'

She started walking by him to return to her horse and

was caught fast in a strong pair of arms. He lifted her against his chest, only to re-ignite her passion.

Against her ear he warned gruffly, 'Later, Sarah. After camp is made and we've eaten. We will give that lust free rein, for however long you desire.'

Before she could catch her breath, or make a sound, he released her and headed back to the camp, leaving her to follow in a haze of desire and need.

Chapter Nine

William crouched down behind a thicket, hoping to catch another hare or two off guard in the underbrush. He'd brought two of the guards along to hunt with him, leaving the other four to protect Sarah.

After a couple of hours they'd managed to catch two hares, but it wasn't going to be enough. He was going to require more nourishment than what they'd brought along and caught thus far, if he was to fulfil his vow to Sarah this night.

His heart kicked like an unbroken rearing horse inside his chest at the thought of making love to her all night. The woman's passions, whether it be anger or lust, flamed swift and hot.

But then, so did his. He'd been painfully aware of that when she'd tried to convince him she was an experienced whore. Had they been secluded, he would have taken her then and there.

There was no doubt in William's mind that this wife of his had stolen his ability to reason. But then, she didn't seem too rational herself at times. And that was fine. He rather enjoyed her heated display earlier. Instead of trembling beneath his anger, she'd thrown it back in his face.

Since it had never happened before, he couldn't help but admire a woman who stood toe to toe with him. Whether it was because she possessed strength of will, or lack of wits, didn't matter. Her plan of attack had worked.

A movement in the underbrush caught his attention, and he motioned toward Paul on his left, and then to Simon on his right. The two guards stealthily crept towards the movement, their arrows notched.

Just as they drew back on their bowstrings a scream split the silence. Birds flew cawing loudly from the trees, the hare darted from the underbrush and disappeared. And William's heart seized at the terror in Sarah's scream.

He reached over his head and slid both swords from the scabbards strapped to his back as he raced toward the clearing. Intent on finding Sarah, he stumbled over the dead body of one of the guards. The other three lay face down in the dirt.

'Sarah!' William's shout went unanswered.

The two remaining guards skidded to a halt behind him. 'Sir William?' Surprise was evident in the high-pitched voice.

William surveyed the perimeter of the clearing. The horses were gone—along with his wife. Two pairs of footprints, one larger than the other, near the log he'd last seen her sitting on led him to believe that at least two people had taken her.

He turned his attention to the dead guards. The arrows sticking out of their necks gave evidence that they'd died quickly.

He winced at the sight of Matthew—this had been the lad's first mission. He shouldn't have had to die so young.

He leaned over the guard's body, rolling him over on to his back and snatched free a rolled missive tucked in the neck edge of his hauberk. The handwriting was little more than a scrawl, but he understood the words. William swallowed hard against the heaving of his stomach.

Arnyll had captured his wife for the slave master Aryseeth.

Memories of his years in captivity, and the living hell it had been, flooded his mind, setting his legs to tremble beneath the weight of his fear. Not for himself, but for Sarah. No one deserved to bear what he had gone through, least of all his wife.

Whatever strength of will she possessed would be stripped from her. The methods employed would quickly have her begging for death.

He'd sooner take her place than leave her to suffer such a fate. An option granted in the missive. A boon that he knew would not be honoured.

Yet, he had no choice other than to journey to Kendal. If he was correct, and Sarah would not be released when he gave himself up, he would take her life before letting her endure Aryseeth's torture.

It would be the only act of love he would ever have the opportunity to grant her.

'My lord?'

William shook the horrors from his thoughts, and turned to the guards, ordering, 'Find the horses.' Before the men left the clearing, he added, 'Stay alert and together.'

While they were gone, he would bury the dead. Once that was done, and he had possession of a mount, he would send the last two guards to find King Henry. And he would go alone to find his wife.

For the first time that he could remember, William dropped to his knees. Without hesitation, he did something that he'd never once done for himself—he prayed for her safety.

'He will kill you for this.' From her seat on the ground, Sarah stared at Richard of Langsford and Stefan of Arnyll through the campfire, adding, 'And I hope he does it slowly.'

She still could hardly believe that these two court lackeys had killed four guards, and then spirited her away from the camp, in a matter of moments. But a tug on the thongs binding her wrists behind her gave credence to the surprise attack.

It was no wonder William had been so intent on finding out what she knew about Arnyll. She now wished that she hadn't avoided Arnyll while at court. Perhaps then she would have had some information to give William.

Sarah closed her eyes at the ludicrous thought. It wasn't as if she'd readily given her husband any information. He'd had to coerce every tiny scrap from her.

'Where are you taking me?'

Arnyll laughed at her question, but provided no answer. He simply nodded to his companion.

Langsford rose from his seat by the fire and approached. The dark snarling hate on his face boded ill.

Sarah shrank back against the tree, wishing she could hide within the trunk. She recognised her error when a smirk briefly crossed his mouth.

Forcing herself to set aside the fear biting at her, she

stiffened her spine. 'What are you doing with the likes of him?' She nodded toward Arnyll.

Richard cracked the palm of his hand against her cheek. 'Close your mouth.'

Shaking the stars from her blurry vision, Sarah ignored his order. She'd been hit harder before and had a crooked nose to show for it. Richard's slap only split her lip. She spat her blood at him, then taunted, 'Do that again and William will crush you with his bare hands.'

Actually, it probably didn't matter if Richard slapped her again or not. There was little doubt that he would live once William found them.

That was her only hope—that William would come looking for her. Surely he wouldn't return to camp, find the men dead and simply ride away? No. She couldn't let herself believe that for a moment.

Even if he came after her only because she was his, and not because of any feelings for her, Sarah would be grateful. She didn't deserve, or expect, any tender feelings from William. Not after the way she'd lied to him and played him false.

Richard grabbed her braid and wound it around his hand. Using the hair as a lead of sorts, he shook her until her teeth rattled against each other. 'After what you did to me, you should be thankful to be alive.'

She knew he was referring to her helping Adrienna escape his clutches. While she was supposed to have tricked the Earl to her bed, Richard was to make certain Adrienna was found in his—even if it had required force. Sarah had realised that Richard would enjoy employing force, and had helped Adrienna escape before it'd been too late.

Langsford's stare seemed near inhuman and she

couldn't help but wonder if she'd be as fortunate. Would anyone rescue her before this man, or his friend, did her serious harm?

Arnyll came up beside him. He placed his hand on Richard's shoulder, and said, 'Do not damage our prize.'

'I deserve to play with her a bit.' Langsford sounded like a snivelling child who'd been denied a treat.

'Oh, I never said you could not play.' Arnyll reached down, grasped the front of Sarah's gown and jerked her to her feet. 'But there are ways to do so without leaving any visible marks.'

Any bravery she'd had when facing William, or even Richard, vanished in the face of this man's soulless gaze. Sarah knew his mind was twisted and sick. She had no wish to test his limits.

'Soon, you will learn to shiver whenever I so much as look at you.'

Dear Lord, she prayed William found her quickly.

Arnyll released her. It was all she could do not to faint in relief. Sarah slid down the trunk of the tree, oblivious to the bark digging into her bound hands and back.

'What do you know about your husband?' Arnyll nudged her with his foot when she didn't answer.

'Nothing.' To her dismay that was the truth. She didn't know anything about him. Not his age, where he lived, where he was born, if he had siblings, or even if parents were still living.

Arnyll's laugh took her by surprise. Sarah looked up at him. 'Did you never wonder how he came by the scars on his body?'

Yes, of course she'd wondered, but she'd never thought to ask. She assumed that some day he would tell her. She wasn't going to tell these men that, though. She hoped that by remaining silent, they would give her some information she could use. If, for whatever reason, William did not arrive to save her, she would need to find a way to escape on her own.

'Lady Sarah, your husband is nothing but a slave. A warrior slave trained to kill on command.' Again Arnyll laughed. But this time it was a cold, calculating sound. 'Bronwyn and his companions escaped from their master.' He squatted down to explain, 'I am tasked with returning them, using you, and the other wives, as bait.'

What companions? The Earl, perhaps?

Richard added, 'You will be able to teach Adrienna all you've learned about being a whore.'

She wanted to scream that she wasn't a whore, it had been a ruse and nothing more. But she held her tongue.

Arnyll stroked her neck, before leaning down and wrapping his fingers around her throat. He smiled, and somehow the expression made him appear more evil. 'You see, you and the other women will share your husbands' fate. However…' he paused to sigh in a show of false concern, tightening his grip enough to make her gasp for air '…your marriages will be voided since slaves cannot wed. But fear not. You will never need worry about sleeping in a lonely bed. Aryseeth will see to that.'

When he removed his hand from her throat and rose, Richard asked him, 'Are you finished?'

'Yes, for now.'

Richard reached out towards her, only to be stopped by Arnyll. 'We're already going to have to answer for her split lip. So, leave her alone, Langsford.'

'But you said—'

Arnyll knocked Richard to the ground at Sarah's feet.

A dagger pressed against his throat stopped Richard from reacting.

'I've changed my mind.' Arnyll's voice was little more than a snarl. 'We will be fortunate if Aryseeth only has us whipped for already marking her. I will not suffer more because you could not control yourself.'

'Fine.' Richard pushed the man away from him. 'I'll leave her alone.'

Arnyll nodded. 'If it will make you happier, you can secure her to the tree for the night.'

After Arnyll reclaimed his seat across the fire from them, Richard retrieved a length of rope from his gear and returned. He seemed to take great joy from wrapping the thick rope beneath her breasts, then adjusting and readjusting, his fingers lingering, or his knuckles brushing, against the softness, until finally, he secured it behind the tree.

He squatted down before her. 'That should do it. You won't be going anywhere.' He glanced at Arnyll, then added, 'Although, I would enjoy it if you tried.'

He wanted to see her struggle against her bonds? Sarah refused to give him the satisfaction. Instead, she forced a smile to her lips and looked up at him. 'No, I think I'm quite comfortable where I am.'

When he left her alone, she leaned her head against the tree behind her. William had been a slave? She couldn't fathom exactly what that meant. Oh, yes, of a surety he had been held captive, but what had Arnyll meant about William being trained to kill on command? Apparently he'd resisted whatever performance they'd requested if he'd been whipped.

She shuddered at the image forming in her mind. The idea of someone taking a lash to her overgrown husband was unthinkable. She knew for certain that they would have had to restrain him in some manner. How had they overpowered him?

Who would do such a thing? What sort of heartless barbarian would abuse another in such a manner?

Sarah swallowed hard, then held her breath in hopes of stopping the tears forming in her eyes from falling. Fear fought for control of her. Fear of what was to come.

Chapter Ten

With grim determination William rode towards Kendal. His steady pace, stopping only when it was too dark to see and starting out again at dawn, had brought him within a day of reaching his destination.

He still feared it would not be quick enough to spare Sarah a taste of Aryseeth's training. The thought sickened him in a manner he could not shake.

He feared his headstrong wife would get herself killed when she opened her mouth to berate the slave master. Or worse, her volatile emotions would burn far too fast and she would be broken too easily.

How many times had he seen that happen to men? They would be brought into the palace dungeon full of spit and fire, running high on their emotions. These were the men Aryseeth would immediately pit against a much weaker opponent to build their arrogance and give them false confidence.

They would then be dropped into a deep, dark hole with the rats and the body of the man they'd just killed. If they somehow survived a week of darkness, solitude, thirst, hunger and encroaching madness, they'd be moved to the cells.

Those were the men who broke the easiest. The ones who had no control over their emotions.

Yet, those who had lived possessed the weight and physical strength to withstand Aryseeth's torture. Sarah had neither. She would be an ineffective, defenceless rag doll in his hands.

William's chest tightened. He shouldn't waste his energy creating horrific scenarios of what might, or might not, happen. There would be time enough for that later.

What he needed to do now was to focus his full attention on getting to Kendal and his wife.

Suddenly another rider blocked his path just ahead. William cursed, jerking on his horse's reins; the animal reared in protest, reaching out its hooves toward the other rider.

Once he had his beast under control, he shouted at the other man, 'God's teeth, Hartford, what the hell were you thinking?'

Guy, the Earl of Hartford, another former dungeon mate, who'd been released along with him and Hugh, smiled at him and said, 'That's a fine greeting.'

William drew his horse closer, cocked his arm and slammed a fist against Guy's shoulder. 'Is that better?'

Guy moved his shoulder about. 'Not really.' He studied William a moment, then asked, 'On your way to Kendal?'

William groaned. 'They have Elizabeth, too?' Even though he'd never met the women, Guy had always talked of his wife—as if doing so would keep him from losing his wits.

'Yes. I take it they have someone of yours?'

'My wife Sarah.'

'Wife? You have a wife?' Guy's eyes widened. 'When did this come about? How did you find anyone willing to wed you?'

William shrugged. 'I gave her no choice.'

Guy's laughter split the air. 'Somehow, I can believe that.'

'Glad that I could amuse you.'

Sobering, Guy asked, 'Were you with Hugh?'

'Not when Sarah was taken. We'd already parted company.' Eager to be on the road again, he suggested, 'Unless there's a reason you can't talk and ride at the same time, we're losing time standing here.'

Guy pressed his horse forwards, wondering aloud, 'And this from the man who always swore controlled patience was the way to win battles?'

'I didn't have a wife involved then.'

'Amazing how that changes your outlook, isn't it?' Guy reached across the distance to cuff William's shoulder. 'Relax, Bronwyn, it will do us no good if you are too highly strung to concentrate.'

William stared at him. 'Relax? I'll do that as soon as Sarah is safely in my arms.'

Guy glanced at the darkening sky. 'We should soon make camp for the night. We can reach Kendal early enough tomorrow to wait for Hugh's arrival.'

'That's assuming his wife was kidnapped, too.'

'Have you ever known Aryseeth to do anything by half-measures?'

'No.' William realised that Guy's assumption was mostly likely correct. 'I wouldn't be surprised if Hugh wasn't already there.'

'Even if he is, at least he's not witless enough to attack alone. Hopefully he'll realise that we'll be arriving shortly and wait.'

William pointed towards the next clearing. 'That's as good a spot as any to stop.'

Sarah crawled to a back corner of the tent, as far away from the entry flap as possible. The chain around her ankle clunked along behind her.

She took a shaking breath. How had William survived captivity? She'd been here only two days and she would gladly take her own life if she had a weapon at hand.

Not that the fat pig Aryseeth had actually harmed her overmuch. It was more that he pounded at her mind constantly. The threats, the verbal descriptions of what he intended to do with her—to her—once William was dead. The man had derived great pleasure from detailing what he vowed would be her husband's death.

At one point she'd been so mindless with fear from the visions taking life in her head that she'd lashed out at Aryseeth. Her wild curses had been silenced with the back of his meaty hand.

While the sharp crack had cleared her mind, the action had fired the slave master's vile lust. Before she realised what was happening, he'd pulled her into a tight embrace.

Thankfully, after doing nothing more than smacking loud, slobbery kisses on her chin and cheek, he'd just as quickly thrown her aside. She wondered how long that would last.

But the incident had taught her a valuable lesson. A display of emotions fed Aryseeth's evilness. Today when she'd been dragged back to his tent, she'd remained as detached from her emotions as possible.

Throughout his threats, and highly suspect stories about William, she'd stood there silent. She hadn't so much as moved a muscle in her face...until later in the day.

While overall her attempt to remain impassive had ended in complete disaster, at least today she'd been able to prolong the inevitable. Maybe tomorrow she'd withstand his verbal, and mental, abuse longer.

Sarah choked on a sob. Tomorrow. How many more of them would she have?

The flap of the tent opened slightly. She jumped and wiped at her face to make certain there was no trace of tears.

A man she did not recognise slipped in through the narrow opening. He approached her, carrying a cloth-wrapped bundle. Coming to a stop before her, he extended the package to her. Uncertain what he was offering, she frowned.

The man shook his head before unwrapping the package to show her the food inside. Her mouth salivated at the sight and smell of the food. She'd not eaten since—she couldn't remember if she, William and the men had stopped for a mid-day meal two days ago or not.

Still, she didn't understand why this man would bring her nourishment. Sarah reached up to take the package, raising her eyebrows in a silent question.

The man patted the top of his head, then lifted his hand as far overhead as he could to signify...sky... height? He brought his hand down and touched his shoulders with both hands, before extending them to about twice the width of his shoulders.

Height...tall...wide...broad... She smiled as it came together in her mind. 'William. You know William?'

He must have understood, or recognised, the name, because he nodded vigorously. At a sound outside of the tent, he pointed at the package and motioned for her to eat rapidly. She did as he suggested. Apparently, he'd brought the food to her without permission and she didn't want him to suffer for his act of kindness.

When she was done, Sarah handed the cloth back to him. 'Thank you.' He nodded before backing out of the tent, bowing repeatedly as he left.

Now that her stomach was full, Sarah felt a little stronger. Perhaps she could make it through one more day. But only one. If William didn't arrive by tomorrow, she didn't know what she'd do.

'There he is.' William hitched a thumb towards Hugh, relieved to know Guy had been correct in his assumption that they'd find him awaiting them.

Even though they'd awakened early and broke camp just as the sun began to rise, it had taken most of the day to ride to Cumbria. They joined Hugh at the edge of a cliff. Flanking him, they too stared down into the valley dotted with Aryseeth's white tents.

Hugh barely glanced at him before asking, 'Sarah and Elizabeth?'

Both William and Guy answered at the same time, 'Yes.'

'What are you planning to do?' Hugh asked in a strangled tone.

Since, in his mind, there was only one obvious course of action, William answered, 'Fight for her freedom. What had you planned on?'

'They want me—I will exchange myself for the women.'

Guy snorted. 'When did you develop such a high opinion of your worth?'

'I will not argue this with either of you.' Hugh picked up his reins.

But before he could ride away, William reached out and grabbed the reins from his hands. 'You are not giving yourself up. We will fight. Together.'

'I have no fight left.'

William rolled his eyes. 'Of course not. That's what happens when you don't train with your men. You become soft.'

Hugh cursed as he unsuccessfully tried to free the reins to his horse. 'You can not goad me out of my decision.'

Guy asked, 'What makes you think Aryseeth will release the women? If you give yourself over to him, not only will he have another warrior for the battle arena, he'll have three new women to add to his house.'

That caught Hugh's attention. 'Then we fight.'

William grunted in reply. 'Are we ready?'

Hugh looked up at the sky and said, 'It is a good day to die.'

To which Guy replied, 'It is a better day to live.'

A servant scratched at the flap to his tent. Aryseeth motioned to a sentry standing guard inside the tent to permit the servant entry.

'Why do you disturb my meal?' Aryseeth snarled, taking pleasure at the sight of the servant's quivering body.

The man crawled into the tent on his knees, keeping his eyes lowered until he was a couple of feet from Aryseeth. He then dropped to the floor, flat on his stomach, his face in the dirt and his arms extended out, waiting silently for permission to speak.

Aryseeth left him in that position until he'd bit off, chewed, and then swallowed a bite of the mutton leg he held. Finally, he asked, 'Well? What?'

'My lord, the men have arrived.'

Aryseeth resisted the urge to shout in victory. He'd known the men would come. Their outrage at having their women taken from them would need to be assuaged. No man would stand idly by at the loss of such fine property.

Isn't that why he had travelled this distance, suffered this inclement weather? All to reclaim the lost property?

The old King Sidatha had been foolish to grant freedom to such warriors. Thankfully, the new King had listened to reason. So when he'd sent Aryseeth to England to negotiate a trade agreement, he'd also ordered Aryseeth to bring these men back with him—and he didn't care how it was accomplished.

Rising from his throne of pillows as if he had all the time in the world, he sauntered across the tent, pausing now and then to take another bite from the mutton leg he still held.

Once outside the tent he saw that the three were armed in the way he'd trained them. They were also dressed in the manner he had dictated for captives. Perhaps they were eager to return to his care. He hoped not, because that would only ruin his pleasure.

The men broke the silence first, asking for their wives. Aryseeth snapped his fingers. As the flaps to the tents opened and each woman was led out by the ropes that bound her, he watched the men intently.

To his chagrin, not one of them so much as moved a muscle. To goad them, he asked, 'What will you exchange for the lives of your women?'

As he expected, Earl Hugh answered, 'We will exchange nothing. We are prepared to take them from you.'

Aryseeth couldn't have asked for a more favourable response. He feigned shock. 'I have fourteen men on hand. You would fight them all?'

Hugh nodded toward Arnyll and Langsford. 'Make that sixteen.'

Aryseeth nodded. 'Sixteen to three. Those sound like fair odds to me.'

Langsford backed away. 'I do not fight.'

Aryseeth motioned to his guards. Two of them flanked Langsford, and then dragged him forwards.

With little feeling, Aryseeth reached inside his robe and pulled out a thin blade. 'Fight or die.'

Langsford shook his head and dropped to his knees. 'I do not—'

The knife slid smoothly across the man's throat. Aryseeth stepped back to avoid soiling his slippers with blood as Langsford fell to the ground.

Hugh said, 'Make that fifteen to three.'

Arnyll rushed forwards and knelt before Aryseeth. 'I am a free man. Have I not served you well in bringing you the others?'

'And you will serve me well in this also.'

'My Lord, they will kill me.'

Aryseeth looked down at the man. 'I would expect no less.' He motioned to his guards. 'Take him and prepare him for the morrow.' With that, Aryseeth turned and went back inside his tent.

William joined Hugh and Guy as they approached their wives. When he got his first close up look at Sarah's face, it was all he could do not to shout in rage.

The sight of her swollen and still bleeding lip, along with the beginnings of a bruise, prompted him to glare at the nearest guard.

Hugh nudged his shoulder. 'Easy, William. Let it rest until morning.'

It would be difficult, but he understood the warning. Aryseeth would use his reaction against him in some manner that would only bring more harm to Sarah. So he dropped his gaze and forced himself to breathe deeply.

While Guy had the luxury of picking his wife Elizabeth up from the ground, he and Hugh were left to take the ropes and lead their wives to the tent.

Since he had told Sarah nothing about his life before returning to England, he fully expected her to soundly berate him once they were alone. He deserved no less for permitting her to become embroiled in this without any knowledge to help her.

Yet, he knew he'd be unable to spend the night in this tent with her. Just the simple thought of entering the shelter made him ill. But he wanted…needed to make certain Sarah was harmed no more than what he could see.

Once they entered the tent, he untied the rope from around her and threw it across the floor before guiding her toward the oil lamp hanging from the centre post. His stomach knotted and his chest tightened at his examination of her injuries.

He cupped her non-bruised cheek. 'Sarah, have you been harmed other than this?'

Her chin trembled, but she blinked back the shimmering tears forming in her eyes. 'What would it matter?'

He stroked his thumb across her cheek. 'Since I willingly risk my life for yours, it matters a great deal to me.'

When she leaned towards him, he placed his other hand on her shoulder to hold her away. William knew it would be a mistake for both of them if he were to gather her close.

She would lose what little strength of spirit she'd so far retained. And he would spend the night in this tent surrounded by memories he'd put to rest, instead of resting for what the morrow would bring.

A hot tear gathered along his thumb. He brushed it away. 'You have not answered me.'

She shook her head. 'No. They have only threatened me with greater harm.'

William knew that if he, Hugh and Guy did not succeed on the morrow, Aryseeth would make good those threats—and worse.

But for tonight she was safe. As long as she remained in this tent, nobody would bother her. The hard part would be convincing her to stay—without him.

William would remain inside these fabric walls not a heartbeat longer than necessary. Already the weight of imaginary chains nearly suffocated him, making it hard to breathe.

It was imperative that he leave this tent—quickly. But he knew she'd not listen to reason. Which left him with two options—either stay and be unable to fight at full strength tomorrow, or make her angry enough to start a fight of their own.

The battle tomorrow would demand his complete attention—mentally and physically. Anything less meant certain death.

But a fight with Sarah could be mended at a later time, when she would be more able to understand his motives. Granted, engaging her on purpose would leave him filled with guilt, but it wasn't as if he'd not experienced that sting before.

He drew in a long breath, preparing to enact the cruellest thing he would ever do, then said, 'They will cause you no further harm now that I am here.'

Her eyes widened as if she found his comment outrageous—it was, but he'd not admit it. Before she could say anything, William led her over to the pallet in the corner.

'You are exhausted, Sarah. Lay down and rest.'

As he expected, she clung to him. 'No. I need you, William. I need you more than I need sleep.'

He pulled her away from his chest, admonishing, 'You may not need sleep, but with a battle in the morning, I do.'

She stretched out on the pallet. 'Fine, then let us both get some sleep.'

'No.' Out of her reach, he backed towards the tent flap. 'I will find no rest next to you.'

Quickly sitting up, his wife stared at him in shock. 'William?'

With his hand on the flap, he asked, 'What, Sarah? What would you have me do?'

'Don't leave me.'

He saw the sheen of tears trailing down her cheeks. And he heard the fear and hurt in her voice, but the crushing weight on his chest urged him to leave. 'Sarah, go to sleep.'

As the sound of her soft, choked cries reached his ears, he forced a sharpness to his voice that he did not feel and ordered, 'You are a warrior's wife. Act as such.'

William lowered the flap behind him, cutting off the sound of Sarah's gasp.

Angry with himself and the situation in general, he

stormed across the campsite. When he and the other men had come into Aryseeth's camp, he'd seen a grouping of boulders near the edge of the creek. That would be as good a place as any to spend the night.

'Stop, slave.' The sharp point of a sword pressed into his back.

William turned around slowly, and stared at the guard. 'Move that weapon.'

The man tapped William's chest with the sword tip. 'Are you giving me orders?'

Wasn't that apparent? 'Move it, or find it planted in your chest.'

The tip of the offending weapon pierced through the links of his mail. A smirk crossed the guard's mouth. 'You seem to have forgotten your proper place.' While pointing at the ground, the man ordered, 'On your knees.'

If that's where this fool wanted to be, it was fine with William. He knocked the sword from the unsuspecting man's grasp half a heartbeat before swiping his legs from beneath him.

William retrieved the sword and held the weapon over the guard's throat. The pounding of feet raced near, making him hold the blade steady rather than ramming it into the quivering man on the ground.

'Stop.' Aryseeth's voice rang clear from the entryway of his ornate tent. The guards racing at William with their weapons at the ready came to an immediate halt.

William dropped the sword, turned and walked towards the boulders. When the men made a move to follow him, the slave master ordered them to leave him alone.

The order surprised him, but William had no intention of questioning this small blessing. He climbed over the boulders and sat in the grass on the other side, using the oversized rock as a backrest.

William picked up a stone and tossed it up and down in his hand. Of all the things to happen, he never would have expected this.

Which had been a mistake on his part. With Arnyll's involvement he should have been on alert for the worst. And now it wasn't just his life in danger, it was his wife's.

His court-raised wife. She had to be terrified, and he had nothing with which to help her. He threw the stone into the creek. He'd sworn a vow to protect her and had failed horribly.

She would have been better off in one of Eleanor's cells than here. Anywhere but here.

It was doubtful that the Queen would have kept her confined to a cell for ever. Once her rage had worn off, she'd have freed Sarah. And while Eleanor's court was nothing more than a prison wrapped in elegance, at least Sarah would have come to no harm there.

Had she remained with the Queen, she could have eventually wed someone of worth. Someone with a title, gold and a grand keep in which to house her. Someone with honour.

Instead, she now knew that she had wed a lowly slave. William gritted his teeth against the pain of knowing he would have to give up this wife of his. She deserved more than a man who had become a murderer in order to survive.

He'd been wrong to think those days were behind him. The guard who had sought to delay him had made that obvious to him. His response to the threat had been to attack the guard. Had Aryseeth not called a halt, William knew he would have rammed the man's own sword through his neck.

It wasn't so much his violent reaction that bothered him. It was more that he'd felt no guilt, only a dark need, a vile desire to take the man's life.

If by some miracle they came through this alive, he would ensure Sarah never faced danger again. More importantly, he would see to it she got everything she deserved.

Even though it meant he would be no part of her future. The one thing Sarah didn't deserve was to be tied to a killer of men.

Chapter Eleven

Sarah and the other two women, Adrienna and Elizabeth, stood along the perimeter of the makeshift arena, waiting for the battle to begin.

Guards had brought them here and the three of them had fallen silent after they'd introduced themselves. She was certain the other wives were as preoccupied with what was to come, and how they would bear it, as she.

This infernal waiting would go far towards breaking their spirits before the horror of battle even began.

The sun was not quite overhead as Sarah scanned the hills, unintentionally wondering aloud, 'There must be a way out of here.'

'Only if your men live.' Aryseeth approached and stopped in front of them. 'Do not count on that outcome. You need accept the fact that you will join my household.'

He went on to describe the women's duties in great detail. Sarah closed her mind to his sick fantasies. Her focus had been fully captured by the three men approaching the arena from the other side of the camp. She was vaguely aware that her mouth had fallen agape at the sight.

William had never appeared more powerful than he did now. His presence—strong, confident, and commanding—made her weak with longing.

He caught her brazen stare and held her captive with his intense gaze. His hooded perusal set her insides to tremble. Her body quickened—along with her breathing.

He caressed her with a blazing hot look that seemed as real as a physical touch. It was all she could do to remain still and keep her moan of longing silent.

In an attempt to distract herself, Sarah broke their visual connection. She tore her gaze away to glance at the other two men. That move had been a mistake, because it provided no distraction.

While the vision of William alone was impressive, the picture of the three men together proved breathtaking.

And when they flexed their biceps and expanded their chests in what was surely a public display of strength, Sarah blew out the breath she hadn't realised she'd been holding, then whispered, 'My, my, my.'

If any here thought these men would lose this day, they would soon see the grievous error of their thoughts. The *hope* she'd had of the men's success had grown into complete certainty. These warriors were not just formidable—they were invincible.

Aryseeth studied the men with a practised eye as they approached the arena. To his satisfaction they had found a way to retain the hard muscle tone and definition that he'd so painstakingly beaten into their bodies.

The men reached the centre of the arena, and stood in a circle with their backs against each other. Hugh waved his sword as if beckoning Aryseeth to give the order to attack.

He moved behind the women and whistled. Ten of

his battle-trained guards raced from between the tents toward the arena. To Aryseeth's disgust, the first skirmish ended far too quickly.

Hugh dispatched three of the guards. The lumbering beast William ended the lives of two men, while Guy had killed one.

So, the warriors had fared well against swords. How would they do against whips and chains?

He whistled again and five more guards appeared. These men were experts with a lash of any type. Each wielded a length of chain in one hand and a long, thick whip in the other.

To his chagrin, William laughed. The laughter turned to ribald curses when Stefan darted around the guards, then wisely turned his back towards the warriors. It was smart of Stefan to keep his gaze on the guards he'd just deserted, as they would not hesitate to take him down like a dog.

Instead of giving the order to do so, Aryseeth shrugged. After such an open act of treachery, it mattered not. If Arnyll survived this battle, he would still die this night for his open betrayal.

Hugh and William dropped their swords, and stepped out of the ring. Guy and Stefan moved so they were standing back to back. Aryseeth knew the two men would fight as one—effectively forming a single unit with four arms. He'd expected that to happen at some point in the battle. After all, it was an excellent way to protect one's back while concentrating on the enemy coming at you.

What he hadn't expected was for Hugh to so easily reach between the swinging lashes to grasp a guard by the throat and snap his neck.

Nor did he expect William to snatch a whip mid-air, and then, hand over hand draw the surprised guard to him with his own weapon. The guard's stunned reaction permitted William the seconds he needed to pull him close enough to grab. The fool deserved to have his neck crushed between William's bicep and forearm.

But it wasn't as if the remaining guards didn't cause any damage. Their whips and chains had laced open the warriors' flesh in many places. Blood ran freely from each of them to pour onto the ground.

When only two of his guards remained, Aryseeth smiled to himself and whistled one last time. The warriors would *not* win their way free from this next attack.

Twenty of his finest men rode down the hill on horseback. They steadily approached the arena. His riders would see to the men's complete submission. The long, sharp-pointed pikes they carried would easily make the warriors see that their freedom, and that of their women, was at an end.

The four men brandished their swords. Each husband looked to his wife as if bidding them farewell before forming their circle for the last time.

They worried for naught. Aryseeth had given his riders strict orders not to kill the warriors, only to maim them so they could no longer fight this battle.

He paced behind the wives. 'Perhaps now you will accept the inevitable. Your men will not win.'

No sooner were the words out of his mouth when the woman called Elizabeth pointed at the hill on the other side of the clearing, screaming, 'Look! Dear God, look!'

Aryseeth swung to look in that direction and cursed. At least fifty men crested the hill. The rider at the head of the line carried a pennant. As they followed the curve of the road, the pennant unfurled in the breeze, displaying King Henry's rampant lion.

So, these men were worth enough to their King that he rode to their rescue? Aryseeth raised his hand, ordering his own riders to halt. He then turned and headed towards his tent.

As far as he was concerned the game was not yet over—only delayed. He could not return to Sidatha without the men and he wouldn't.

It would require more time, more gold and a new plan of action. But no matter what it took—he would *not* fail his lord.

He stopped at the tent flap and hitched a thumb towards the escaping Arnyll. Someone had to pay for this setback and this fool was expendable. Two of his guards took down Arnyll, quickly dispatching him to his maker.

William rushed toward Sarah, pausing only to witness Arnyll's death. A moment of regret swept over him. He had wanted to be the one who took Stefan's life.

But the regret was short lived and he turned back to Sarah, only to see her slowly crumple. William caught her in his arms before she landed on the ground.

'William…' Sarah breathed his name on a broken sigh.

He gently wiped the tears from her face, vowing that this would never happen again. From now on, she would be safe.

King Henry paused beside them. 'Bronwyn, are you well?' The King was staring at the blood still dripping from a gash on William's side. 'Do you require assistance?'

William glanced down at what appeared to him as little more than a scratch. 'No. 'Tis nothing. Most of the blood isn't mine.'

Just then Sarah looked up at the King. 'Thank you for coming to our aid, Sire.'

Henry's eyes widened. 'Lady Remy?'

'Bronwyn,' Sarah corrected. 'William and I are wed.'

The King's surprised stare swung to William. 'You married my wife's informant?'

'Yes.'

Before the King moved on to the other men, William asked, 'May I beg a few moments of your time before we part company?'

Henry nodded toward Aryseeth's camp. 'I will be here a couple of days. Come find me before you leave.' He glanced over his shoulder, adding, 'If there are any supplies or food you require, the wagons will be along soon.'

William bowed his head. 'Thank you.'

Sarah rested her head against his chest. 'What business have you with the King?'

'Nothing that concerns you,' William lied. His discussion with the King would concern nothing except Sarah. But he didn't want to hint at what he'd planned until after he spoke with Henry.

For now, he wanted nothing more than to find some place private to be alone with his wife. And soon—before simply holding her close would no longer be enough.

William released her. 'Stay right here, don't move.' He raced to where he and the other men had stashed their supplies. He retrieved the leather bag containing food, an empty skin, and rolled up a few covers to take along also. If Guy or Hugh needed anything, they could sort through what was left, or, as the King had said, gather what they needed from the supply wagons.

William returned to Sarah and led her to the place where he had spent last night. They scrambled over the natural wall of boulders and rocks, to the grassy area between the rocks and the stream.

He dropped their supplies on the ground and pulled his wife into his embrace.

Sarah wrapped her arms tightly around him and buried her face against his chest. 'I am so angry at you I could scream.'

He stroked her hair and, because he couldn't blame her if she did rail at him, said nothing. Instead, he picked her up and, after sitting on the grass, his back against the boulder, held her on his lap.

She leaned away from William's chest and stared up at him. Never had she been so glad to see anyone in her life as she had been last night. To know that he'd come for her meant more than she could ever explain.

From what she'd learned from Aryseeth and Arnyll, William had spent many years in captivity. How anyone could have endured such a life, without becoming an animal, was beyond her comprehension.

Yet, this huge, strong man had always treated her with tenderness. Even when he was raging angry, he'd not physically harmed her.

She rested her cheek against his chest and stroked his arm. 'How long were you held captive?'

'Fifteen years.'

Sarah frowned at his distracted tone of voice. But she forged ahead. 'How did it come about?'

William shrugged. 'My parents had—died, and the new lord of the keep had me put out. Some men found me wandering along a stream and hit me on the head with a fallen log. The next thing I knew, I was aboard a ship heading for the other side of the world.'

'The new lord put you out? Why?'

'Because he was my father's brother and he had lied to the King, telling him that I had also perished, when in truth he had murdered my parents in hopes of gaining control of the keep.'

Aghast that someone would treat him so, Sarah asked, 'Why didn't you go to King Henry when you returned?'

'Stephen was the King when my parents died. Bronwyn was loyal to Stephen instead of Henry's mother Matilda. Both sides needed men and gold desperately. I doubt if Henry cared that Bronwyn came to their side through treachery.'

She would see that was rectified as soon as possible. For now, she asked, wanting him to tell her, even though she already knew the answer, 'What did you do as a captive?'

'Killed men.'

Sarah didn't need to see the expression on his face to know how deeply just saying the words affected him. The tensing of his muscles beneath her fingers, and the quickness of his heart pounding beneath her cheek, told her of the lingering anger.

'William, you had no choice. You did as you were commanded.' She now understood why he'd once used that word to describe her relationship with the Queen.

But in her experience there was a vast difference between being ordered to do a task and being commanded. Disobeying an order had consequences, of course, but it usually involved being disgraced for a time, or, at worst, a visit to a cell. Disobeying a command meant instant death—as Langsford had discovered yesterday and Arnyll today.

Her husband's chest heaved with a sigh. 'There are always choices.'

'Death is not a choice. Even if it were, you were too young to make such a final decision.'

'But had I made that decision I would not have so much blood on my hands. I would never have become a beast who lived only for the battle, and the killing.'

His voice was gruff and Sarah looked for a way to prove he was not a beast, not a killer at heart. She reached up to cup his cheek and stroke his lips. 'Perhaps, but you never grew into the beast Arnyll was. It is apparent he liked the battle, and the killing, far too much.'

William's derisive snort surprised her. 'Aye, he liked the killing, but never the battle. He was no warrior and never could be. Arnyll was more of a murdering informant released upon his fellow captives to spy for Aryseeth.'

Shame thickened in Sarah's throat, making it hard to breathe and near impossible to swallow. What could she say in response to that comment that would not fall back on her acts for Queen Eleanor?

Nothing. So she forged ahead. 'You once told me that sometimes little bits of information end in death. Why?'

William's body shook. She felt his stomach knot against her hip. Sarah wrapped her arms round him, whispering, 'No, William, there is no need to speak of it. Just let it die in the past.'

They sat in silence for a long while. Finally, she felt him relax. Soon, his heart and breathing slowed to a normal rhythm. What she didn't feel was his arms around her.

The sick feeling that something was dreadfully wrong made her lean back and look up at him. 'William?'

He looked everywhere but at her. She touched his cheek. 'What is wrong?'

When he didn't answer, she slid her hands behind his

head, but no amount of forcing would make him look down at her.

She lowered her arms and folded her hands in her lap. Dear Lord, what had she done? Maybe it was the comparison between her and Arnyll. 'William, I am sorry I spied for the Queen. So, very sorry. I never meant any harm. I only—'

He placed a finger against her lips. 'Hush. You did what you had to do to survive. After all you've seen, all you've heard, do you still think I don't realise what that means? Nothing you did could ever compare to Arnyll's vile spitefulness.'

Perhaps he was right, she might not have committed vile acts, but many were quite spiteful at times.

'Where did you go last night?'

He circled an arm around her, coaxing her back against his chest. 'Here. I slept here.'

'Why? How could you have so easily left me alone, knowing how frightened I was?'

William rested his head against the boulder and sighed. 'Sarah, I could not breathe in that tent. Every man who had ever died at my hands haunted me there. Every scar caused from a lash burned anew. I chose to run from the memories instead of facing them.'

She could understand running away. How many times had she pushed memories aside rather than deal with them?

She reached up and touched his face. 'So angering me was the easy way to make good your escape?'

William brushed his cheek against her palm before drawing her hand to his lips for a kiss. 'Yes. Can you forgive me?'

'Oh, William, I thank you.'

'Thank me? For what?'

'You came for me. I could never ask for more.'

He rubbed a lock of her hair between his fingers, brushed a hand across her cheek. 'You are my wife, how could I not come for you?'

'You could have let Aryseeth take me from England, then told all that I had died. None would be the wiser.'

'Oh, aye, that would have been honourable, would it not? Especially since I know well the torment you would suffer.'

'Honourable? Is honour the only reason you came?'

He crushed her to his chest. His lips were demanding against hers, leaving her breathless and wanting so much more. He broke the kiss to bury his face against her neck, asking, 'What else is there?'

If Sarah didn't know better, she'd think that her warrior husband was near tears. Surely she'd only imagined the tremor in his voice. She longed to argue with him, to rail that he could have come because he desired her. Or because he cared enough about her as a person that he couldn't let her die. Something— anything other than his honour.

But this moment wasn't the time for arguments or harsh words. It had been a long night for both of them and a brutal morning. So, instead she stroked his hair, taking great comfort in the fact that he was alive and was holding her. 'I still thank you.'

He lifted his head to whisper against her ear, 'You are welcome.'

Sarah closed her eyes and relaxed more fully against him. 'I am so tired. I could sleep right here for days.'

His hands closed on either side of her waist before he lifted her from his lap. 'There is a cure for that.'

She shook out the skirt of her gown, complaining, 'I was not looking for a cure.'

'We have all night to sleep.' He rose. 'Right now, I want a bath.'

Sarah walked to the stream and dropped to her knees at the edge. With a deep sigh, she splashed water on her face.

'Is it cold?'

She shook her head. 'Not very.'

'Good.' William unrolled one of the covers on the grass, leaving two more draped over a boulder. He then sat down to tug off his boots, before he rose to strip free of his clothes. He wanted more than just the feel of water splashed against his skin. He wanted to sink into the stream and let the current cleanse away the filth, the blood and the feverish anger that still beat inside his chest.

Sarah gasped loud as he walked past, naked. 'William!' She looked over her shoulder. 'What if someone sees you?'

He'd lost all sense of modesty many, many years ago. It surprised him that she hadn't. There couldn't have been much, if any, privacy in the Queen's court. 'I possess nothing the others haven't already seen on their own bodies.'

Once the water reached his hips, William sank down on to the bottom of the stream. He closed his eyes as the water swirled around him to carry away the stench of Aryseeth's evilness and his own blood-drenched sins.

'Is it cold?'

He opened one eye, then turned his head to see Sarah pacing the bank. Was she thinking about joining him? 'It hasn't changed temperature since I asked you that same question.'

'I only had my hands in the water. Is it cold against...your body?'

She *was* contemplating joining him in the stream. Had the water been cold, her intention alone would have warmed it considerably. That thought was enough to make him shiver—but not from any chill. He was still fresh from a battle—did she not realise what that meant?

Any patience that resided within him had been pushed away. Didn't his need to be up and about make that clear?

Ah, but possessing her would go far towards calming the lingering battle lust. 'No, Sarah, it's not cold.'

'But it is deep.'

He would stand up and turn around to show her how deep it was if he was certain she wouldn't dash off like a frightened rabbit at the sight of his arousal. 'I'm sitting down.'

Again, she eyed the water with longing. 'I can't swim.'

'I can.' Although, if she joined him, there would no swimming.

'Do you have any soap?'

Soap? That request took a few heartbeats for him to understand. She actually wanted a bath? William scooped up a handful of sand from the bottom of the stream and held it up. 'This will work just as well.'

She tugged at the unbroken side of her lower lip. 'You won't let me drown?'

That had to have been the most witless question she'd asked thus far. Unconcerned about her response, William rose, the water sluicing off him as he stalked toward her. Once on the grassy bank, he hauled her up on to a boulder and removed her soft boots, stockings and girdle.

'Aye, Sarah, after risking my life in a battle to the death for you, I will most assuredly let you drown.'

Before she could respond, he slid her off the boulder and pulled her gown and chemise over her head.

She crossed her arms over her breasts and shivered as the air brushed against her. William lifted her in his arms and carried her out into the stream. When he waded back out and sat down, she squeaked, clinging to his neck. 'You lied. It is cold.'

Cold? With her wet flesh pressed against his, her legs wrapped tightly around his waist, he was far from cold. He was on fire.

And if she wasn't, then he was doing something wrong. William pulled her arms from around his neck. 'Turn around.'

'What?'

He scooped up a handful of sand. 'You wanted a bath.'

She relaxed her legs and slid down on to his lap. Sarah's eyes flew open wide. 'Oh.' A seductive smile slowly curved her mouth as she swayed her hips back and forth against him. 'Can the bath not wait?'

William paused, then blew out a breath at the sultry tone of her voice and the friction of her movements. He could so easily take her now. But he wanted more than a hard-and-fast release. He leaned down to kiss her neck, then to nuzzle her ear. 'If you don't take it now, I can't promise you'll get one.'

She frowned as if debating. Unwilling to wait for her to make up her mind, he grasped her around the waist and pulled her to her feet before him. Rising up on his knees, William gently scrubbed her body with the gritty sand. He ran his palms over her arms, shoulders and neck before lowering his hands over her breasts, then down to her stomach and hips.

Sarah grasped his shoulders and closed her eyes, obviously enjoying his ministrations almost as much as he. He suddenly realised that this would be one of the moments he remembered when they parted. A memory that would burn against his heart, only making him miss her more.

He could save himself the coming pain by pushing her away. But he could not deny himself the feel of her soft skin beneath his hands, or the sound of her sighs against his ears.

Unable to speak past the sudden thickness of his throat, William motioned for her to turn around.

He scrubbed her back, sliding his hands down to caress the roundness below. With her feet spread apart to keep a solid footing against the slight current, she was open to his touch. From the ragged sound of her breaths, he knew she was anticipating the feel of his hand.

William smiled to himself. He had every intention of being selfish and no intention of rushing through this night.

He rubbed the gritty sand along the length of her legs, then rinsed the sand away before skimming his fingertips up the inside of her thigh. The tender flesh quivered beneath his teasing touch.

Her small gasp of surprise, followed by a soft moan, urged him on. But when she made a move to turn in his arms, he held her still. With a hand on her shoulder, he whispered against her ear, 'No, Sarah, stay there.'

Chapter Twelve

Anticipation shook the earth beneath Sarah's feet. William's deep, husky voice, the words whispered hotly against her ear, made her long for things she could barely imagine.

His strong hand on her shoulder kept her steady when she wanted to lean back against his chest for support. The slow teasing touch, drawing tiny circles up her inner thigh, assaulted her senses.

It wasn't just the quickened drumming of her heart. Nor was it simply the heated flow of her blood. In their short time together, she'd come to expect those pleasurable rushes of feelings whenever he touched her.

This was as if a lover—her lover—sought to learn her body, one agonising speck at a time. He drew his tantalising circles with just the tips of his fingers, until the nerves beneath her skin shook. Then he'd still the quivering flesh with a stroke of his palm, before moving higher.

By the time his touch slid up once again, his breathing was as ragged as her own. As he leaned over to place his lips against her neck, his warm breath raced hot across her ear, sending more sparks of desire to trip down her spine.

Ready to become his wife in more than just name, she gave herself over to the passion he coaxed to life. Sarah tipped her head, giving him yet more flesh to tease. She loved the way he made her feel, the first burning rush of desire that gave way to the tense wanting and anticipation. Even now, when the maddening need that built until she thought she'd scream in frustration made her feel wanted and alive.

And just when she thought she could stand it no longer, he turned her around and lifted her high in his arms. The cool air puckered her nipples, but he chased away the cold, suckling first one, then the other as he carried her quickly to their makeshift bed.

Without words he worshipped her slowly, thoroughly with sure touches and demanding lips. She cried out his name as the unrelenting need burst into fulfilment.

Desperate for something more, Sarah reached for him. Instead of coming into her embrace, William grasped her wrists with one hand, holding her captive.

He left her no choice but to submit. And after a brief moment of panic at the fierce, possessive expression etched on the hard planes of his face, she willingly surrendered to his passion.

Yet every touch, each caress of her over-sensitive flesh, sent needy hunger soaring hot to her core. Arching toward him, she begged, 'William, please…please, I need you.'

Before her cry could end, he released her wrists and came over her, whispering hoarsely, 'Shh, hush, I am here.' He filled her with a heat that matched her own.

She clung to him, frozen, as a sharp pain flared, only to subside just as quickly.

William paused, shook free of her hold to raise up on his forearms and stare down at her. Anger flicked across his hooded gaze.

She knew he'd finally realised for a certainty that the Queen's whore was no harlot. He could rail at her later. Be as outraged as he wished.

But right now—right now he could chase away this madness overtaking her body. She arched her hips up against him. 'William, please.'

He groaned, and for a moment she thought he'd pull away. Instead, he gathered her tight against his chest. Sarah held on as he possessed her, claimed her as his. She gasped as he took them over the edge of a seemingly bottomless chasm and into satisfied fulfilment.

Spent, and breathing hard, William rolled on to his back, carrying her along to rest atop him. She felt the hard, rapid pounding of his heart against her damp cheek.

He gently stroked her hair, asking, 'Did I hurt you?'

She had no idea why she cried. No clue where the tears had come from, or when they'd started. She raised up, her forearms resting on his chest, and looked at him. 'Only a little and only for a moment.'

William swiped his thumb across her cheek. 'Then these are what? Tears of…guilt?'

She arched an eyebrow at him. 'As far as you're concerned, that would be the appropriate response, wouldn't it? What did you think I would do, William? You told me that you had willingly wed a harlot, so that's what you expected. How could I admit that even that much was a lie?'

'A simple "I'm a virgin" would have sufficed.'

At his harsh tone, Sarah started to move off him, but he held her fast. 'Is there anything else I should know, Sarah? Anything?'

Since she had every intention of convincing Queen Eleanor to change her mind, Sarah most certainly wasn't going to tell him that his death had already been planned.

She stroked his cheek, following along when he twisted his face away from her touch. 'Yes, William, you should know that I am glad you thought I was a whore. Had you known your wife was an inexperienced virgin, would you have so readily brought me to this pallet?'

Before his frown could fully form at her answer, she added, 'Perhaps my tears were not from guilt, but from the most indescribable moment of...joy...I've ever known.'

'Joy?'

Sarah's cheeks flamed. She drew circles on his chest and looked down at her hands. 'Lust, perhaps?'

'Perhaps?' He caressed the fullness of her hips. 'I would think there was little question in the matter.'

She laughed softly at his arrogance, then kissed his sweat-slicked chest. Pushing herself up, she nodded towards the stream, suggesting, 'If you have any strength left, there is some cool water nearby.'

William stared up the darkening sky. Sounds from the camp drifted over the boulders, punctuated by the rush of the stream and Sarah's even breathing. Their second bath had been playful, albeit quick due to the sudden chill of the air. Once dried and dressed, they'd eaten.

He absently curled a finger around an errant lock of her still damp hair. She'd been so exhausted that she had nodded off in between bites of food. He'd easily coaxed her to bed, and his arms.

Now that she slept, the time to speak with the King was nigh. Yet, he had no great wish to leave her side. For when he returned all would be different.

William closed his eyes, only to be overwhelmed by visions of Sarah—laughing, crying or in the throes of passion. What madness had fallen over him? How had such a little bit of fluff come to affect him so?

He would give his life for her. And she knew that. A knowledge that would only make the days ahead that much more difficult. This *little bit of fluff* would surely make his life a living hell.

The fact that until this day she had been a virgin changed things slightly. Now, because she'd once again lied, he would have to wait a few weeks to fully implement his plans.

But in the end, she would be safe from the dangers his world had already wrought upon her. That certainty alone would give his convictions enough strength to sustain them.

Slowly easing his arm from beneath her, William leaned over her and dropped a kiss on her forehead. 'Some day, Sarah, I pray you forgive me.'

He released her from his embrace and then rose. As he knew they would be, a couple of guards were stationed nearby on the other side of the boulder. He motioned one aside and requested they keep an eye on his wife.

Certain the men would keep their word, William headed to the camp.

'Bronwyn.'

William swung around, and bowed his head. 'My lord. If you have a moment.'

'Of course I do. Walk with me.' The King offered him a goblet of wine that William waved off. Henry tossed the contents before asking, 'What is so important that you leave your new wife's bed?'

William watched Aryseeth, accompanied by four of the King's guards, cross the camp. Ire fired his blood and he clenched his fists to keep his hands from shaking in rage.

At his hesitation, Henry turned his head to follow William's line of sight. He turned back and grasped William's shoulder. 'Bronwyn, I wear no crown at this moment. Speak freely.'

Through gritted teeth, William nearly spat. 'That man should be dead.'

'Of course he should. I do not disagree. But if you remember correctly, you and Wynnedom brought him to me with an offer of trade that I could not refuse. If I have him killed now, how will we seal the agreement? How will I know how best to rescue the others still in captivity? Do you not still want their release, too?'

'Of course I do.'

'Then what do you expect me to do, Bronwyn? If I have him and his men killed, there will be no chance for negotiating the release of the others.'

'You need do nothing. I will gladly take his life.'

The King nodded. 'Fine, you do just that. Not only will you jeopardise the lives of the others still held, but what do you think Sidatha will do when he discovers his slave master's demise? Do you believe he will suddenly see the error of his ways and free the remaining slaves?'

When William looked down at his feet, Henry continued, 'Or do you perhaps not agree that he will simply find someone to replace Aryseeth? Someone who could possibly be even more evil?'

William doubted if a more evil man existed, but he

knew the truth in the King's logic. Still, it did nothing to calm the helplessness and outrage he felt. Henry stepped in front of him, preventing William from taking another step. 'I have seen firsthand the man's evilness. Before my eyes, he killed his own servant for an infraction so minor, I remember it not. And then, as if nothing untoward had occurred, he sought to engage me in an agreement to trade spices and gems for the lives of men to use in his sick games.'

'My lord, there is a difference between seeing the evilness and living it.' In an attempt to clear the darkness from once again entering his mind, William heaved a sigh. 'Hugh and I vowed to see to the freedom of the other men. We promised them we would not rest until they were released.'

'And you assume that you alone are responsible for what happens to them?' Henry resumed his walk. 'I know well what responsibility is, William. I am responsible for the lives and well-being of all those who reside on my lands. Do you believe that I take their oath of fealty lightly?'

'No, but—'

'But what? What is the difference? You made a vow to free the other men. I made a vow to keep my people well. To keep them safe. Some of the men still in Sidatha's cells are my subjects. I will not forget them, William. That is the only reason I lower myself to deal with the devil Aryseeth. So, until I can secure the safety of those men, I cannot permit you to kill the man.'

And William knew that until Aryseeth was dead, the slave master would not stop trying to get him back into captivity. Every moment Aryseeth lived, there would be danger—for him and for Sarah. He stopped and swallowed hard. It was now more imperative than ever to see his plan put into action. 'I seek a boon, my lord.'

'As long as it doesn't involve Aryseeth and blood, ask away.'

'I would request that you petition the Church for an annulment of my marriage.'

'What?' Henry swung around, his eyes wide with surprise. He rubbed his forehead, then dragged his hand down his face. 'On what grounds?'

'As long as Aryseeth lives, Sarah is not safe.'

'You seek to bargain with me?' Henry's voice rose. 'I will not barter his life for your marriage.'

William knew he needed to explain, quickly. 'Nay, my lord. I truly seek only to see her safe. I would see her back in the Queen's court. Free from me, and free to wed someone worthy of her hand.'

Henry stared at him a few moments, frowning as he appeared to digest what he'd heard. 'You are worthy of her hand.'

'No. I could not even honour the vow to protect her.'

'William, it was not your fault that she was taken.'

'Yes, it was.' He had promised to protect her, to keep her safe, and had failed. If it was not his fault, then whose?

'So, instead of trying harder to protect her, you feel it would be safer to give her up?'

If that's the way the King wanted to look at it, William wasn't going to argue. Not if it meant Henry would approach the Church.

'She would be safer among people of her own background than she would be with a former warrior slave.'

For a moment, when Henry narrowed his eyes, William thought he would refute that fact. But the King rubbed his chin and asked, 'What grounds do I use?'

Something didn't seem quite right; this conversation was going far smoother than he'd expected. Unable to work out what caused his unease, William answered, 'She was forced, my lord. Neither the Queen, nor I, gave her any other option.'

'But did she not stand before the Church and vow that she took you of her own free will?'

'Aye, but it was that, or face a cell,' William explained.

'She didn't appear to me to have the look of a woman who wed a man out of fear.'

William snorted. 'Sire, I had come to free her from Aryseeth's clutches. She would have worshipped any man who'd done the same.'

'Perhaps.' Henry nodded towards the camp. 'Even if I agree to this, I do not have men to spare. I cannot see her safely back to Eleanor.'

William hadn't expected him to do so. 'It is my responsibility. I will see her to the Queen.'

The King's shrug gave William pause. The feeling earlier that something wasn't quite right had strengthened. Henry raised a hand as if he had given up without a fight. 'I will send four men along with you and a missive to my wife explaining the situation. It will go far towards easing Sarah's entry back into the court.'

The relief that William had expected didn't come. Instead his chest tightened as if someone had punched him. 'Thank you, my lord.'

'Is there a possibility that she's carrying your child, William?'

William coughed, nearly choking on his own spit. He'd already taken that into consideration. 'Yes, there is. And if it proves the case, I will keep her as my wife.'

Henry nodded as if he completely understood. 'Then

here's what we'll do. You escort Sarah back to Queen Eleanor. I'll send a missive ahead, so that she expects you. I will also send along a missive for the Church, instructing Eleanor to include her fervent apology in forcing Sarah's hand before she directs the petition to the Church. In the meantime, you will remain at court.'

'Sire, I can't do that.'

'Oh?'

'I told Wynnedom that I would see to the training of his men.'

'Wynnedom will have to do with someone else. I have men capable of training his guards. He's not that far from here, I'll have one of the guards explain the situation to him.'

The last thing William wanted to do was to linger at the court, with Sarah in such close proximity. 'But—'

'But nothing. That's the offer, Bronwyn. Take it or not. The Church will take some time before answering the petition. And if Sarah has already conceived, it is your duty to be there to see the petition withdrawn.' Henry laughed and clapped William's shoulder once again. 'Do not look so horrified at the thought of being at court. It will not be for long.'

Regardless of the number of days, William knew they would feel like an eternity. Not willing to lose the King's good humour and help, William nodded. 'I accept your offer.'

Under his breath, Henry mumbled something William couldn't hear. But at full voice, the King said, 'Good. I will have all ready at first light. For now I bid you a goodnight and wish you well in explaining this to Lady Sarah.'

After taking his leave, William took his time returning

to the small camp beyond the boulders. It might be better to explain all to Sarah after they'd set out on the morrow. He wasn't certain how she would welcome the news.

It was possible Sarah would balk at this forced change of plans, and it could prove difficult to get her to see reason. He would essentially be setting her aside. He doubted if any woman would take such a slight rationally. Especially after becoming as intimate as he and Sarah had.

His wife relied far too much on her emotions rather than logic or reason. If she took offence, she would argue endlessly.

On the other hand, she'd been forced into this marriage. An annulment might prove to be the answer to her prayers. He had no way of knowing for certain.

He was still lost in thought when he arrived at the boulders and silently dismissed the guards. William climbed atop a flat rock and stared down at Sarah.

How hard would it be to trick her into believing that since they didn't care for each other, an annulment would be the best course of action for both of them. Any feelings he had were based solely on lust, while hers were from nothing more than gratitude and misplaced desire.

William knew that lying was a mortal sin, but he wondered how much his intentional plotting would add to the sin. The fires of hell did not frighten him. He'd already survived hell.

Nor did he fear living the rest of his life in solitude. All he knew for certain was that her safety was of more importance to him than anything else.

What he feared was that she would be affronted and fight him blindly. And in the end miss the opportunity to have the life she deserved.

He regretted very little in this life. But what he'd

done to her was unforgivable. To be unable to protect his wife was a deed worse than merely a mortal sin. He'd been left alone and unprotected in this world and he'd not have those terrors visited on anyone, most especially not his wife.

But since the King saw fit to send Aryseeth away instead of killing the man, William would have to look over his shoulder every day of his life. That knowledge only added to his determination to see Sarah safely away from him.

'What are you thinking about, William?'

He jumped at the touch of Sarah's hand against his chest and the sound of her words crashing into his thoughts. He'd been so lost in his gloom that he'd not heard her rise.

William took her hand from his chest and shook his head. 'Nothing,' he replied harshly, as if her presence bothered him, when in truth he longed to take her into his embrace. 'I think of nothing except the welcome silence that was about me.'

She backed away a step. In the light from their raging campfire, he saw the confusion register on her face. While it pricked at his heart, he did nothing to stop her worries from taking on life.

'William?' Sarah started to reach for him, but drew her arm back at his hard glare. What had she done? What had happened while she'd slept?

She walked to the fire, holding her hands above the warmth to thaw the iciness filling her veins with an unknown dread. She silently cursed her sudden timid nature. If she permitted words and a sour disposition to cow her so easily now, what would happen a week, or a month, from now?

She turned back to her husband. 'Has something happened?'

He glowered at her, making her think he'd not answer. But eventually, he said, 'No. Nothing. Go back to bed.'

How did one go so easily from being a passionate lover to surly if nothing had happened? She strode back to him, determined that he shake off this sudden dark cloud enveloping him. 'Come, now, William. It is quite apparent that something has happened to cause such a change in your mood.'

She reached up to touch his cheek. With a speed she hadn't expected, William grasped her wrist. 'What happened?'

'That is what I asked.' Sarah tugged her arm, trying to break free of his shackle-like hold. 'William, you are hurting me.'

He released her by pushing her arm away. 'After all this day has wrought, am I not permitted a moment's peace?'

'Peace? You want a moment of peace?' She stared up at him, meeting his glare with one of her own. 'Fine. I am going to bed. Join me when you've rid yourself of your surly mood.'

Before she ruined her fine anger with tears, Sarah lay down on the covers and pulled a blanket over her.

Chapter Thirteen

Sarah gritted her teeth against the pain throbbing behind her eyes. Between the constant jostling of the horse beneath her, and the glaring, relentless sun, she was certain her head would burst.

She gave her silent litany of woes pause and cautiously lowered her hand from her forehead to peek up at the sun. It was warming the wrong side of her face. They were headed south. But Wynnedom's land was north and east. By the Saints above, her husband was lost.

They hadn't spoken to each other since taking leave of the King early this morning. But she'd no wish to spend more time on the road than necessary and prodded her horse to a quicker pace. Coming up behind her husband, she called out, 'William.'

'What?' He didn't even turn to look at her and his mood was no better than it had been last night.

Sarah took a breath, fighting to keep her own temper in hand. 'We are going in the wrong direction.'

'No. We aren't.' His tone sounded like one she'd use with a petulant child.

'Yes. We are,' She corrected him in the same tone, adding, 'Wynnedom is north and east of here.'

'I know where Wynnedom is located.' His tone darkened further. 'I don't need you to tell me.'

The four guards that King Henry had ordered to ride with them increased their distance from her and William. Their intentional move made her aware that something was wrong. Something the guards knew. And if their sudden distancing was any indication, it was something she wasn't going to take lightly.

Apparently, William wasn't the only person who thought she could be a shrew.

Sarah narrowed her eyes, as much from the pain, as from distrustful contemplation. 'William?'

'What?'

Again, his anger-laden voice set her more on edge. She twisted the horse's reins, taking her frustration out on the thick leather rather than on the infuriating man ahead of her. 'Where are we going?'

'Poitiers.'

His one-word answers were coming close to getting the... She blinked, letting her thought trail off. *Did he say Poitiers?* Certain she'd misheard, Sarah asked him again, 'Where?'

'Poitiers.'

She pulled up sharply on the reins. Her horse reared to a halt. William kept riding until he obviously realised she no longer followed. He turned to face her.

The instant impression of facing an opponent in the lists flitted through Sarah's mind. Her hand itched for a lance, blunted or not, with which to challenge him. Unfortunately, she was left with nothing but her voice. 'What do you mean, Poitiers?'

'I am taking you back to the Queen's court.'

'Oh, you are? For what reason, pray tell?'

William waved the guards to move away even more before he answered, 'This was a mistake, Sarah, for both of us. I am returning you to the Queen's court for your own safety.'

'A mistake?' Confused, she asked, 'What was a mistake?'

'Our marriage.'

A fist driven into her stomach couldn't have hurt any worse. And the knowledge that his obvious rejection did hurt so, took her breath away. When had she let him slip far enough into her heart that it mattered? How had he sneaked past the walls she'd so carefully erected against any intrusion?

Confused by her own response and angry with him, Sarah asked, 'What did I do wrong? Did I not perform well enough in your bed?' She couldn't have calmed the heavy sarcasm evident in her tone had she wanted to.

He shook his head. 'That has nothing to do with my decision. You did nothing wrong.'

Her mind was filled with such a whirl of thoughts that she barely heard his answer. 'And how will our returning to the court correct this *mistake*?' She flinched at her own use of the word.

'King Henry has promised to petition the Church for an annulment of our marriage. You will be free to wed again.'

She knew her mouth was hanging open, but she didn't care if she looked like some crazed fishwife. A part of her realised from the rigidity of her body, the conflicting rush of ice and fire racing the length of her spine, and the sudden urge to choke William, that she was in shock.

But her heart and her head were in so much pain that the only thing she could think to do was to scream at him. 'What the hell are you babbling about? Annulment? Have you lost your mind? Did one of Aryseeth's men beat you about the head?'

'Sarah—'

'No!' She held out her hand as if to stop his words. 'Shut up, William.' All traces of courtly behaviour deserted her as memory of them making love raced through her mind. A memory that now seemed to laugh at her. 'You have taken from me the only thing I had to give and now you think to toss me aside like a gnawed bone?'

Sarah paused just long enough to take a deep breath. *'Trust me, Sarah.'* She mimicked his words from only days ago. 'Trust you? For the love of God, why? So you could steal my heart like a thief, only to trounce on it?'

She looked away, searching for the slightest shred of dignity she could find. Unable to grasp even a thread to pull about herself, she admitted, 'Dear Lord, William, I was such a fool to trust you.'

She had taken the risk and discovered, yet again, that it was not worth the price. When would she learn? How many times would giving her trust, and her heart, be thrown back in her face before she stopped opening herself up for the hurt?

Sarah stared across the distance at him. The barest trace of a smirk slanting one side of his mouth cut her as deeply as his words had. 'Are you enjoying this, William? Will memories of the hurt you caused me humour you until you find the next woman foolish enough to believe your softly spoken lies?'

He crossed his hands over the pommel of his saddle, appearing for all the world like a man at peace with his life. His uninterested look choked Sarah's questions off in her throat.

She closed her eyes tightly and clenched her jaw. *Please, Lord, please, do not let me cry now. Later, perhaps, but not now.*

Nearly certain she could get through the rest of this day dry-eyed, she stiffened her spine, squared her shoulders and glared at William. 'You were correct. This was a mistake. Let us make haste to Poitiers, my lord.'

To her satisfaction, the art of duplicity easily returned. Lying to him, and herself, was the only method of self-defence she had. It would be the only way she could get through the next few days.

William nodded, but he said nothing. He waved at the guards, beckoning them to rejoin the party before he turned his horse around to continue their journey.

More than willing to make this the shortest trip possible, Sarah hadn't complained about being on the back of her horse until it was too dark to see the road ahead. But now, the only part of her body that did not burn, throb, or ache was her feet.

The covers beneath her provided little cushion between her sore body and the hard ground. She tried to focus on the stars overhead, but her mind kept drifting to the one thought that had plagued her most of the day.

What had she done?

Two familiar hands carrying food—an apple, cheese, bread, dried meat—blocked her vision of the stars. 'Eat.'

She pushed William's hands away. 'I am not hungry.' That much was the truth. The thought of putting food into her stomach made her queasy.

He didn't leave as she'd hoped. Instead he sat down beside her. 'You have to eat, Sarah.'

'I don't *have* to do anything.' To be even more contrary, she asked, 'What difference does it make to you?'

'It would make no sense to get ill from not eating.'

'Why did you bother coming to rescue me from Aryseeth? Would it not have been better...easier...to just leave me there?'

She'd goaded him on purpose. There was no reason he shouldn't be as angry as she. But she hadn't expected him to grab the front of her gown and jerk her upright.

'Stop this. You will eat if I have to force the food down your throat.'

Vile curses were on the tip of her tongue. 'Go to...' But the profanity she wanted to spew at him lodged in her throat. 'Leave me alone, William. Just leave me alone.'

'I will. Once we are no longer wed. Until then, you need do as I bid.'

Sarah turned her face away and swallowed. She wanted to rail at him, wanted to beat her fists against his chest. But one word, one question kept pushing all else aside. *Why?*

A day ago, she would have done his bidding with a light heart—or at least with little argument. A day ago, he'd teased her, held her, made love to her. Why now did he want to set her aside? But she feared the answer to her question, so she held it inside.

She looked up at him, searching for any emotion, any hint that he might think of her as something more than a temporary responsibility.

No emotion was evident on his features. Nothing that would give her a clue to his thoughts. She looked closer as light from the dancing fire illuminated his eyes.

Sarah studied his hard, unwavering gaze. She'd seen the golden flecks shimmer beneath the throes of passion. She had witnessed the glittering flash caused by anger. And the barely perceptible twinkle when he'd teased her.

But this dull, muddy brown stare held no trace of life or emotion—not passion, anger, nor light-hearted jesting.

Even through the rage slamming inside her, tearing her gut to pieces, she realised that something—something she couldn't yet name—was dreadfully wrong.

Something so dreadful that he'd decided to set her aside rather than face whatever tormented him. Until she knew what that something was, she would be unable to help him, or to help herself.

She held his gaze, hoping to catch sight of life, as she picked up the apple. 'I don't have a knife.'

William released her, frowning. He didn't trust her abrupt change in demeanour. It could only mean that she was plotting.

He didn't want her to think she could form a plan of attack that would change his mind. He wanted her to believe that he no longer desired her as his wife. It rankled that he'd underestimated her.

William jerked his dagger out of the scabbard and handed it to her. The weapon was a little overmuch to use as an eating knife, but it would have to do.

Sarah stared at the weapon, then shifted her attention to his chest. From her perspective he most likely deserved to have the blade planted in his chest. However, it wasn't on his agenda this night. He leaned back, warning her, 'Do not consider it.'

She blinked, then stabbed the apple. 'Consider what?'

The blade flew through the apple, barely missing her

fingers. He swore and grabbed both away from her. 'Do not consider slicing off your fingers.'

When her eyes widened with surprise, William realised he'd made a mistake. She'd been paying too close attention to his expressions. And perhaps to the tone and cadence of his voice.

Sarah might not be a battle-hardened warrior, but she'd learned to pay close attention to her opponents. He'd forgotten that, as the Queen's spy, she would be skilled at reading a person's emotion by their movements, the shifting look on their face, or the subtle differences in the way they spoke.

If she thought she would be able to outflank him by watching and waiting, so be it. He might have unwittingly given away a trace of emotion this night, but he'd not make that mistake again. From now on, he'd simply have to maintain tighter control over his features and voice.

A feat that might prove easier said than done.

He sliced the apple and handed the pieces to her. Using the bottom of his tunic to wipe the blade clean, he then sheathed the dagger and rose. 'Eat and go to sleep. We leave early on the morrow.'

She snapped off a bite of the apple slice and gazed up at him. 'That anxious to be free of me, are you?'

'I see no reason to delay.'

He turned away, and as he left, he heard her softly say, 'You are a very poor liar, William.'

It was all he could do not to stop in his tracks. No. He'd kept his tone even. And hadn't let so much as a frown mar his expression. So, what had she seen? What did she think she heard in his voice? Was it simply wishful thinking on her part?

Sarah watched his back stiffen for a fraction of a

heartbeat and knew he'd heard her. That had been her intention. Let him focus his attention on making certain she couldn't see through his lies. The harder he tried to hide his expressions, the more she would see.

She hadn't been the Queen's spy for naught. It never failed to amaze her that people didn't take the briefest flash of their eyes, the slightest spike in the tone, or rhythm, of their voice into consideration. They thought that if they masked the features on their face, or stilted the movements of their body, that none would be the wiser.

With some people, an emotionless look, or a stiff immobile body were the first clues that something was not quite right. And others spoke faster, or slower, or changed the pitch of their voice when attempting to hide something.

Then there were those like her husband. The easy ones, who had mirrors for eyes. All else could be in perfect harmony, giving nothing away by the look on their face, the way they moved, or the sound of their voice. But the slightest difference in the hue of their eyes, or the size of their pupils, gave away more than they realised.

Perhaps he didn't care for her. And perhaps he truly believed she'd be better off at court. But she didn't believe either was true. And while even the slight chance that either was the case hurt her more than was acceptable, that wasn't the information she needed. There was only one question and one alone that, when answered, could provide her with a way to fight this decision of his.

Why?

How she was going to discover that was unclear. Some sleep might help. And, yes, some food might, too.

She did, however, notice that he'd become wary

when she had stopped asking questions and seemed to resign herself to his will. He'd obviously expected more of a fight from her.

Sarah turned her face away from the group gathered around the campfire and smiled. Oh, he'd get his fight, but not the kind he wanted. He had once told her that he could tell when she was plotting something. Good. She would give him something to worry about.

If he worried about her plotting, it was only because he feared falling victim to her plans. And if he feared that, then he wasn't as single-mindedly determined to set her aside as he tried to make her believe.

If so much wasn't at stake, she would almost feel sorry for him.

Chapter Fourteen

William glowered at the road ahead. Even though the journey from Sidatha's Palace to England had taken over a year, it hadn't seemed as long as this one. Because he was unfamiliar with the area, he'd let the guards talk him into taking this alternate route. They'd vehemently insisted that it would make for a shorter trip.

Shorter in distance, perhaps, but not time. This badly maintained, winding road covered a terrain proving much more rugged.

If he didn't know better, he'd think that the woman riding behind him, laughing and talking with the guards, was happy to see this trip prolonged. Perhaps not exactly happy, but she didn't seem distressed in the least.

It would take someone much duller of wit than he not to realise she was up to something. Of course she was—how could he have expected less of her?

This worrying about whatever she plotted was making him half-crazed. Which was probably part of her plan. She'd make him lose his mind, then declare they couldn't have the marriage annulled because he lacked full reasoning capabilities.

Considering the way he wanted to throttle Henry's guards, her plan might just work.

'William?'

He bit back a groan at the sound of her voice. He turned his head to look at her over his shoulder. 'What?'

She tipped her head to the side, smiled at him and pouted her lips. Then asked, 'Are we stopping for a meal break soon?'

He forced his mind away from the idea of kissing the teasing look from her face, and answered, 'I told you to eat something this morning.'

'I did not feel well then. But now I find that I am famished. If it will delay us too much...'

'Of course it will delay us. But it would be rather hard to gain the good graces of the Church if I let you starve to death.'

His answer wiped the teasing expression from her face. Now, she appeared ready to curse. He faced forwards and said, 'I smell a cooking fire. Perhaps there is a small village just ahead, we'll stop there.'

He hoped it was a village. A public area would provide the perfect place to stop. There would be less chance for either of them to have much contact. At the moment, he preferred not being alone with her.

It would be all too easy to get into a heated argument that he knew would not end in his favour. He was too angry, in truth, far too filled with jealousy at the thought of her marrying another, to be rational. This was something he needed to overcome soon. The question was—how? Perhaps the more important question should be—why?

Before he could find the answers, they were in the

centre of a cluster of huts. Close enough to a village for him. William dismounted, then helped Sarah from her horse, before any of the guards could offer their assistance.

With his hands round her waist and hers on his shoulders, he lowered her towards the ground. When her head was near his, she leaned forwards, brushing her cheek against his.

He paused, momentarily revelling in the slight touch, before reasoning took over. 'Sarah, don't.'

To his amazement, she did as he asked, without arguing. Once he'd lowered her to the ground, she rested her palms against his chest. 'Why are you doing this to us?' Not waiting for an answer, she walked away.

King Henry's guards gathered around the small well-house. The two younger ones were going out of their way to make certain Sarah was comfortable. One procured an empty barrel for her to sit on, while the other brought her water to drink.

William clenched his jaw as a wave of irrational anger whipped over him. It was doubtful that he would be able to completely avoid her at court, so this was something he needed to get used to. Otherwise, he'd find himself in a cell the first time he pounded one of her admirers into the ground.

An elderly man approached him, just as a small commotion broke out near the well-house. One of the older guards stumbled to a nearby copse of trees and bushes and fell to his knees, retching.

Of course, regardless of her own health, his wife saw fit to rush to the sick man's aid. Clearing the distance between them in a few long stride, William shouted, 'Sarah, get away from him.'

Too late. She was already kneeling at the man's side, checking his face for a fever with her hand.

'Get up.' William grasped her arm. 'Let the other men see to him.'

'William, he needs help, he's sick.'

'Aye, and you have no knowledge of what sickened him. Yet you put your own health at risk.'

But did she see the wisdom in his concern? No. She shook off his hold, jammed her fists on her hips and glared up at him. 'He didn't seem to be feverish. It was most likely something he ate, or drank, this morning that has disagreed with him.'

William took a step closer to her, intentionally seeking to intimidate her. 'I thought you were the Queen's spy—not her physician. Leave the men to deal with him, Sarah.'

Someone smaller and weaker would have listened to him. A grown man would have followed his order. His wife, on the other hand, tossed her head back and warned, 'You gave up the right to order me about any more. So don't tell me what to do.'

He reached out and captured her chin in his hand. 'I have never harmed a woman in my life, but, Sarah—'

To his complete amazement, she cut him off with a laugh. Then said, 'Nor will you now.'

The only thing worse than her ignoring his orders was knowing she was right. He tugged, drawing her closer as he lowered his head. And the only thing worse than knowing she was right was realising how much he admired her audacity.

He felt the tension drain out of her, as she fluttered her eyelids closed. Her breath was warm and inviting against his lips.

Before he could touch his mouth to hers, a scream of abject horror tore them apart. William released her and shook his head, trying to clear the treacherous haze of desire, then turned to see who had screamed and why.

A white-haired woman, with the contents of her now-empty basket strewn about her feet, stared at him in shock. She let the basket fall from her limp fingers, then made the sign of a cross before muttering what could have been, to William's ears, a prayer or a curse.

The elderly man who had approached him before the guard became ill once again came to his side. He tore his hood from his head, twisting it in his hands, as he asked, 'My lord, are you he?'

'He who?'

Sarah slapped a hand over her mouth to mute her giggle at his inability to form a decent question. He spared her a warning frown, before asking the man, 'Who do you think I am?'

'Are you Lord Simon's son?'

Nearly seventeen years fell away as if they'd been nothing but a nightmare. William swayed on his feet, while the memories that he'd buried unearthed to whirl violently through his mind.

Sarah touched his arm, giving him the anchor needed to steady his suddenly weak legs. An anchor that he realised would sorely be missed. He swallowed past the lump in his throat and asked, 'Gunther?'

Frail arms embraced him. 'We thought you were dead.'

William returned the embrace, looking over the man's nearly bald head to the guards. Oddly enough, the sick guard now appeared hale and hearty. The King's men had duped him about the road to get him here intentionally. He was certain it'd been done at their Sire's order.

He glanced down at Sarah. The glint of unshed tears pooling in her eyes spoke of her innocence in this ploy.

When she moved to back away from him, William instinctively reached out to keep her near. 'No, don't go.'

Gunther released him and stepped back. 'Ah, William, it does this old heart good to see you.'

The woman who had screamed joined them. She stood just behind Gunther and silently peered at William.

It took him a few moments of searching his memories to be able to ask, 'Berta, is that you?' The woman nodded, then burrowed into Gunther's arms, sobbing.

William nodded at Sarah, who stood at his side. 'This is Lady Sarah, my wife.' He paused, wondering why the introduction fell so easily from his lips when it would soon be untrue. 'Sarah, this is Gunther, my father's steward, and his wife, Berta.' He leaned over and in a mock whisper added, 'Be careful, Berta has a wicked right fist.'

Laughter soon chased away the woman's tears, and she moved away from Gunther. 'You've come home.'

William looked around the small cluster of huts. 'It appears that way, but I don't remember any of this. What has happened?'

'Your father's brother relieved us of our duties soon after you disappeared.' Gunther shrugged. 'We had nowhere to go. And he didn't seem to care if we claimed this little plot for ourselves.'

William curled his lips in a snarl. 'And how is dear Arthur these days?'

Berta hissed, then answered, 'Just where he should be. Dead.'

'Now, now, Berta.' Gunther patted her shoulder. 'He passed away unexpectedly nearly ten years or so ago.'

'The keep?'

'Remains empty.'

'My lord.' The miraculously cured guard approached, holding out a long leather pouch that would likely contain a scrolled missive. He kept his distance, extending the scroll from the ends of his fingers. 'King Henry directed me to give you this upon our arrival.'

William snatched it from him. 'Anything else I should know about?'

The guard hesitated before shaking his head. 'No.'

'No? Or, no, not yet?'

With a quick turn, the guard went back to join the other men. William groaned at the hasty exit.

He was almost afraid to read the missive, certain it would contain a directive he'd not like. His stomach knotted as he removed the scroll from the pouch, then scanned the message.

Bronwyn Keep and the surrounding lands were his to hold, rebuild, fortify, and protect—for Lady Sarah of Bronwyn. Upon the deaths of the lord and lady, the property would pass to their oldest living child—son or daughter. However, in the event Lady Sarah's child was not of Bronwyn blood, the property reverted to the Crown.

By the third time he reread the missive, the words swam on the page.

Sarah touched his arm. 'William?'

With great care, he rolled the missive, slid it back into the leather pouch and tucked it into his tunic. 'We will discuss this later.'

Much later—after he'd had enough time to clear the red haze of outrage from his vision.

Ignoring her questioning look, he turned back to Gunther. 'You said the keep had remained empty? Why?'

'At first we knew not what to do and waited for the King to send a new lord. When none arrived, Lord Arthur's men left and the keep was far too much for the few of us to maintain.'

William understood that. He'd already noted that this village contained little more than a dozen people, and half of them were past their prime.

'And then…' Gunther paused, a confused look marring his brow. 'A few years ago, strange things started happening at the keep.'

Berta piped up, 'It is haunted, my lord.' She nodded vigorously as if the motion gave credence to her absurd statement. 'By spirits.'

Well, of course it was haunted by spirits. What else would haunt it? William closed his eyes, keeping his sarcasm to himself, and rubbed the bridge of his nose.

To make the explanation even worse, Gunther added, 'We all thought it was your spirit finally come home. But since you obviously aren't dead, perhaps it is your parents who walk the floors.'

At the moment, humouring them seemed the easier choice. 'Do they haunt during the day?'

Berta looked at him as if *he'd* lost the ability to reason. 'Of course not.'

'Then I will have a look at the keep.'

Gunther shuffled from one foot to the other. 'My lord?'

'Yes?' William heard the tightness in his voice, at his increasing impatience.

'There is not much to see.'

Bronwyn had been naught but a timber tower keep. After all these years *not much to see* could mean anything from overgrown vegetation, to a burnt-out shell, to something in between. 'I still want to see it.'

Gunther led him down a narrow walking path through a woods populated mostly with fallen dead trees and bramble. Sarah and the four guards followed.

What passed for a forest opened out to an overgrown field separating them from a…keep?

William squinted. That couldn't be Bronwyn. Not even on its worse day had it looked as bad as this. He squared his shoulders and cleared a path before him with his sword, hacking at the weeds and brush as he went.

Once near the keep, William shook his head. While the gate and the twin gate towers still stood, the rest of the wooden palisade forming the wall had fallen. Nature had waged war on Bronwyn and, apparently, was winning.

He and the two younger guards hacked away at more weeds in the bailey. The stables to his right had burned to nothing more than blackened rubble. The central well-house had fallen over and into the well.

The stone-lined steps leading up the motte to the tower seemed to still be intact. At least they didn't crumble beneath his feet.

However, the wooden steps at the base of the keep were rotted away, leaving no visible method of entering the tower from this side. William cocked one eyebrow, and ordered the others, 'Stand back.'

He rammed the pommel of his sword against a rotten section of the keep's wall. The wall fell apart and he peered inside.

To his confused surprise, the inside appeared to be lived in. He pulled back out and looked at Gunther. 'Someone is staying here.'

Gunther and Bertha answered in unison. 'Ghosts, just like we told you, my lord.'

William's temples throbbed. This day seemed to

keep becoming more and more of an ordeal. A wife
who disobeyed him at every turn. Guards who tricked
him into taking a different road. A village and people
that brought back more memories than he'd ever
thought to recover. A missive from King Henry saying
in effect that he could have his keep, or his annulment,
but not both. The missive was a sad jest. And the keep
was nothing but a decaying haunted tower that had
been taken over by weeds, brush and, according to
Gunther—ghosts.

What next?

He vaguely heard Sarah's sudden gasp of breath,
before she folded into a faint at his feet.

'Sarah, wake up.'

William's voice seemed to be coming at her from
a great distance. She willed herself to do his bidding,
but couldn't find her way out of the fog surrounding
her.

'Sarah.' The bed beneath her dipped with his weight.

Bed? Where was she? Fighting the urge to fall back
to sleep, she turned her head from side to side and forced
her eyes to open. Only to quickly close them against the
glare of the torch light.

'Are you awake?'

She shielded her eyes with her hand. 'I think so.
Where are we?'

'Bronwyn.' He pulled her up, plumped the pillows
behind her and let her relax against them.

'What happened?'

He handed her a hunk of bread. 'I forgot to feed you.
So you fainted.'

'Oh. I was feeling rather queasy.' She glanced around

the chamber. 'For a keep in such disrepair, this room is rather...well kept.'

'I'm sure we can thank the ghosts for that.'

She nearly choked on the bread and he handed her a goblet filled with water. 'William. That's not possible. Ghosts are just spirits, it isn't like they can sweep and dust.'

'Aren't you amusing?' He moved to sit on a bench alongside the bed. 'Apparently, someone is tricking the villagers in order to live here.'

Between bites, she asked, 'So, what are you going to do about it?'

'Me? It's not up to me.'

'How can it not be up to you?'

He leaned over, retrieved the scroll from the floor, then handed it to her. 'Here, read this.'

She tore off another bite of the bread and popped it into her mouth before unrolling the missive. William held the goblet out to her.

By the time she'd read the last line, she was choking on the bread. She grabbed the waiting goblet from his hand. When the bout of coughing had eased, she read the missive again.

'This has to be a cruel jest.' Sarah turned to him. 'William, I had nothing to do with this.'

He took it from her hand and put it back into the pouch. 'I never thought you had.'

Sarah frowned. While he was being polite, and acting concerned, there was still something missing. She searched his face.

'What are you doing, Sarah?'

Quickly turning her head, she said, 'Nothing.'

He leaned back on the bench. 'I am exceedingly tired of your games.'

'Games?' She twisted the covers beneath her hands.

'You heard me. You search for something in my face. Something that makes you believe you know what I'm thinking. What do you look for?'

She had to give him credit. Not many people realised what she was doing. She wasn't yet ready to tell him that she looked to see if any flecks of golden specks glimmered in his eyes. If she divulged that secret, he would only find a way to completely avoid her.

So, she said, 'I was simply trying to determine if your frown was from being tired, or from anger.'

He could hold himself stiff, and ignore her, in an attempt to deceive her. But he could do nothing to change the reaction of his eyes. She would always see the enlarged pupils and the golden shimmer of passion, or the sparkle of teasing, and even the glint of anger.

'And how did you think to discover which was the case?'

She shrugged. 'I thought that if your eyes were red, then you were tired. And if not, I would assume anger made you scowl so.'

At his intent stare, she added, 'That is my only game, William. I don't claim to know your thoughts. I can only claim to know if you're tired or angry.'

Before she could take another breath, or form another lie to distract him, he knelt on the bed and leaned over her. 'What about your eyes, Sarah? How do they change with your moods?'

Her heart pounded so hard she found it difficult to breath. She wanted him to caress her—to kiss her. She needed his touch, his lips on hers desperately. But not if weeks from now he would set her aside.

She stared up at him, knowing this could hurt more than anything thus far. 'You are welcome to discover that for yourself—once you vow to have the petition to the Church withdrawn.'

and so at the board he may not be to serve of it has will and some
a surging there has. You are a vicious to you must
another, thought is up you go to hope the positive
as much a substance.

Chapter Fifteen

'That I will not do.' William rose.

Sarah had known this would not be easy. But she needed to know what had changed. Before he slipped away—physically and mentally—she curled her fingers into the fabric covering his chest and held him near the bed. 'Why not, William? What has changed to make you dislike me so strongly?'

'Did I say that?' He disengaged her fingers from his tunic, and then sat back down on the bench. 'I don't remember saying that I disliked you.'

To be honest, at the moment she couldn't remember either. 'Even if you did not use those words, you have made it plain that it is true.'

'It would be easier for you to believe it so.'

'Why? Don't I at least deserve to know why I am being cast aside?'

He touched her cheek briefly, his hand warm against her flesh. 'Would this discussion not be easier at court, surrounded by people you knew, rather than here alone, in a bedchamber?'

'No, William. It would not. I do not want an audience, and I cannot bear another day, another breath of wondering what I did that was so wrong.'

'What *you* did?' He stared at her. 'Sarah, you did nothing wrong.'

She wasn't certain if she wanted to laugh or cry at this absurd discussion. He obviously felt something for her. And she knew that she could so easily come to care for him deeply, if given time. Yet, they were discussing the annulment of their marriage.

'So, you claim not to dislike me and insist that I did nothing wrong. William, those are not reasons to have our marriage vows absolved.'

'It is hard to explain.'

'You must try.' He had to realise that he couldn't do this to her without some kind of explanation.

'Sarah, you don't deserve this.'

'You will get no argument from me on that.'

'I meant that you don't deserve to be married to someone who possesses nothing. No title, no wealth, nothing.'

She suddenly understood the danger of marrying someone without the benefit of a betrothal, or courtship. There'd been no time for them to learn of each other. No time to discover what the other thought, or dreamed of, or of what they hoped for the future.

The only things they'd had the opportunity to discover during their short marriage was that they greatly enjoyed touching or kissing each other, making love and how to tease, or goad, the other person into, or out of, rage. That obviously wasn't enough for him.

'William, I am no longer a child with a little girl's dreams. I care not about a title, only about the man.'

As she said the words, she realised they were true. While she'd used that very excuse against wedding him, now a title, and all that went with it, no longer mattered.

'And you do have something.' She waved a hand, encompassing the chamber. 'You have this keep.'

'Even this is not mine. It is yours to command.'

'You know full well that King Henry did that only to convince you to change your mind. Or to at least get you to stop and think.'

Henry would no more hand a keep over to her than he would to an enemy. Land was land—ramshackle or not, it had worth. And worth was too important a bargaining tool to give away without reason.

'You could have died. Or worse.'

Now they were getting to the crux of the problem. She heard the anger and dismay in his admission. 'And I didn't because you came for me. You saved me from the horrors Aryseeth had planned.'

'It was my *duty* to do so.' He rose to face away from her. 'Since it was my fault you were captured to begin with.'

His duty? She chose to ignore that part of his explanation, for now, focusing instead on the last. 'How was it your fault?'

'I left you alone.'

No, he hadn't. 'You left me with four armed guards.'

'Who had not been trained.'

She countered, 'Who had just successfully defeated Arnyll's men.'

'Obviously, they were unable to do so a second time.'

Sarah sat forwards, trying to make sense of his argument. 'Let me see if I have this. Since you feel that you failed in your duty to me, you have decided to make amends by setting me aside?' She shook her head at the lack of logic.

'No.' He turned and looked down at her. 'I am making amends by giving you the opportunity to wed someone who will better serve you.'

No one could better serve her than William. But she was curious to know his thoughts. 'Better serve me how?'

'It is doubtful that Aryseeth will cease his quest to return Hugh, Guy and I to captivity until his last breath. That puts you at risk, too. A risk I am not willing to take. You need to wed someone who can keep you safe, Sarah.'

'Regardless of what I think of this decision?' She understood his concern about the slave master. It was a shame Henry had not ordered the beast killed. Even so, she could not imagine anyone better suited to keeping her safe than William.

'You are not in a position to be rational about this decision.'

She couldn't be rational? And he thought *he* was? 'And why is that?' She really did not want to hear his answer, but she'd come this far.

'You would feel indebted to anyone who had come to your rescue.'

'Indebted is the last thing I feel for you.'

'If you are referring to what we shared in bed, let me assure you that lust is not particular about the parties involved.'

Her temples pounded. Sarah had to swallow her ire at his callous assurance. 'Meaning I would moan and writhe for any man?'

His eyes blazed, but he nodded.

If he thought he was angry, he truly had no idea how outraged she was at his calm, albeit completely irrational comments. Unfortunately, she knew that she was fast becoming as irrational as he and was powerless to stop it.

The arrogant, all-knowing, smug look on his face sent her over the edge. She fisted her hands on the bed and glared up at him. 'Perhaps, husband, we should test the truth of that assumption.'

William grabbed a handful of fabric on the front of her gown and pulled her up on the bed. With their noses level, he nearly growled an order, 'Rid yourself of that idea.'

'Or what?'

'You are still my wife and will act as such.'

'Your *wife*? I am naught but your responsibility. Your duty. So what difference does it make what I do? In a matter of weeks, the vows we spoke to each other will be struck from the records.'

'By God, woman, as long as I am your husband, you will do as I say.'

She contemplated her response for less than half a second; knowing it could end badly, she weighed the odds. Sarah pushed against his chest. 'Get your hands off of me, and leave me alone.'

'You think to give *me* orders?' His voice deepened further.

She matched the level deadliness of his tone. 'You heard me.'

He released her abruptly. She fell back on to the bed, with him pinning her wrists to the mattress. She intentionally tried to buck him off of her.

'Stop it.' He held her face between his hands. 'You are weaker than I, Sarah. You have not the power to fight me. I will take my hands off you when I am good and ready.'

'Then you best be good and ready now.' She yelled at him, 'Leave me alone.'

He cut off her shout with his mouth hard against hers, sweeping her away, giving her no choice, demanding a response.

It was all she could do not to smile in triumph beneath his lips.

Too soon he broke the kiss; sliding his mouth to her ear, he hoarsely whispered, 'You are such a brazen wench.'

'What else could you expect?' The laugh she'd fought to hold inside escaped.

He released her wrists. 'I was right. You do have all the makings of a shrew.'

Sarah clasped him to her. 'And I am wed to a brute who thinks to order me about at whim.'

'That was a dangerous game to play.'

'Oh, William, you worry for naught.' She brushed her cheek against his. 'Just because I can goad you into mindlessness does not mean you would lose control and harm me. You have more honour than that.'

He stiffened and his withdrawal chilled her as effectively as being doused with ice-cold water. She caught the ragged edge of his sigh before he pushed off of her. 'Come, it is time to return to the village.'

Sarah narrowed her eyes in thought. So that was it. Not only did he believe that he'd failed in his duty to her, he seemed to think that, by doing so, his honour had been besmirched.

Sweet Mary, as a warrior, duty and honour were all. She understood duty, but how was she, who knew nothing about battle and little about men's honour, to convince him he was wrong?

He was right. They did need to return to the Queen's court. Not for an annulment, but because Eleanor was the only woman she knew who might be able to help her.

That is, if after this last failure, the Queen would even speak to her, let alone help her work out a way to keep her marriage intact.

Sarah reached up and took the hand William offered. He pulled her up from the bed and brushed the wrinkled and bunched skirt of her gown, muttering, 'You know what they'll be thinking.'

She nudged her shoulder against his arm playfully. 'That we were doing those husband-and-wife things.'

'No doubt.'

The corner of the tapestry hanging on the far wall seemed to move. Sarah blinked, not certain the movement had actually happened. It did so again. She placed a finger over William's lips, then pointed towards the threadbare wall covering.

Once again, the corner billowed out as if pushed by an unseen hand. She moved closer to William. But he edged her aside and tore the tapestry from the wall.

The sound of rushing feet and squeaks of fear echoed from behind an open door set into the wall.

'Stay here. I think we've discovered Bronwyn's ghosts.'

Sarah sat on the edge of the bed, waiting for him to retrieve the miscreants who'd frightened the villagers into not returning to the keep.

She didn't have to wait long. William came back through the door with a young male dangling from each hand. A young woman followed close behind.

He dropped the boys to the floor. 'Explain yourselves.'

To Sarah's open-mouthed shock, the young woman—little more than a girl—slipped her gown from her shoulders, letting it pool on the floor around her feet.

The girl approached William, her hips swaying from side to side. 'If you let them go, you can have me.'

Sarah's eyes widened in speechless shock at the girl's brazen proposal. This half-grown child might have been of an age to wed—barely—but where had she learned such wanton behaviour? By her sinuous movements, seductive gaze and softly beckoning tone, she was either temptress born, or completely lacking in judgement.

While the girl amazed her, it was William who drew her attention. What healthy male would turn away one as desirous as this girl? Sarah's ears buzzed with anger. The longer her husband stood rooted to the floor with his unblinking stare nailed to the vision before him, the more heated her ire grew.

Finally, he responded to the girl's proposal. 'And what would I do with you?' He pointed at the gown on the floor. 'Put your clothes back on.'

His response wiped away Sarah's anger, until the woman-child ignored him, moving closer to place her hands against his chest. Before one word could leave the seductress's parted lips, Sarah rose. 'Perhaps his order was not clear enough.'

She grabbed the gown from the floor and jammed it into the space between the girl and William. 'Get dressed.'

The girl's face reddened under Sarah's scrutiny, and she quickly scrambled back into her gown.

William turned to confront the boys. Huddled together against the wall, they shrank beneath the glare of the man towering over them.

Sarah felt a moment of pity for the lads. They were terrified of what surely appeared to them a predator ready to pounce on its helpless prey. The moment passed quickly when she remembered Gunther, Berta and the others living in hovels.

William crossed his arms against his chest and did nothing more than stare down at them. Which was enough to cause one of the boys to bolt for the door. He'd underestimated William's speed. Anyone who equated his size to slowness had either never seen him move, or lacked a brain. The boy was guilty of both.

He hadn't taken his second step when a large hand clamped down on his shoulder, bringing him up short. 'You were not dismissed.'

William swung him around and pushed him next to his partner, accusing, 'The three of you are Bronwyn's ghosts.'

Since they'd not been asked a question, the boys wisely held their tongues. The girl, however, wasn't as wise. 'You are strangers here. What does it matter to you?'

For her stupidity, Sarah pushed her over to join the boys. Let William deal with the three of them, because she was suddenly too tired to care. She dropped on to the edge of the bed.

William looked at her, as if torn between coming to her side, or seeing to the three ghosts. Sarah waved a hand at him. 'I will be fine. Continue.'

He turned back to face the three. 'How long have you been tricking the villagers into staying away?'

The girl tossed her head, sending her unbound hair over her shoulder. 'We don't have to tell you anything.'

'That's where you're wrong. You have to tell me everything.'

'Why? Who do you think you are?'

Sarah's eyes widened at the girl's belligerent tone of voice. Didn't she realise how dangerous it was to speak to an adult man, a stranger no less, with a sword and dagger strapped to his waist, in such a manner?

She turned her head away to hide her amused smile as she remembered herself at that age. Of course the girl realised that. She was frightened, and her mouth was the only form of bravado she knew. Especially since the man had already turned down the offer of her body, and, with the jealous wife still present, she'd probably realised making him another offer could prove dangerous.

'Who do I think I am?' Impatience deepened his voice. 'I am the Lord of Bronwyn and you will tell me what I want to know.'

Sarah looked back at the group, curious to hear their answer.

The taller of the two boys squared his shoulders and took a breath before beginning, 'My lord, I am sorry, we didn't know. We've been here in the keep...' He paused as if uncertain. 'A long time. Maybe three, four winters now. It was right after our parents died in the stable fire.'

The shorter boy moved closer to the girl, as if seeking comfort. She draped an arm across his shoulders.

Sarah gasped softly, trying not to interrupt. Three or four years? Not one of them appeared to be over fifteen years old. They'd only been children when they had first started this charade.

'Why didn't you go to the village?'

The girl answered, dragging her toe back and forth across the floor. 'They didn't know we were here. Our parents always warned us to stay away from the village. They said that the people there must be mad to live in the woods instead of the keep, so we avoided them. That's why we pretended to be ghosts. It kept the people away.'

'We slept most of the day.' The boy next to her pointed at the bed, adding, 'Here. Then, at night, we would light fires and make funny sounds if anyone came near.'

William shook his head. 'How old are you?'

The taller boy nodded toward the others. 'Joyce is sixteen. Alfred is ten. I'm Charles and I'm fifteen.'

'Well, Joyce, Alfred and Charles, you are coming to the village with us for the night. You will see that you were mistaken. The people are not mad. We'll decide what to do with you in the morning.'

'But, my lord, won't they be angry that we've tricked them?'

'No.' Sarah rose to join them. 'Not after we explain, they won't be angry.' She looked up at William. 'Shouldn't we return before it gets too dark?'

He agreed and put his hand on her waist to escort her from the room. Sarah caught a glimpse of Joyce's hard, speculating stare and knew she'd need to speak with the girl tonight—before the child did anything foolish to get herself hurt.

Sarah had only guessed that the villagers wouldn't be angry with the children. So, she was greatly relieved to discover she'd been correct. Since Gunther and Berta had instantly taken the three under their protection, the rest of the villagers followed suit.

The two boys were now living with a younger couple who already had a twelve-year-old son—right between Charles's and Alfred's ages—while Joyce was going to stay with Gunther and Berta. Even though the three siblings wouldn't be living under the same roof, they would be less than ten yards apart.

William leaned back from the small table in Gunther's hut. 'Berta, I had forgotten the taste of good food. Thank you.'

The older woman blushed as she flapped her apron at him. 'You don't appear to have gone hungry of late.' She turned to Gunther. 'There is a jug of cider and a fire waiting outside.'

Sarah laughed at how quickly the two men headed outside. 'That's one way to clear the hut.'

'It's all in the training, my lady. Besides, the offer of Bronwyn's cider is too tempting for many to ignore.'

Under normal circumstances Sarah never would have chosen cider to quench her thirst. The drink was too bitter for her taste.

But Gunther and Berta had gone out of their way to be hospitable. They'd shared their food and offered to put the hut next door to rights for their use.

Sarah lifted the cup to her lips. She frowned. 'Is that cinnamon?'

'Yes. Cinnamon, cloves and honey.'

Perhaps it wouldn't be too bitter. She drank the cider and slowly put the cup on the table. 'I don't know anything about making cider, but there are some monks in Normandy who could benefit from your secret.'

Berta laughed and poured them both another cup. 'The secret is the apples. Some sweet, some tart and few crab apples added to the process makes for a hard cider that is neither too sweet, nor too bitter.'

'It must have taken years to figure out the right combination.'

'No, only a few. At first, Lord Bronwyn, William's father, made small batches. He kept track of the ingredients until he found one that suited him.'

Sarah polished off the cup. 'The man obviously had good taste.'

'Yes, he did.' Berta filled their empty cups. 'But remember, if you drink Gunther's cider, it won't have the honey or spices. I add that to mine because I like it that way.'

'So, is that what William's family did? They grew apples?'

'Yes. We've kept the orchards up as best we could. But Gunther is slowing down and the lads aren't interested in staying here. So, last year's crop wasn't as successful as other years.' Berta sighed, then added, 'It was heartbreaking to watch so much of the crop rot on the trees.'

Sarah's knowledge of trees, crops and harvesting was non-existent. But there was a royal decree that essentially put Bronwyn in her hands.

'Did William help in the orchards as a child?'

'Sometimes, but not often, my lady. His father was determined to see his son educated. William spent most of his days with the village priest, or looking for ways to avoid his lessons.'

'So, he was a typical boy.' Sarah poured herself another cup of cider.

Berta warned, 'Careful, Lady Sarah—while it may be smooth going down, it kicks like a goat when you least expect it.'

The woman was correct. The cider did go down smoothly. She set the half-full cup down. From the warmth in her belly, Sarah worried she'd be right about the kick, too.

'I wouldn't say William was a typical boy.' Berta frowned silently for a moment, before continuing, 'He was more giving, kinder than most other boys his age. I always thought it was because of his size.'

'What do you mean?'

Berta leaned forwards. 'Promise you will never tell him.'

'Not a word, Berta, I swear.'

'He doesn't know I saw him, but once when he thought no one was watching he slipped into the stables with his dog. She had just delivered a litter and William was so intrigued by the tiny puppies that he couldn't resist holding them when no one watched.'

Berta paused to glance at the doorway. Certain they were still alone, she said, 'His father had ordered him to leave the bitch and her pups alone until they were big enough to handle. But he didn't listen.'

Sarah closed her eyes, knowing this story was going to end badly.

'That day, his father came into the stables, surprising him. Instead of putting the pup down and admitting he'd disobeyed, he quickly shoved the tiny thing behind his back.'

'Oh, no.'

'Oh, yes, my lady. When his father left the stables, William discovered that he'd accidentally hurt the puppy's hips. The poor little thing could barely walk and William was devastated—terrified his father would have the pup put down. I'd only seen it happen because Gunther and I had been making use of some free moments up in the loft.'

Sarah's heart ached for the little boy. 'And you didn't go down to him?'

'Good heavens, no. The child wouldn't have talked to me, so I sent Gunther down to him.'

'How old was he?'

'William was only five or six then. He didn't harm that puppy on purpose. The lad would have broken his own arm or leg before harming the pup. But after that, he was more careful of everything. He wouldn't so much as touch a thing if he thought he might cause it harm.'

Sarah's stomach churned. Her chest burned. And this boy had been forced to kill men to stay alive? She stared out the open door towards her husband and asked softly, 'What happened to the pup?'

'When William's father learned what had happened, he took a strap to William's backside and then forced him to care for the animal. The thing grew up to be the best hunter in the keep.'

Berta rose from the table and stood at the door a moment before adding, 'When William turned up missing, the dog looked for him for weeks before going to sleep one night and simply not waking up. Gunther buried the dog next to William's parents.' The woman twisted her apron in her hands. 'It was one of the saddest days of our life. We felt as if, by burying the dog, we were also burying Lord William.'

'Thank you for sharing that, Berta.' Sarah wiped at her eyes.

'My lady, will the two of you stay on at Bronwyn?'

Not wanting to give the woman false hope, Sarah answered truthfully, 'I would like to, but I don't know, Berta.'

'Is there anything Gunther or I can do, or say?'

Sadly, she didn't have an answer to that either. 'These last few days have been hard for William. For the moment, I think he would benefit from being here for a time.'

She crossed to the door and took Berta's hands in her own. 'I promise nothing, but I will talk to him. Perhaps he will see the sense in remaining here for a while.'

Chapter Sixteen

William tossed a broken stick into the fire. He felt Sarah's stare upon his back and looked over his shoulder to see her approach. She stopped behind him and placed a hand gently on his shoulder.

Without thinking, he reached up and laid his hand over hers, asking, 'Are you tired?'

'Very.'

He rose, then, after bidding Gunther and the others a good evening, led her to the hut.

William wanted nothing more than to stretch out on a bed with Sarah at his side. To listen to her even breathing as she slept would be a comforting end to this day.

But he knew it would be impossible to lie next to her and not hold her, kiss her and touch her. He could be selfish and think only of his own needs and desires— but not with Sarah. She didn't deserve to be so badly used by him.

Besides, with the grace of God and the Church, a few months from now she would be wedded to another. He already possessed enough memories that would tease him mercilessly; he needn't add more.

When they reached the doorway, he stopped and stroked the back of his hand across her cheek. William forced a calmness he didn't feel to his voice. 'I wish you pleasant dreams, Sarah.'

She stared up at him, her frown warning him she wasn't going to end this day quietly. 'Pleasant dreams?'

He pushed the door open. 'Go to bed. I will see you in the morning.'

She didn't move. 'I am not sleeping alone, William.'

'Since I am not sleeping with you, I would have to disagree.'

Sarah narrowed her eyes, crossed her arms against her chest and leaned against the door jamb. 'You told all here that I am your wife, did you not?'

'Yes. But—'

She raised one hand, cutting him off. 'But nothing. We are still wed.' She spoke quietly so no one else could overhear her words. But he heard the steel beneath. 'Until that changes I am not sleeping alone. So, either come inside with me, or I swear, William…'

Sarah let her warning trail off, leaving him to fill in the missing words for himself.

'For someone who had no wish to wed me in the first place, you are acting like—'

'A shrew,' she completed his sentence. 'You should be glad I do not stomp my feet and wail. I can, though, if you wish.'

He glanced towards the centre of the village. At least a dozen people were still gathered around the fire. 'You wouldn't.'

Sarah lifted one leg and opened her mouth. William nearly shoved her inside the hut, swiftly closing the door behind them.

He leaned against the door. 'Anything else you'd care to demand?'

'Yes.' She pointed at a chest in the corner of the one-room hut. 'You can light the lamp, then close the shutters.'

When he didn't move, she sighed. 'William, you need not act as if I am going to ravish you against your will. I simply wish not to sleep alone in a strange place.'

No matter how hard he tried, be it holding his breath, or biting the inside of his mouth, he couldn't stop the laugh from choking him. Dear Lord, he would miss this woman's outspokenness.

'Does anything frighten you, Sarah?' He lit the oil lamp, then placed it on the table nearer the bed. 'Anything at all?'

She sat on the edge of the bed and pulled off her boots. 'Yes, many things frighten me. But you causing me bodily harm is not one of those things.'

Then she was an oddity among women. As an adult, he'd not yet met a female who wasn't terrified of his size. They feared him without knowing anything about him.

He sat next to her on the bed. 'Do you not think that might be foolish?'

She turned, presenting her back to him. 'Unlace me, please.' She started to unplait her hair before she finally answered, 'No, William, I don't think it's foolish.' Sarah glanced over her shoulder. 'The laces?'

Hesitantly reaching toward her, William plucked at the lacings. He pulled them through the small slits exposing more and more of her flesh with each tug.

'What I don't understand is why you seem to act like you want me to fear you. I feared my father and quickly learned that being afraid only seemed to make him desire to hit me more.'

William's hands shook. His heart hammered in his chest. He swallowed hard, hoping the action would enable him to speak past the building desire. 'So you assume that if you don't show fear no one will harm you?'

She shook her head. Her unbound hair fell over her shoulder to brush against his hands. The soft strands curled around his wrists like silken chains binding the two of them together.

'I am not an imbecile, William. I realise that some men are more prone to causing harm than others. If I thought you were one of those men, I would tread far more carefully.'

He pulled the laces free. Dropping them to the floor, he leaned forwards and brushed her hair aside to press his lips to the base of her neck. 'Since you fear me not, you think it acceptable to say, or do, anything you want regardless of my wishes?'

She sighed softly, then leaned back into his touch and reached up to push her gown from her shoulders. 'Tell me of your wishes, William. Tell me what you want me to do.'

What did he want her to do? Nothing. But that didn't mean he wanted to do nothing in return. While the notion of conceiving a child was a risk he would not take, and the idea of not touching or kissing her at all would now be impossible, there had to be a middle ground.

William smiled as the answer occurred to him. Of course, it was possible that she might not agree with his wicked proposal.

He trailed his lips to the soft flesh of her now half-bared shoulder and slipped his arms around her. 'I want you to let me touch you, kiss you, without expectation of more.'

When she moved as if to turn around, he held her in place. 'No. I don't want you to move, I don't want you to do anything, Sarah.'

'I…I don't understand.'

He moved his lips across her shoulder and neck, savouring the taste and smell of her. When he moved up her neck towards her ear, she shivered and he paused to whisper, 'Sarah, I want to make a memory to carry with me the rest of my days. Just one memory that will last for ever.'

Her breath hitched. The flesh beneath his lips convulsed as she swallowed. 'But, William, we can have more than just memories to last for ever.

He hooked his fingers in the neck edge of her gown and pulled it and her chemise down to her elbows. While skimming his fingertips along her exposed skin, he once again reminded her, 'I will not change my mind, Sarah. You are returning to court.'

She dropped her head forwards. 'Do you not care for me at all?'

William sensed her hurt feelings and knew that wasn't what she wanted to ask. Not stopping his gentle exploration of her body, he tried to explain. 'I care a great deal for you. If I didn't, I wouldn't now be asking for your permission, I would have already had you on your back on this bed. Nor would I be so concerned for your future.'

Her shoulders trembled and he knew she was trying to hide her tears. William pulled her across his lap and cupped her cheek, brushing at her tears with his thumb. 'There is no easy way to say this, Sarah. If you are asking me if I love you, then the answer is no.'

She pushed against his chest. 'Let me go.'

'No.' He caressed her neck, before stroking the line of her collarbone. 'I care for you more than anyone in the world. I want you to be happy, to be content. More than that, I want you to be safe and secure. I need to know you are free from danger.'

She stopped struggling and rested her head against his shoulder. 'Is that not love?'

His heart stuttered as he circled the curve of her breast. 'No, Sarah. Love is selfish and weak.'

The sound of her unsteady breaths filled the silence in the hut. Sarah ran her tongue along her lips and closed her eyes. 'Is this not selfish on your part?'

He brushed his thumb across the pebbling flesh. When she shuddered at the contact, he asked, 'How can it be selfish for me to give you pleasure?'

Sarah had no answer for him. She could barely think past the lust clouding her mind. To keep from crying out for him to stop this torment, or to keep from begging him to continue, she said, 'Love is not selfish.'

'No?' William stopped his teasing and remained silent until she opened her eyes and looked up at him. 'What was the first thing your father said to you after your mother's accident?'

'He accused me of killing her.'

'Did he? Or did he accuse you of killing *his* wife and *his* unborn child?'

'You said yourself that those were just words spoken in grief and anger.'

'And I'm certain they were. That does not negate the fact they came from his heart. Harsh, selfish words proclaiming *his* hurt and *his* loss.'

She couldn't argue his logic. At the moment, she couldn't clear the fog of desire enough to argue anything.

His palm was warm against her skin as he stroked a hand over her shoulder and arm.

'Did the Queen ever ask you to do a thing for love of her?'

'Yes, she...' Sarah frowned, then closed her eyes when she realised he could possibly be right.

'And when you completed that task for her, did you not feel weak and perhaps used?'

Sarah nodded.

She felt him move beneath her. 'Sarah...' his breath was hot against her ear '...Sarah, let me care for you without expecting more from me. Let me show you pleasure, without asking for anything else. Let me create my own memory.'

Sarah opened her eyes and studied him through the blur of tears. William was not forcing her. He was not teasing her. Golden flecks blazed against his eyes. Her breath caught in her chest at the passion shimmering from their depths.

If she was unable to convince him that setting her aside was a mistake he should not make, this might very well be the last time he would let his passion rule his actions.

Unable to speak, she relaxed in his arms and nodded.

He laid her on the bed and quickly removed her clothing. But when she plucked at his shirt, he pushed her hand away. 'No.' Looming over her, stroking her face, kissing her lips, William said, 'Do nothing, Sarah. Nothing but let the sensations overtake you.'

Feeling foolish, she closed her eyes and just lay there as he asked. But doing nothing was hard. Especially when she wanted to clasp him to her, to touch him. She wanted to feel his flesh beneath her fingers, to trace the scars on his back. And she longed to taste the pulse beating against his chest.

She wanted to do everything to him that he was doing to her. But was uncertain she could even if he'd permit it.

Could her touch convey as much desire, as great a reverence, as his? When she shivered and a soft moan escaped, William slid down the length of the bed to explore the sensitive skin on her legs.

Sarah grasped the cover beneath her, curling her fingers into fabric.

Could her lips skim as much heat into his body as this? She was afire from the hungry kisses he trailed up one leg, then the other.

She arched her back, seeking release from the madness. And when he relented, bringing her the fulfilment she craved, she cried out for him to hold her.

And he did. William held her in his arms, kissing her until the trembling ceased and she felt as if she could collapse.

When he rolled on to his side, she followed, clutched against his chest, burying her face to hide the tears that she could not hold back.

She couldn't let him take her back to court. This wasn't supposed to have happened, but it had. She wanted no one else. No one. It mattered not how grand their title, how large their chest of gold, or how rich their keep.

She would rather live in this one room hut with William than anywhere else.

And if she couldn't make that happen, she would rather live the rest of her life alone. She could hold her memories to her chest and be content.

What was she going to do?

* * *

William gently slid his arm from beneath his sleeping wife. The oil lamp had long burned out. Everyone had left the fire, seeking their own beds hours ago.

He sat up and brushed the hair from Sarah's face. She'd sobbed herself to sleep and he could only guess at the thoughts in her mind.

There was no doubt that she would now set about seeking a way to force him into changing his mind. If nothing else, he knew how single-minded his wife could be when she set her heart on something.

He smiled sadly. It wouldn't matter how great his feelings for her were, he would not subject her to the life he could offer. Not when it was within his power to give her something better.

His only regret was that he didn't feel sorry for creating this situation in the first place. How could he? Had he not demanded this marriage, he never would have discovered a passion, or a hunger, so intense that it made him feel alive for the first time in his adult life.

Sarah was to thank for that gift. And he would do everything to ensure he paid her back a thousandfold.

William rose from the bed and crossed the hut. He stopped at the door and opened it before he looked back at the bed. His throat tightened. If he believed in love, this would be the woman he would want to share it with.

He stepped out into the night air, closing the door behind him.

But love didn't really exist—not for him. And she deserved more than he could offer.

Chapter Seventeen

'Pull!' William bellowed. The older men flapped their shirts and yelled at the six horses yoked to another section of the fallen wall.

The horses dug in their hooves, straining against the yoke, and slowly the section rose. He, the remaining men, and some of the younger women, raced to place timber supports in front and behind it. They would shore up the wall, once they had a brief respite.

William wiped the sweat from his brow. Construction on an ill-kept keep was not for the faint of heart. But he wanted to see the villagers living inside the walls before he escorted Sarah back to court.

It would be easy enough, and less difficult on his mood, to have King Henry's guards take her. However, the King had ordered him to do so. Thankfully, a time frame hadn't been discussed.

Wagon wheels clattered as Sarah and Berta hauled another load of debris from the tower. They nodded and drove by, headed toward an area by the river that had been cleared to use as a place to burn the broken and rotten bits of timber and other rubbish.

William shook his head as the wagon passed. Two of Henry's guards rode on the back. From their glum expressions, it was apparent that they'd once again lost the who-would-drive-the-wagon argument with the women.

It was their own fault. They should have just taken the reins to the horse and been done with it.

'My lord.' Gunther pointed across the partially cleared field. 'The others are coming.'

At the sight of almost twenty people headed to Bronwyn, William dropped his shirt over his head. There was no need to make a spectacle of himself to strangers. It had taken Gunther half a day to cease staring at the scars criss-crossing his back. And another half a day to stop asking questions William would never answer.

When Gunther took a step back, William beckoned him forwards. 'I don't know these people, Gunther. I would appreciate your help.'

He hadn't told the older man that he would be stepping back into his role as overseer of the keep in William's coming absence. His reasoning was that he needed to make certain the man was still capable of the responsibility. But these last two days had shown him the man was still more than capable.

The group stopped before William. After doffing their caps, one man stepped forward. 'You are Lord William?'

Would he ever get used to being called Lord? Doubtful. He corrected the man. 'Sir William.'

Gunther huffed. 'Forgive his lordship, Timothy, he is not yet accustomed to the formality.'

'My lord.' Apparently this Timothy would heed Gunther with no difficulty. 'We are from the other village. The old lord considered us outlaws for deserting our posts.'

William couldn't fault them for that. He hadn't been

here to see firsthand whether they'd been treated justly or not. However, from what little he remembered of his father's brother, it was doubtful if any of these people had been treated justly.

He clasped the man's forearms. 'I see no outlaws before me. I see only people who were forced from Bronwyn. They are welcome to return home if that is their desire.'

Sighs of relief rippled through both groups of people. William glanced over his shoulder and saw that those from Gunther's village had lined up behind him. The men dropped the shovels they'd held. And the women all let a rock fall from their hands.

Surprised at such a show of aggression, he addressed Gunther. 'Is there a problem I should know about?'

The older man glared at the group. 'No. After all this time it seems they have forgotten their manners is all.'

William relaxed as looks of sheepish guilt crossed their faces. He directed his attention back to the man called Timothy. 'I apologise for their zealousness.'

'There is no need. We have also been too long without the company of others and likely would have done the same.'

From the corner of his eye, William watched the beginnings of a new friendship. Alfred, now the youngest of the group, was challenging a boy about his size from the newer group.

William cocked his head in the boys' direction. Timothy and Gunther watched with him as the two lads sized each other up.

Alfred made the first move, tackling the other boy, who appeared to have no intention of backing down. The two tussled, rolling about on the ground while throwing a random punch now and then.

As William had known would happen, the fight was over before it truly began. Seemingly unaware that the adults had been watching them, the boys ran off towards the keep together.

William turned back to the men. He studied them, speculating if perhaps a good tussle might bring the two villages closer together.

'No, my lord.' Obviously his thoughts were plain to see. 'I am not going to roll around on the ground with Timothy or anyone else.' Gunther rubbed the back of his neck. 'Unless, of course, it will get me out of clearing the bailey.'

William waved toward the wall. 'If you wish not to clear the bailey, you are more than welcome to help shore up the wall.'

Gunther snorted. 'I'll take the bailey, thank you.'

'Where would you like us to start, my lord?' Timothy asked.

Since now was as good a time as any, William said, 'When the women return, we are going to break for the noon meal. Gunther is more than able to decide who is best suited for what task. Since you know your peoples's skills, you can help him.'

'My lord...I...are you sure?' Gunther scratched his head. 'It has been a long time since I've overseen something as large as Bronwyn.'

'Has anyone else here had the responsibility before?' When no one spoke up, William said, 'Then, Gunther, it is up to you.'

The clattering of the wagon's wheels announced the women's return. The sound caught everyone's attention.

Timothy whistled softly, before saying under his breath, 'Now there is a fine-looking woman.' He asked

Gunther, 'Have you kept her hidden in your village all this time?'

The man looked at Sarah as if he'd like to have her for his mid-day meal. With restraint, William tapped his shoulder, instead of knocking him to the ground. 'Don't let appearances deceive you. That *fine-looking woman*, with the dirt streaked down her cheek, only appears to be a hard-working villager.' He stepped forwards to assist Sarah from the wagon, then turned back to Timothy. 'However, she is my wife.'

Beneath her breath, Sarah muttered to herself, 'Strange, I don't feel much like a wife.'

William glanced down at her, one eyebrow winging up to disappear beneath the hair falling over his forehead. Had he heard her? Maybe it would be a good thing if he had. She smiled up at him. 'Isn't it nearly time for a break?'

He frowned. But before he could say anything, Berta hussled past. 'Come, it is time to eat.'

Sarah felt sorry for the woman. A week ago, Berta had found Sarah crying over waking up in the hut alone. She'd been miserable from crying herself to sleep, then again upon waking.

The older woman had offered comfort until the tears subsided. Then she'd offered a few lessons in training husbands.

The lessons were welcome more as a few brief moments of humour than anything else. Some of the suggestions Berta offered wouldn't have been tolerated even if William hadn't decided to set her aside.

Somehow Sarah didn't see William falling in line simply because she refused him sex. In fact, she was fairly certain he would either quickly see to it that she

ended up begging him to take her in his arms, or he
would demand his rights and be done with it.

Nor did she see him fretting about her moods or disposition because he didn't find a meal awaiting him
upon returning to the hut in the evening. William would
be more likely to leave her to her mood while he went
to hunt and cook his own food to fill his belly.

But listening to Berta talk of these things went a long
way toward lightening Sarah's day. It let her know that
other couples had their own strange oddities that they
accepted as normal. Even couples who had been wed
for more years than they could remember.

She enjoyed watching Gunther and Berta tease each
other like they were newly-weds. And she could tell by
his smile, and easy manner, that William found it
amusing too.

It had been a week since he'd last held her, or kissed
her. While she missed his touch, and those moments
of closeness at night, she had few if any complaints
about the days.

After that first day, when they'd taken great pains to
avoid each other, they'd fallen into an easier manner with
each other. They shared meals with Gunther and Berta.
They worked on Bronwyn's restoration side by side all
day and sat next to each other around the fire at night.

He'd even gone so far as to tease her about the dirt
streaking her courtly face. Which had led to an awkward
moment when he'd wiped the dirt from her face and his
touch had lingered on her cheek. But that moment of
hesitation had let her know that he longed for her as
much as she did for him.

William fell back from the others and waited for her
to catch up on the path back to the village. He took her

hand in his as if it were the most natural thing in the world. 'Have I told you how proud I am of you?'

Determined to keep this moment light, Sarah laughed. 'Proud? Why, because I can now drive the wagon without tipping it over?'

'Well, yes, there is that. But, Sarah, I don't know any court-raised ladies who would pitch in and help the way you have.'

Why wouldn't she help? This was, after all her keep was it not? And even though she might not ever be living here, her children would some day. But Sarah kept those thoughts to herself. 'If I didn't help, I would be sitting in the village alone all day talking to myself.' She glanced up at him. 'Can you imagine how boring that would become?'

'If the weather holds as it has been, we should be done within the next week.'

Sarah's heart tripped. 'Bronwyn won't be restored in a week.'

'No. But it will be completed enough for the villagers to move into. Once the wall is up, I'll be able to leave long enough to escort you to court.'

She dug her heels into the ground, coming to a halting stop. All thought of easier manners and being companionable fled. 'I beg your pardon?'

He released her hand and turned to stare at her. 'Sarah, you didn't believe anything had changed, did you?'

'No, my lord, why would I have thought that?'

'Sarah…'

'No.' She glared at him. 'Don't you dare explain to me how you are doing this for my own good, or my safety. I am not that gullible. Besides, I am an adult, I can make decisions on my safety, and what is good for

me on my own. You are taking me back to court because
you don't want me as your wife. For God's sake,
William, be man enough to admit it.'

He scowled, his eyes glimmered with rage. 'I never
said that.'

'No. Not in words you haven't.' She threw her hands
up and headed towards the village. As she pushed past
him, she gritted her teeth and added, 'A wife would
require you to assume responsibility.'

He grabbed her arm and swung her around to face
him. 'What did you say?'

'You heard me. If you remained wedded to me, you
would be honour bound to be responsible for my
welfare. You would be responsible for the upkeep and
maintenance of this keep.' Angry and beyond rational
thought, she added, 'You would be responsible for my
keep, William. Mine.'

He released her as if he'd been burned. 'I have never
shirked my responsibilities. Never.'

She'd come this far, she wasn't turning back now.
'Oh, haven't you?' Taking a step closer to him, she
crooked one eyebrow and asked, 'What about the responsibilities you have in our marriage bed?'

His eyes widened briefly before he narrowed them
and smiled down at her. 'Is that what this is about, Sarah?'

She fought the urge to pound her fists against his
chest and scream at him. Instead, she grabbed the front
of his shirt, twisting the fabric in her hand. 'Yes. You
took from me the only thing I had to give to a husband
and then threw it back in my face because you thought
you'd wed a whore, not a virgin.'

He wrapped his fingers around her hand. But when he
parted his lips to respond, Sarah shouted, 'Listen to me.'

William raised his hands in the air. 'I'm listening.'

She relaxed her hold, but didn't release him. 'You taught me the meaning of lust, showed me the heights of desire and passion. You talked to me. You listened to me. You protected me.' Her voice caught in the thickening of her throat. She swallowed hard. Feeling the fight drain out of her, she admitted, 'William, you made me believe it was possible to care for someone without fear of being hurt.'

He closed his eyes against the pain in her voice. He'd never wanted this to happen. He hadn't meant to hurt her so deeply.

'Sarah, I am sorry.'

She released him. 'Save your apology for another.'

He watched her walk away. Bereft of words, choking with emotions he couldn't sort out enough to name, he turned and struck a tree.

The tearing of his flesh and the shattering of knuckles was a welcome relief from the searing pain in his chest.

Dear Lord, what was he going to do?

Gunther walked up the path towards him. The older man looked at William's hand and shook his head. 'Berta sent me to get you. Come, William, come and eat.'

'I'm not hungry.' William shook his head at the petulant tone of his voice.

'Of course you aren't. If I'd lost an argument with a tree, I'd not be hungry either. But you must eat. Come.'

Puzzled, William looked down at the older man. 'How does she know?'

'Who? What?'

As they headed toward the village, William wondered, 'Berta. How does she know when to send you?'

Gunther laughed. 'I don't know. I don't ask. When the woman tells me to go after someone, I go.'

'And you've remained married after all these years?'

With a shrug, Gunther answered, 'My lord, one day you'll learn that there are battles just not worth fighting.'

William lifted his gaze from the dirt path and met Sarah's brilliant blue stare. 'Oh Lord, Gunther, you might be right.'

The older man only snorted in reply.

Chapter Eighteen

From her bed, Sarah stared up at the hut's ceiling. She'd stared at it so long, that she could pick out which reeds needed to be replaced. Her stomach rolled and she pressed her hand tighter against it. This fifth morning of waking up ill went a long way toward confirming what she'd begun to suspect two mornings past.

She wouldn't be certain for another week or so, but if her suspicions were correct, she was carrying William's child. Normally, that would not be a cause for grief. However, under the current circumstances, the knowledge was daunting.

She couldn't tell him. She refused to use a child as a means to force his hand. Although there was little doubt in her mind that eventually, the King, or the Church, would do so once her condition was apparent.

Sarah knew she had little time to try to find another way to change William's mind about the annulment. She wanted him—no—she needed him to stay because he cared for her more than his misplaced guilt and worry. Somehow he had to realise that his honour was intact.

He had protected her as best as anyone could. There would always be some things in life he would not be able to control.

She couldn't help but worry that he would feel trapped once he learned of the child. Granted, they had made love once, so he had to have realised the possibility existed.

While he had moved back into their hut, they did not share the bed. He'd offered no explanation and she'd not asked. To be honest, they'd both fallen on to their respective covers exhausted at the end of the day.

Which was a good thing, because it left her little time to long for the warmth of his body before falling asleep. But now she wondered if part of his reasoning had been to avoid conceiving a child before the annulment.

The rickety door of the hut creaked open, breaking into her thoughts. William filled the doorway, blocking out the sun. 'Why are you back in bed fully dressed? Are you feeling unwell?'

Outlined by the door frame and the sun, even with his head bent to fit into the space, he made such an imposing figure. She longed for him to enter the hut, and lie down beside her. But Sarah knew that would not happen.

Until she could figure out a way to crack through the will of steel he wrapped around himself, there would be no hope of being enveloped in his embrace.

'I am fine, William. I was up, but the crispness of the breeze made me decide it was a perfect morning to lie abed.' She doubted if he'd had a great deal of prolonged intimate relations with many women during most of his adult years thus far and didn't worry about him discovering her secret.

She worried more that Berta would soon tell him.

Yesterday, the older woman had started giving Sarah the sly *I know your secret* look repeatedly. Soon, she would have to take the woman into her confidence just to keep the secret hidden a little longer.

'The wagons will be here soon.'

She sat up and closed her eyes against her stomach's objection to the quick movement. William immediately stood over her. 'You are not well.'

No matter how she longed for his embrace, now would not be the best time. Not if she wanted to keep her condition a secret. 'Will you cease worrying like an old woman. I am fine.' To lend truth to her words, she stood up. 'See. I am just tired. Court life didn't prepare me for moving a village.'

If she read the incredulous look on his face correctly, he didn't believe her. To keep him from questioning her, she pushed him out the door. 'Go. I will gather our belongings and be along directly.'

Thankfully, he didn't linger to argue with her. More thankfully, Berta came into the hut carrying an empty pot, water and some bread crusts. The older women pushed Sarah down on to a bench, handing her the pot. 'You look rather green this morning.'

Unable to speak, Sarah hung her head over the vessel while Berta untangled and then braided her hair. 'You will have to tell him soon, my lady.'

'Not yet.' Sarah took a long drink of the water, praying it would stay down. 'I pray you not to tell him either.'

'I think it is a mistake, but it is not my place to tell your husband anything. Eat this.' Berta handed her a bread crust. 'It may help if you would take a few bites before rising in the morning. Keeping a little something in your stomach usually does the trick.'

Between small bites, Sarah asked, 'How long does this last?'

'A few weeks. A few months. It is different with each child.' Berta sighed. 'With my last one, the only day I wasn't sick was the day he was born.'

That was disheartening to know. Sarah wondered aloud, 'Why on earth do women have more than one child?'

'Because the making is far too much fun to avoid for long.'

The hard bread lodged in Sarah's throat. She held up a hand, choking out, 'Enough.'

'You and William have recently wed.' Berta flapped a rag at her. 'You still embarrass too easily.'

'Yes. Very recently.' She changed the subject before it became even more personal. 'Did you find the keep's kitchen to your liking?'

'With a little elbow grease, it will do.'

That was a relief. She and William had inspected the different rooms in the keep a few days back. The Great Hall had been filthy and reeking of rotting rushes. But thanks to Berta and some of the other women they'd managed to make it livable, if not presentable.

The one bedchamber was passable with little work required, the other two were a different story and would take many more days of cleaning and scrubbing. Thankfully, overall the keep appeared sound.

As far as she'd been able to tell, the corridor connecting the separate kitchen buildings to the keep required small repairs—a board here or there, a patch or two on the roof. But the kitchen, buttery and pantry had seemed usable.

However, it was the first kitchen she'd spent any

amount of time in since she'd been a child and Sarah didn't trust her judgement. Berta and her daughters would be the ones using the kitchen; it made more sense to have them see for themselves.

'What about the well?' The men had been working on it for two days now. Sarah disliked the idea of moving the people so far away from a water source if the men discovered they couldn't repair the well.

'The structure has finally been repaired. When I left this morning, Charles and little Alfred were dangling from ropes, cleaning the debris out of the well.'

'Dangling from ropes?' Worry sent Sarah's voice an octave higher. 'Inside the well?'

'Rest easy.' Berta patted her arm. 'They are fine. It proved easier for the men to hold the ropes with boys attached than it would have been for them to hold your husband.'

Sarah couldn't argue that point. She agreed with the idea that William would be too heavy to hold aloft, adding, 'He most likely wouldn't fit inside to begin with.'

Wagon wheels clattering over the rough road announced the arrival of the other villagers. Berta's wide smile, and the deepening of the crinkles around her eyes, made her face shine with joy.

She rushed to the door. 'They are here.'

From the look on the older woman's face, the excitement in her voice, Sarah knew that William had been correct. His idea of moving the two small villages to Bronwyn was a good choice. Families, by blood or friendship, shouldn't be apart the way these people had been.

Where Gunther and Berta's people had been forced from Bronwyn, the others had escaped the previous lord's heavy hand. They'd hidden in the hills and forests, living like hunted outlaws.

William had instructed the guards to carry word to the others in the area that the new Lord of Bronwyn would gladly welcome their return. The people had shown up at the keep the next day. The task of blending the groups of people into one had proved easier than anyone had imagined.

In reality, the move served a dual purpose. Their combined numbers at Bronwyn would make their lives safer. And the keep required work that many hands would make lighter.

Her husband might not have had experience running a keep, but he was obviously no fool. He would make a good lord for Bronwyn.

Joyce stuck her head inside the hut. 'My lady, we are ready to leave.'

'Thank you, Joyce. I'll ride with the men.' She handed the girl the last bundle-wrapped package of belongings for her and William. 'Have Charles put these in the wagon.'

Instead of leaving, the girl came inside the hut. 'My lady, I…I wanted to apologise again for my brazen behaviour. I had no right to act in such a manner.'

Sarah couldn't help but pull the girl close. 'Joyce, we have been over this. You only did what you felt you must. Your mistake wasn't that you felt compelled to protect your brothers. It was that you failed to take your opponent's size and experience into consideration.'

'I still don't quite understand. How am I to know of an opponent's experience?'

'Fear not, you will learn. For now, just know that you, Charles and Alfred are safe.'

'I thank you for that.'

A young man stepped into the door way. 'Joyce, we need to go.'

The girl's eyes lit up like candle flames, a flush tinted her cheeks. And with the way she quickly bobbed her head in farewell and raced out of the hut, Sarah knew that William was but a distant memory in the girl's mind.

Stepping out of the hut, Sarah headed to the shelter that protected the horses from the rain. The three-sided lean-to had been hastily erected, but it kept the animals dry.

Glad that someone had seen to having the beast saddled, she reached for her horse's reins. But before she could touch the leather, a hand covered her mouth.

A voice whispered close to her ear, 'Lady Sarah, I am from the Queen's court. Do not scream.'

Realising that it wasn't Aryseeth come to recapture her, she nearly fainted from relief. She nodded her understanding and the hand lowered. 'You near frightened me half to death,' she exclaimed, turning to face the man.

'I apologise, but I knew not how else to approach you unseen.'

For a moment confusion kept her silent. She then closed her eyes and sighed. Eleanor had told her that she'd be sending men to relay messages. Her heart skidded to a stop, before jumping frantically. The Queen had also promised to send men to kill William.

Which task had this man come to accomplish?

'What news have you for Queen Eleanor?'

She didn't recognise this man. If he was from Eleanor's court, would he not at least be a little familiar to her? 'None I wish to share at the moment.' Sarah slowly took a step backwards, toward the opening of the shelter, while speaking. 'But we will be returning to court in a matter of days. I will speak to her then.'

'I have my orders, Lady Sarah.'

'And what would those would be?'

He glanced outside the shelter. 'I have not seen the Earl of Wynnedom or his wife about.'

She knew that if she told him they were no longer travelling together, that William's life would be in jeopardy. So, she lied and took another small step, trying to keep the man from noticing her retreat. 'An Earl and his wife do not help with the packing and moving of a village. They are already at Bronwyn.'

'How strange.' Eleanor's man shook his head. 'I ran into the Earl of Wynnedom and his wife two days ago. They were travelling north, towards his castle.'

Sarah moved closer to the opening. 'I will explain all to the Queen when we arrive back at court.'

'And you will. Sooner than you think.'

Before she could scream, or turn to run, he slammed his fist against her chin.

Certain all was in order, William rode to the rear of the group nearing Bronwyn. What was keeping Sarah now?

He'd seen Berta enter the hut, but she was now on the first wagon. So, where was his wife? She didn't have much left to pack. It wasn't as if they'd brought along that many items to begin with.

'My lord!' Gunther ran around the last wagon towards him, shouting.

William dismounted, catching the breathless old man before he dropped to his knees. 'Lady Sarah—your wife…' Gunther panted, trying hard to catch his breath. He waved back at the village. 'She…has been…taken.'

At the sharp, hard pain twisting in his gut, he let the man slip to the ground. 'When?'

Gunther shook his head. 'I know not—' He gasped for air. 'Charles saw...he waits...go'

William swung up on to his horse, shouting for the King's guards. Only three of them arrived. He had not the time to wait for the other man. He ordered, 'One of you stay with the villagers. I care not who. The other two ride with me.'

Without question, one of the older guards went to help Gunther, while the remaining two followed William back to the village. As they rode, he explained, 'Lady Sarah has been taken.'

'Where was Randolph?' one of the men asked. 'He was to see she was guarded.'

'An answer I'd like to know.' William snapped back in response.

Randolph's whereabouts became obvious when the men rode into the village. Charles knelt over the unconscious man, trying to shake him awake.

William ordered the boy, 'Leave him be. Fetch Berta and have her see to him. How many were there and which way did they take Lady Sarah?'

'Just one man that I saw.' The boy pointed south. 'He took her that way.'

'Was she walking?'

'No. He had clipped her on the chin, so he was carrying her, on foot.'

Anxious to find his wife before she was taken too far away, William nodded at the guards. 'Get the details, then follow me.'

He set off down the road. They weren't that far ahead of him. And, if the man had left on foot, William had a better chance to catch up with them.

How had this happened yet again? One of them,

either he or Sarah, was cursed. Both times she had been guarded. And both times, someone had made off with her. What were the chances of that happening to someone else?

More to the point, what was the chance of him preventing it from happening again?

Slim to none.

He had to get her back to the Queen's court. At least there she had never been in danger.

William hadn't ridden an hour before he caught the sound of Sarah's voice. He slipped off his horse, tying the reins to a tree, and cringed at the anger of her tone. He knew by her outraged tone that she'd not been harmed. These captors were most likely cursing their luck at having captured her.

Cautiously sneaking through the denseness of the forest, William crept toward the voices.

Sarah glared at the man who had taken her from Bronwyn, as another one of the Queen's guards tied her hands together. 'You know he's going to find us. And when he does—'

'Woman, shut your mouth.' The man in charge, the one who had spirited her away, raised his hand as if to slap her, then lowered it, snarling, 'I tire of listening to you.'

'How happy is Queen Eleanor going to be when she learns of how you've treated me?'

He stepped against her and smiled. 'About as happy as she will be to learn you've not followed her orders.'

Did he think her witless? He was trying to trick her into giving him information to use against her. 'You don't know if that's true or not.'

He moved away, glaring. 'It is fairly obvious that you no longer travel with the Earl.'

'That doesn't mean I have disobeyed her orders.' She would lie to these men without a trace of remorse. Anything to keep them from harming William.

'If you had obtained the information the Queen wanted, you'd have given it to me.'

'Why would I do that when I knew I'd be delivering it myself in a matter of days?'

'Because you knew Queen Eleanor was sending someone to relay the message. You expected me.'

'I also expected to be treated as a member of her court.' Sarah tugged at the bindings. 'It seems I was wrong. Perhaps you were also.'

The man laughed at her and lifted a wineskin toward his companion. 'The men were right. She is rather obstinate, is she not?'

'Aye, that she is.' He rubbed his shin where Sarah had kicked him more than once. 'There is a way to settle her right down.'

Sarah narrowed her eyes. While she would fear such a threat coming from one as vile as Aryseeth, these men instilled more loathing, than fear, in her.

She warned, 'The Queen would see you dead.'

'True.' The man in charge walked back to her and stroked a finger along her collar bone. 'It might be worth it, though. I have yet to decide.'

Before she could say anything, he removed his touch. 'But I need see to your husband first. Then you and I can have a good tumble.'

Sarah lunged toward him, catching him off guard and knocking him to the ground. She caught her balance before she too hit the ground, and kicked him. 'How's that for a good tumble?'

The other man rushed over, grabbed her bound wrists, swung her around and slammed her against a tree. 'Are you seeking to get yourself killed?'

Rising from the ground, the man grasped her chin. 'You will pay for that. When I return, my hands will be covered with your husband's blood. We will see how brave you are when I wipe them clean on your body.'

This imbecile would be lucky if he got within striking distance of William and lived. 'You won't get close enough to touch him. Just take me back to the Queen and leave well enough alone.'

'No. Since you helped plan this with the Queen, you knew this was going to happen. All so you could end up with some rich lord.'

'You've been listening to children's tales.'

'No. I think not.' He shook his head. 'It takes a special kind of woman to be that devious. You are heartless and shrew enough to plot your own husband's death. Especially if it means the promise of gold in your coffers.'

'How much of that wine have you swallowed? You are out of your mind.'

'Am I? You cannot tell me that you and the Queen did not have this all plotted out before you left the court. It would be a lie. Otherwise, I would not be here to see Bronwyn dead.'

The other guard approached carrying a rope. He pushed her to the ground against the tree, then bound her.

'You just sit there and think about it while I am gone.' He squatted in front of her. 'And you think about being nice to me when I return.' He touched her cheek. 'You truly do not want me telling the lords at court what a murdering bitch you are before you can choose your next victim.'

Sarah opened her mouth to respond. But before the first word could leave her mouth, the blade of a dagger slid across the man's throat. Just as quickly, a sword slammed through the other man's chest.

She screamed and closed her eyes, waiting for her own death. But when moments passed and it did not come, she slowly opened her eyes and looked up into William's blazing glare.

Sarah breathed a sigh of relief. 'William—'

'Do not speak to me, Sarah. Ever. Again.'

She didn't have to ask how much of the conversation he'd overheard. 'William, the man was seeking to goad me. He wasn't telling the truth.'

He didn't respond. In fact, he acted as if she hadn't even spoken. She shivered at the cold dread creeping down her spine.

Three of the King's guards skidded to a halt behind him. William pointed at her. 'Get her out of my sight.'

Stunned, the guards scrambled to do his bidding, and cut her free of the bindings. One helped her from the ground. 'Come, my lady, we'll take you back to Bronwyn.'

'No!' William bellowed. 'Do not take her back there. Head toward the Queen's court.'

Sarah jerked free of the guards and ran to William. She grasped his arm, 'William, listen to me.'

He pulled out of her hold and walked away. 'Save your lies for your next husband. This one is done with you.'

He shouted at the guards. 'Take her away from here.'

The guards hesitated as if uncertain what to do. One took a deep breath and then grasped Sarah's arms. He held on tightly, forcing her to come with him as she struggled against his hold.

'Damn you. Release me,' she screamed, then kicked him. Frantic for William to know the truth, she dug her fingernails into the guard's arm until he swore.

A large, strong hand wrapped around the back of her neck and dragged her off the guard. 'He has done nothing to harm you. Stop.'

She swung around, grabbing the front of William's tunic, and cried out, 'William, I swear to God his words were false.'

He stood as unmoving as a mountain, refusing to look at her, stared over her head and asked, 'Did the Queen plan to have me killed?'

Sarah's heart shattered into pieces. She could not lie to him. Not any longer. But telling him the truth would ensure their marriage ended. 'Yes, but—'

He cut off her answer with a snarl. 'And all this time you knew of this plan?'

'William—'

He shoved her away. 'You sicken me.'

Sarah stumbled backwards. Tripping over a tree limb, she landed on the ground. Defeated, she stayed there, on her knees, sobbing for what she'd lost.

He stood over her. 'Did you obtain the information Eleanor wanted?'

'No.' Her reply was little more than a choked whisper.

'I can't hear you.' William raised his voice. 'Did you?'

He already knew she'd been spying on him and Earl Hugh. But he'd never asked why. Not even now did he demand to know the reason, because to him reasons no longer mattered. She swallowed hard against the thickness in her throat, to answer, 'No.'

'Was the man right? Were you promised a titled lord for your co-operation?'

Unable to speak, she could only nod. 'Since you failed, I am sure your next husband will be no more, or less, than what you've earned.' He clenched his hands into fists at his sides.

She couldn't blame him if he beat her for her past actions. She deserved it. And a part of her would welcome the physical pain. It might lessen the pain in her heart.

But she couldn't let him hurt the baby. Sarah curled into a tight ball, protecting their child. Between shuddering sobs, she cried out, 'Please, William, have mercy. I am pregnant.'

Chapter Nineteen

William stared down at her, swaying on his feet as her fear hit him hard enough to suck the breath from his body. He recognised her terror, had witnessed the same cowering fear in men who had experienced their first taste of Aryseeth's lash.

But to have his wife cower from him in such terror, to know he had caused this fear, made him ill. He pushed aside his anger; it would still be there to cloak his pain later. Right now she needed to be assured that she wasn't in danger of physical harm. He slowly knelt in front of her, careful not to make any sudden moves that would frighten her more.

'Sarah.' William lowered his voice, fighting to keep his rage and hurt from making it over-harsh. 'Sarah, stop this. You know you are in no danger.'

When she didn't respond, he added, 'Sarah, physically harming you would not ease my pain. It would only make the pain worse.'

Hesitantly, she raised her head and looked at him. William took one glance at the trepidation in her gaze and the trembling of her lower lip and wanted to curse, wanted to scream in frustration for what would never be.

Instead, he extended his hands, palms up, towards her. 'Sarah, come here. Take my hand.'

When she placed one trembling hand atop his, William gently tugged her closer. He stroked her cheek with the back of his fingers, wiping away the still-falling tears. She would shed many more of them in the days to come. Who would wipe them from her cheeks?

She came up to her knees slowly and lowered her gaze. William clasped both of her hands, brushing his thumbs across her skin. 'Sarah, we cannot go on like this.'

Partners in a marriage were not always compatible. He knew that. At court he'd witnessed many couples who had little use for each other. Had he not wanted that same type of arrangement himself? Wasn't that why he'd demanded Sarah of Remy, the Queen's whore, wed him to begin with?

He was the one who'd desired a wife who would not bind his heart in any silken threads. He was the one who'd wanted a simple arrangement—a woman to bear his children and see to his household.

Why then did his chest hurt so? Why were his emotions so overwrought he could barely think? Why did he want to pull her into his arms one moment and push her from him the next?

He'd been caught firmly in a trap of his own making. And he'd left himself only one chance of escaping the chains tightening around his heart.

When she remained silent, he edged closer and rested his forehead against hers. 'Are you certain you carry a child?'

She nodded, whispering, 'Yes.'

William closed his eyes. There should be a great measure of joy at such knowledge. And while a part of him felt a smug sense of accomplishment that he was certain every man experienced, it was tempered with a heavy sadness.

If their child was a boy, who would teach him how to ride and wield a weapon? Who would be there to guide him into manhood?

And if it was a girl, who would protect her and cherish her? Who would see to her future?

These were his responsibilities and could be his only joy. There had to be a way to see to these things. He didn't know how, but there was time yet to figure it out.

'Sarah, I swear to you that I will not leave you to fend for yourself. I will see that you and the child are always cared for. You will want for nothing that I can provide.'

'You are all we need, all I want.'

While it would be kinder to lie to her, enough lies had been told and he wouldn't give her false hope. In the end, nothing would change and it would only add to the untruths that already lay between them. William caressed her cheek. 'I know you think that now. But, Sarah, I cannot trust you. And you have made it plain that you cannot trust me either. If we are unable to talk to each other, or come to each other with the truth—no matter how painful—we have nothing and we never will.'

She leaned into his touch. 'I have nothing else to hide.'

William placed a finger over her lips. 'No. Sarah, don't. The time for trusting, for being honest, is gone.'

Her lips trembled beneath his touch. 'And crying will change nothing either.' He sat back on his heels. 'The King has given you Bronwyn. As long as we remain wed, it will one day belong to our child. But until the keep is repaired and I have trained enough men to see to your defences, I want you to return to court. You will be safer there.'

'What will you do?'

He saw no other choice. Once all was in order, he would leave. It made no sense for him to stay here. Doing so would only torment both of them.

'For now I'll oversee the repairs at Bronwyn. After that...' he shrugged '...I will find my way.'

'Find your way to me, William.'

He threaded his fingers through her hair and drew her closer for what he'd meant to be a gentle kiss of farewell. But once their lips met, any thought of gentleness was forgotten.

His heart raged. This woman was *his*. He had claimed her, body and soul. Just as she had laid claim to him. She carried his child and she belonged with him. They belonged together.

William released her, then rose, warning, 'Don't wait for me, Sarah.'

He nodded toward the guards. 'See that she arrives safely at the Queen's court.'

William swallowed hard as he walked away from what might have been. He wanted to shout, wanted to make something hurt as badly as he did.

How could he have been so foolish as to believe she had given up keeping secrets, stopped lying to him, and trusted him even a little when, in truth, she knew the whole time that his demise had already been planned? Why had he started to think about withdrawing his petition so they could build a life together, here at Bronwyn?

Now, he would complete the renovations on the keep.

He would train the guards. But he couldn't live under the same roof with her.

He would ensure her safe arrival back at Poitiers. That too was his responsibility. And he needed to see the King so he could explain why he had to stop the annulment. He feared a missive could be too easily misconstrued and William wanted to be certain the King and the Church understood the change in plans.

Then he needed to see to Bronwyn. But after that—he didn't know what he'd do. He couldn't think that far ahead.

For this moment, the only thing he wanted to do was to drown out the sound of his wife's broken cries.

Gunther, Berta and Timothy stared at him as if he'd spoken in a foreign tongue they didn't understand. William leaned his forearms on the trestle table set up in the Great Hall of Bronwyn and tried to explain one more time. 'Lady Sarah will be returning to Queen Eleanor's court for a time. She will reside there until the repairs on Bronwyn are made and men are trained to see to the keep's defence. Since the King has given Bronwyn to Lady Sarah, once all is completed, I will reside elsewhere.'

'Begging your pardon, my lord,' Berta interrupted him, 'you already said that. I asked why.'

A part of him wanted to tell Berta it was none of her business. Another part felt he owed them some type of explanation. After all, while they might not have shared a bed, or any intimate moments of late, he and Sarah had worked well together as lord and lady of the keep.

And just because he'd chosen not to be intimate with his wife, didn't mean he'd been content with the idea. He'd missed her touch and the sound of her voice more than was comfortable.

'My lord?'

William snapped his attention back to those gathered at the table. There was little reason to conceal the truth from them; eventually they'd find a way to discover it. He'd rather the information came from him and not from one who would embellish the tale. 'Sarah was forced by Queen Eleanor to wed me. The joining was not her choice and, to be blunt, it has not worked well for either of us.'

They again stared at him as if he hadn't spoken in a language they could understand. William explained further, 'Even though that is an acceptable arrangement between nobles, I am not of noble birth. She should have been given the opportunity to decide for herself.'

Berta slapped the table and chortled, before she asked, 'A little late for that, isn't it?'

Apparently the woman knew Sarah was carrying his child and so did the others, which explained why his explanations seemed to be falling on deaf ears.

Gunther leaned closer to his wife. 'Berta, do not be so disrespectful.'

She looked at him and shot back, 'Lady Sarah is pregnant.' Her questioning glare drifted to William. 'Who is being disrespectful?'

William cringed. Another man, or someone less familiar, would not get away with speaking so to him. He wouldn't have hesitated to tell them to mind their own business, or to put them in their place.

However, this was Berta. And she'd boxed his ears enough times in the past to make him realise she had no qualms about taking him to task. The woman didn't care if he was bigger, or stronger, nor did the mere fact that he was the Lord of Bronwyn hold any weight in her opinion. At least, not when it came to Sarah.

That might have evolved differently had he grown up at Bronwyn. But the only memory Berta had of him couldn't be very different than his own. He'd been an adolescent in an overgrown boy's body when last they'd seen each other.

And if he remembered correctly, she'd shooed him from her kitchen for sneaking fruit meant for a pie. Later, when one of her pies had come up missing, she'd dragged him bellowing across the courtyard by his ear.

No, he was never going to get this older woman to see him as anything but a boy in need of a sharp crack across his knuckles. William paused. How dangerous would it be to have his cook championing his wife? Especially when he was intent on leaving said wife?

'Berta, do I need hire a food taster?'

Apparently she understood his meaning, because she shrugged and then said, 'Not if you get your head out of your —'

'Berta!' Gunther shouted, stopping her comment mid-sentence.

Although William, and most likely everyone within hearing, knew exactly what the woman had been about to say. And he agreed. He had a keep to rebuild, and then fortify. And a good likelihood of a child to support.

The thought of a child, be it a brawny boy or a tiny bit of a girl, made the pain of loss ease a little. He didn't have time to be wool gathering about what might have been. Instead, he needed to be figuring out a way to make this strange arrangement palatable for both him and Sarah.

William reached across the table and took Berta's hand. A twinge of guilt that he couldn't even trust his wife on this was easily pushed aside as he asked, 'How certain are you that she is with child?'

Without looking at her husband, she said, 'As certain as I am of my husband's outrage at my behaviour.'

He glanced at Gunther. Berta was right. The man scowled so hard at her that his outrage was nearly tangible.

She squeezed his fingers. 'My lord, aye, Lady Sarah is most definitely carrying your child.'

In gratitude, he dipped his head. 'Thank you.' Then pushed his chair back from the table.

'I need be on my way.'

'To where?' Gunther and Berta both stared at Timothy. It took him but a heartbeat to rephrase his question. 'When will you return from court, my lord?'

That was a good question—one he had no answer for. 'Soon, I hope. Once I am granted an audience, I will need only a few hours to speak with the King and then be on my way back here.'

As he turned away, Berta asked, 'And Lady Sarah?'

William shook his head. He had no answer for her. Even if he could get Sarah to speak with him, there was no guarantee they would be able to come to a solution acceptable to both of them.

Once Sarah eased back into court life, she would most likely discover it suited her more than living at Bronwyn. She was used to the finer things in life. Granted, the keep wouldn't always be rundown, but he would always be a former slave and Bronwyn would always be in the middle of nowhere.

He headed for his small chamber behind the Great Hall to change and gather his weapons. He buckled the second sword belt across his chest and slid the swords into the crossed scabbards resting against his back.

He adjusted his habergeon and made certain his swords stayed put, before sheathing a dagger on either side of his belt. After stashing his only set of court clothing into a saddlebag, he flung the pouch over his shoulder, grabbed a smaller bag from atop the wooden chest and returned to the hall.

Activity in the Great Hall came to a dead halt as, one by one, each pair of eyes stared at him. William scowled. Had they never seen anyone prepared for battle before?

He ignored the stares, and moved toward Gunther, only to be stopped by Charles and Alfred.

Alfred stretched up on his toes to poke at William's biceps, asking, 'Where'd you get those?'

'I purchased them at a local fair.'

To which Charles replied, 'He is but teasing you, Alfred. You cannot buy muscles. You have to build them.'

The younger lad pulled up his sleeve and stuck out his arm. He bent it at the elbow and stared at his own undeveloped muscles. 'Can I make some, too?'

William ruffled the boy's hair. 'We will work on it when I return.'

Charles moved closer, nearly salivating as he investigated William's weapons. 'Can we work on those, too?'

His question made William pause. At fifteen the boy was nearly a man. Yet he'd had no one to teach him the things a man needed to know. He was too young and inexperienced to be out on his own, and too old for William to foster out to another keep.

Besides, he didn't think Alfred or Joyce would fare well if they were separated from Charles this soon. Which meant the task of Charles's education and training fell to him.

'Yes, Charles, we will.' The boy's gratitude was evident in his wide grin.

William turned to Bronwyn's steward. 'Gunther?'

The older man approached. 'Yes?'

'I have to find guards for Bronwyn. While I'm at court, I'll see if the King has any suggestions. In the meantime, see if any of the men, or older boys, desire to train for the position. For those who do, make sure they are put to the heavier tasks. Let's start getting their muscles built up a little.'

He handed the man the small pouch. 'I know that the nearest marketplace is two days' ride from here. But I don't how long I'll be gone and I would rather you not run out of supplies. There should be enough gold in here to purchase whatever supplies you deem necessary to repair and stock the keep.'

William leaned closer, and lowered his voice. 'Since the men are too busy with rebuilding the keep, purchase some wooden swords for the lads, including these two here. And remember, we have more than a few growing boys in the keep, so make certain Berta has extra supplies to fill the larder.'

Gunther looked inside the pouch. His eyes widened. He held the pouch tightly to his chest, glancing around to make sure no one else could see what was inside. 'My lord, there is enough here for—'

'Whatever we need, Gunther. And you have to admit, we need everything. Send Timothy with the wagons and a couple of the men.' He slung an arm around the man's shoulders. 'If that isn't enough gold, there's more in my chest.'

He understood Gunther's gasp of surprise, since he'd done the same thing when the chest had arrived at Bronwyn yesterday morn. Apparently, the trade negotiations between Sidatha and King Henry were going better than expected. And the King was making good on his promise of gold.

William hoped the negotiations for the release of the others still held in captivity was going just as well. Otherwise, the gold he was using to rebuild the keep was little more than blood money. He didn't think he could live with that lingering on his soul. He mentally shook the thought away. Surely King Henry would be successful.

'For right now, we'll do the repairs we can. Later, we'll have to hire the rest of the work done.' Thinking to his child's future, he mused, 'One day we'll rebuild in stone and I'm certain that will come at a much higher price.'

Gunther nodded, then looked toward William's chamber. 'I am locking that chest up some place safe.'

'I trust you'll do whatever you think is required.' William lowered his arm. 'I need to be on my way if I am to catch up with Sarah and the guards.'

Instead of heading out the newly installed doors at the front of the hall, William headed toward the kitchens. On his way through, he passed behind Berta and reached beyond her to break off a hunk of cheese, knowing full well it would cost him.

She turned to snap a rag at him. 'Be gone with you.' The kitchen maids giggled, which only made the older woman snap the rag at him again. 'Are you happy now? Distracting these innocent girls from their work.'

William rubbed the red mark on his arm in mock agony. 'Old woman, you have grievously injured your lord.'

'Aye, and if he doesn't take himself from my kitchen I'll grievously injure him more. Now go.' She set the rag on the table and handed him a sack, then cupped his cheek. 'This is for Lady Sarah, it helps her in the morning. Now, go, see what the two of you can work out together.'

'Berta, I don't know if—' Uncertain what to say, he let his words trail off.

She shook her head. 'Just try, my lord.'

Sarah wanted nothing more than to fall from her horse, curl up on the ground and sleep for at least a fortnight. But she forced herself to stay in the saddle through willpower alone.

Something was wrong. This sickness plaguing her stomach and head had nothing to do with a child. The pains were too sharp. Every sound, no matter how soft, threatened to split her head in two. The smallest trickle of sunlight streaming through the leaves blinded her. And the sweat pouring down her was not from the heat of the day. Nor were the chills racking her caused from any breeze.

When bright lights and halos distorted her visions, she recognised the symptoms and feared it was one of her sick headaches. The kind that made her blind, and ill, for days. She hadn't experienced one since her menses had first started years ago. This was not the time for them to return.

The horse's ears danced and Sarah grabbed the high pommel of the saddle as she swayed. Her head throbbed so painfully that she wanted to cry, yet knew doing so would only make the pain worse.

Why had she bothered to get out of bed this morning? Had she simply told William that she hadn't felt well, none of this would be happening.

She wouldn't have been taken by the Queen's guards. William wouldn't have overheard the guard's comments. And she wouldn't now be headed back to court without the company of her husband.

It wouldn't have mattered if he'd have been angry or not. At least she wouldn't have been on the road, and he would have been near to help her.

And she so needed help. Sarah's eyes closed, and suddenly, she no longer cared.

'For the love of God!' William's shout startled the guards riding before and behind his wife as he raced by them to catch Sarah before she fell from her saddle.

He'd intended to get just close enough to make certain all was well before falling back so he'd not be seen. But he'd instantly noticed that Sarah was weaving on her horse, and had come closer to see what was wrong.

He glared at the men. 'How long has she been like this?'

All three of the men shook their heads. 'We don't know, my lord. She never complained of feeling unwell.'

Holding her in his arms, William kneed his horse to a stop and slung a leg over his saddle to drop to the ground. 'Get me some water, some blankets. Now.'

While the guards raced to do his bidding, William sat on the ground, against a boulder. 'Sarah.' He placed a hand against her cheeks, then her forehead, and felt his heart skip. She was on fire.

William cursed. Then he prayed. His medical skills were limited. Like every other warrior he knew, he could crudely sew a wound and reset a disjointed limb. Other than that, he knew nothing.

Did you warm a person who had a fever? Or did you cool them off? He didn't know.

Henry's guards hadn't even noticed anything was wrong. It was doubtful if they would be of any help. When they returned, carrying the supplies he'd requested, he set them to work building a lean-to tent.

What they lacked in building skills, they made up for in speed. William hoped it didn't rain any time soon. The hastily built shelter would barely hold out the morning dew, let alone rain.

Once he settled his wife inside the abode, he told the men, 'The other guard and two of Bronwyn's men should arrive soon.' Impatient, he'd left them behind a couple of hours ago.

'When they get here, we're going to need a fire, food and a supply of water. But I want three men guarding this camp at all times. Is that understood?'

At the men's nods, William crawled into the shelter with Sarah. After stripping the damp garments from her, he tossed the gown and chemise outside, ordering, 'Hang these up to dry.'

He grabbed his tunic from his saddlebag, wet it with the water and wiped the perspiration from her limp, un-resisting body. He had no idea if he was doing more harm than good, but he had to do something.

Before he finished, chills overtook her, shaking her so hard that her teeth chattered together. William stripped off his weapons, but kept them close at hand, then removed his clothes before stretching out on the pallet next to her. He draped another cover over them, pulled her close and held her tightly next to his flesh.

William rubbed warmth into her back and arms. He brushed the hair from her face. 'Ah, Sarah, this is what I meant about not trusting me. Why did you tell me that you were well this morning if you truly weren't?'

Sarah lifted her arm to feebly bat at his hand. 'Stop.' Her voice was as weak as her movements. 'Don't touch me. It hurts.'

'Sarah, I—'

She groaned, then whispered so softly he had to lean closer to hear. 'Hush.' She flinched as if talking was painful. 'Don't speak.'

Slowly, she curled into a ball on her side. Her uneven breathing eased as she rocked herself to sleep.

William sighed. Whatever afflicted Sarah seemed familiar to her. Which meant she had most likely known what was happening to her this morning.

He would berate her later. Now, he could only wonder why she intentionally sought to make their life together difficult.

He shouldn't have hesitated this morning. When he'd had the fleeting impression she was lying about being found back in bed, he should have badgered her. He shouldn't have walked away until she'd admitted to feeling ill.

This was not how he wanted to spend the rest of his life.

Sarah moaned in pain, then began rocking herself again. The sound chased away his questions, and put his slight anger to rest.

He could lie here placing blame all he wished. It would not change the fact that his wife, the mother of his child, was sick.

Even if the only comfort he could offer her was the warmth of his body, that is what he would do. He wasn't leaving her until he knew for certain that she, and the babe, would be well.

William stretched out his legs, seeking comfort for what he suspected would be a very long night.

Chapter Twenty

Sarah stretched her arms and legs, then froze. She was prone on a pallet, with the covers over her twisted every which way. Worse, she was naked beneath them. Her hands flew to her stomach. Was the babe still safe? Dear Lord, how would she know for certain?

Before opening her eyes, she lifted her hand to shield them from any light. A move she didn't regret when she saw the sun streaming into the tent.

How had she got here? The last thing she remembered clearly was that she'd felt terrible as the headache overcame her. She remembered feeling so bad that she wished William had been near.

Instead, she'd been alone with three of King Henry's guards. And now she was naked inside a dilapidated tent?

She jerked upright and choked as her stomach rolled violently. Sarah lay back down, grateful for the proof that she was still with child. Apparently, her sick headache hadn't affected the babe.

With a quick glance around the tent, she found her

clothes. Slowly, so as not to induce a bout of retching, she sat up and dressed.

How was she going to leave this tent and face the guards? But it wasn't as if she could stay in here for ever. Sarah took a deep breath, hoping the action would fortify her before crawling out of the tent.

Six men sat around a small campfire. She didn't know when or why two of Bronwyn's men had joined their party. She would discover that soon enough. For now, she glared as best she could at all of them, silently daring them to say anything. They looked too sheepish to open their mouths, let alone make any comment.

She notched her chin in the air, knowing from experience that a measure of arrogance would help get her through the embarrassment sweeping through her.

'You might want this.'

She didn't have to look towards the voice to know it was William. Relief wiped away her embarrassment. The guards hadn't undressed her.

She walked over to where her husband sat on his horse, a sack dangling from one finger.

'What is that?'

He shrugged. 'A gift from Berta. She said you might want it in the morning.'

Sarah took the sack of bread crusts. 'Thank you.'

'Don't thank me. Thank Berta.'

'I will when next I see her.' Sarah placed a hand on his thigh. 'But that isn't what I meant. I was thanking you for being here when I was sick.'

'I don't know what you are talking about.' His eyebrows rose. 'Have you been sick? I just got here. You heard me ride up.'

She looked at the men. They pointedly ignored her. Shifting her gaze back to William, she said, 'You lie.'

Swinging down from his horse, he said, 'You should know.'

His words stung, but she could hardly refute them. When she remained silent, he grasped her chin, forcing her to meet his stare. 'The next time someone asks you if you are ill, try telling them the truth. You have more to think about than just yourself. You were sick for two days. What would you have done, how would you have felt, had you lost the baby, Sarah?'

She gasped at the thought, but said nothing. There was nothing to say. As much as it galled her to admit it, he was right.

William cupped her cheek briefly, then asked, 'Do you understand me?'

'Yes.' He needn't treat her like a child. 'I understand.'

'Are you feeling better?'

She nodded slowly, since quick movements unsettled her stomach further. 'For the most part, yes.'

'Good. Then you should have no difficulty returning to Bronwyn.'

She frowned. 'But I thought I was to reside at court?'

'Is that what you want?'

Sarah stared at him, only to watch him look away. He ensured she would be able to tell nothing by his gaze. He'd learned to mask his features long ago. And now that she'd foolishly let him know of her tricks, he made certain she'd be unable to read his stare.

What did she want? For one thing, she certainly had no wish to return to the Queen's court. Where life had been difficult before, it would be more so now.

She'd failed in completing her task for the Queen.

For a time, Eleanor would make her life more miserable than it already was at present.

More than that, she had no wish to be parted from William. She realised that he didn't trust her—she'd given him little reason to do so. But it would difficult—nigh on impossible—to rectify that if they were living apart.

'Is it that hard to choose, Sarah?' His harsh tone and the return of his glare alerted her to the fact she'd hesitated too long.

Yet again, he was giving her a choice—something that she would never have at court. 'No. Oh, no, William. I want to return to Bronwyn.' She moved closer to him, seeking a way to make him understand that the only thing that mattered was that he would be there, too.

But he stepped back from her. 'Then that's where you will go.'

'And you?'

The hard edge to his glare softened, but not in a manner that spoke of any feelings for her. He glanced away, then turned back to shake his head. 'No. I need continue on to Poitiers.'

'No!'

William's eyes widened at her shout. 'What do you mean, no?'

Sarah twisted her hands together. 'William, the Queen will see you dead.'

'Why does that bother you now? Isn't it what you intended all along?'

'No, it isn't.' She shook her head. 'I disagreed with the idea from the first. Even when I did not wish to wed you, I never wished for your death. I thought I would somehow find a way to convince the Queen not to see the plan through.'

'I should let you worry. But you need not fear. King Henry was headed to Eleanor's court after he saw to Aryseeth. I will come to no harm, Sarah.'

But they would still be apart. Sarah swayed on her feet at the sickness churning in her gut.

William held her upright. 'Are you still unwell?'

For a moment she wanted to lie. Instead she asked, 'If I say yes, will you stay with me?'

'You would still play such games?'

'Yes.' Sarah gazed up at him. 'If it would keep you by my side, yes, William, I would.'

'You would not feel guilty for doing so?'

'Of course I would. But at least I'd not be alone.'

'Alone? Bronwyn is not empty. There are plenty of people there to keep you company.'

Perhaps, but she didn't long for their company. 'That isn't what I meant.'

William retrieved the reins to his horse. Once on the saddle, he looked down at her. 'I know. But it's the best I can offer you.'

She placed a hand on his leg. 'William, why must you go to court? Can this not wait?'

'You know it can't.' He flicked the reins and left her standing alone at the side of the road.

William gritted his teeth hard enough that he feared they would shatter. If the woman seated to his left at the table flinched away from him one more time, he would leave the table in disgust.

He hated being at court. Why he'd told the King he would stay until the week's end baffled him. William wasn't certain he could stomach three more days at court. He should have fabricated some excuse to leave immediately after his audience.

Audience. The King had kept him waiting eight days for what turned out to be nothing more than a charade. King Henry had already surmised the petition for the annulment wouldn't be needed. While the petition had been drawn up, it had never been presented to the Church. The King took great pleasure in handing the document to William to destroy.

Henry took even greater pleasure in letting William know that the Queen would not be interfering in Sarah's, or William's, life again. Even though he had seen the well-measured look that passed between the King and Queen, he was relieved to know the decision had been made, but he didn't want to know what had brought it about.

'Lord Bronwyn, you have not told us of your wife. How is Lady Sarah?' The woman at his right asked the question in a tone that said she really didn't wish to know, but was asking simply to make conversation.

'She is well, considering her condition.' The moment the words left his mouth he knew he'd made a mistake.

'Condition?' The woman glanced towards one of her friends across the table. Both women rolled their eyes and made a face. 'It is a little soon for her to be in any *condition*, is it not?'

He couldn't have heard her correctly. And if he had, he wanted to see just how bold this woman would be. 'I beg your pardon?'

The jealous woman shrugged and leaned closer as if sharing a secret. 'You have not been wed long. Surely, even you are aware that Lady Sarah—'

'What?' William cut her off. After setting his eating knife down, he asked, 'Lady Sarah what?'

The woman across the table laughed and shook her head. 'Please, Lord William, there isn't a soul alive who doesn't know about the Queen's whore. No matter how she tricked you, surely you didn't believe you were her first?'

The insinuation that Sarah might be carrying another man's child was more than enough for him. William rose and looked towards the high table. He raised his voice loud enough to be heard over the din, and called out to the King, 'My liege?'

Henry lifted a hand, bringing all chatter in the Great Hall to a stop. He then motioned William forwards.

But instead of approaching the King, William remained where he was. He glared at the women until they trembled in their seats. Only then did he turn his attention back to the King. 'I pray you forgive my insolence, but I have had enough of court gossip that holds no truth.' He backed away from the table and bowed. 'I seek my leave.' Standing upright, he added, 'Now.'

The Queen turned a frown toward her ladies. King Henry's eyebrows rose briefly before he finally nodded his consent. As William headed to his chamber to gather his belongings, Henry called out, 'Wish Lady Sarah well and let her know she is welcome any time.'

William only raised his hand in reply. But he smiled to himself at the sound of instant chatter breaking out amongst those gathered. The King's last comment, his open invitation, would not have been offered to one held in low regard.

As he took the stairs two at a time, he hoped the women who had found so much pleasure in tormenting his wife choked on the knowledge.

It mattered not, for he would not be around to witness the event. He was going home.

William paused inside the chamber, realising that the thought of returning to Bronwyn made him feel oddly at ease. How could that be? Especially when he'd already decided that he wouldn't be living in the keep. He planned to reside in one of the now-empty huts.

William tore off his court tunic and shirt, tossing them into a leather satchel before donning his battle dress. While lacing the mailed habergeon, his mind played over the women at the table.

It wasn't so much what *they* said that captured his attention. It was his immediate response to their words. His muscles had tensed, his senses went on alert and his heart had raced as if he'd been under attack.

Yet, he'd not been the target of their malice. His wife had. And every fibre of his being had jumped instantly to her defence. His body had reacted before his mind had taken offence to their remarks.

William shoved the rest of his belongings into the satchel, then strapped on his weapons. He'd logically decided that he and Sarah couldn't live together. He couldn't trust her. How could he live with someone he couldn't trust?

Certain the answer to that question lay at Bronwyn, not here at court, he raced from the chamber towards the stables, anxious to be on the road.

Before the sun set this day, he wanted to cover as much ground toward Bronwyn as possible.

Chapter Twenty-One

The sun was just beginning to set as William rode through Bronwyn's gates. He was exhausted from four days on the road and still frustrated from the three days of waiting for the channel to calm enough to cross.

A bustle of frantic activity in the bailey took him by surprise. This time of day, the comings and goings should have been nearly over. He would think the people would be settling in for the night.

William headed toward the nearly rebuilt stable only to be stopped by Timothy's shout. 'Lord William!'

The tone of the man's voice made the hairs on William's neck stand upright. He swung from his saddle, checking the walls for an enemy while reaching for his crossed-swords. 'What is wrong?'

'Lady Sarah is missing.'

His concern for the safety of the keep turned to ice-cold fear. 'What do you mean—missing?' He headed for the keep with Timothy on his heels.

'We have not seen her since last night.'

William pushed through the doors to the Great Hall and stormed inside. 'Where is Berta?'

'Right here.' The woman skidded to a breathless stop at his side. 'Lord William, I'm sorry, I don't know what happened or where she is. When she didn't come down for the morning meal, I went up to her chamber and it was empty.'

William turned on his heels and took the steps two at a time. Berta caught up with him in the chamber.

He glanced around the room. 'Is anything else missing besides Sarah?'

'A gown. Her comb and hair clips. I think there is a cover missing and so is her heavy cloak.' Berta scratched her head, frowning, and added, 'I haven't seen Charles or two of the new guards either.'

'Good.'

Berta blinked. 'Good?'

'Hopefully, it means she wasn't taken. Instead, she left of her own accord. If none of the horses is missing, she is on foot and can't be too far, Berta. And since it appears the guards and Charles followed her, she isn't alone or unprotected.'

The older woman threw up her arms, then shook her head. 'The village. I was too frantic to think straight. While we checked the forest and orchards, she went to the old village.'

William was halfway out the door when he answered in agreement, 'That is my thought, too.'

'My lord, wait.'

Impatient to be on his way, William paused. 'What?'

'It is likely none of you has eaten, the men can eat here on their return, but take some food for you and Lady Sarah. It will take but a moment for me to fill a sack.'

William saw the wisdom in her suggestion. 'You head for the kitchen and I'll meet you there in a moment.'

After Berta went down the stairs, he returned to the chamber. He pulled a blanket from the bed and rolled it up before securing it with a hair ribbon Sarah had left on the chest at the foot of the bed.

He and Sarah wouldn't be coming back to the keep tonight. There were too many things they needed to discuss—in private.

She'd once claimed that wealth and title no longer mattered to her. He didn't know if he believed her or not, but during his time away he did know a few things for certain.

He knew that while he didn't completely trust his wife, he didn't completely trust anyone. For so long he'd been shown time and again that trusting someone earned you the lash, or death.

He hadn't trusted the King about the gold, or the keep, yet he now had both. Perhaps it was time to take the chance on trusting people, starting with his wife.

He also knew the full details of what Sarah and Queen Eleanor had planned. Sarah had told him the truth. The Queen admitted that his wife had balked at the idea from the beginning and had been threatened into accepting the plot.

Most of all, he knew for certain that he didn't want to go another day without holding Sarah in his arms. He'd been a fool to desire a marriage without ties. While not having emotional ties to a wife might be of benefit to some, he feared it would soon prove a boring and lonely existence.

He'd rather have someone working at his side who he could tease into a fury. A righteous anger he could then spend all night soothing.

But in the end, the choice had to be hers. Eleanor had

said she could return to court any time she so desired. William hoped she didn't still desire such a life. But it was something he needed to discover.

Regardless of all else, Sarah was his wife. She carried his child. And it would be a cold day in hell before he gave her, or the child, up without a fight.

Sarah jerked awake, frowning. She'd nodded off earlier and something had startled her from sleep. Light from the oil lamps flickered across the semi-darkened hut. As she rose from the bed, the smell of a campfire wafted through the shutters.

While she'd come here to be alone with her self-pity and misery, she'd quickly realised she hadn't been alone. Earlier she'd heard a couple of the guards whispering to each other from the bramble outside the hut. Knowing they were only doing their duty by seeing to her safety, she hadn't sent them away.

But so far they'd remained hidden, as if they knew she wished not to be disturbed. So who was here now?

Shaking off the trepidation, she opened the door and peered outside.

'Took you long enough.' William didn't turn away from the fire. Over his shoulder he groused, 'I thought I'd have to sit out here all night.'

Sarah gasped in surprise and forced herself not to run across the small distance separating them to throw her arms around him. She approached as slowly as she could and took a seat on the log next to him.

'You could have come inside.'

William nodded toward the path and called out, 'You can show yourself now.'

Not surprised, she watched as Charles, flanked by two of the guards, stepped out of the woods.

'You aren't surprised?'

'Why would I be? I heard them in the bushes earlier. But how did you know they were here?'

William poked a stick into the fire, rearranging the now charcoaled logs. 'The woods were too silent—quiet enough to hear the impatient shuffle of feet.'

After dismissing the men to return to Bronwyn, he rose and reached out to assist her to her feet. 'You frightened Berta half to death.'

'I didn't mean to.' She'd been certain the older woman would know where she'd gone to be alone.

'You didn't mean to do a lot of things, Sarah. But you did them anyway.'

She neither wanted, nor needed, any further pain. To stem the flood of hurt, she let the anger beneath flare to life. Regardless of all she'd done, he wasn't blameless either. How could he have just ridden away like he did?

She was still outraged that he'd left her behind. Yet Sarah knew that the mourning lurking in the background would quickly wipe away any spark of rage. Would her grief for their lost marriage ever lessen? Would there come a time when grief gave way to anger? If so, would the anger also fade away with time?

She would rather feel nothing than this overwhelming sense of loss and pain. Had anyone ever told her that caring for someone could hurt this badly, she'd have laughed at them. But they'd have been correct.

She sighed. 'William, I am in no mood for this.'

'No? Feeling sorry for yourself, Sarah?'

'I am not—' She stopped mid-sentence. Yes, she was feeling sorry for herself. 'Why shouldn't I? I have a keep and no husband. I will soon have a child with no father. I have every right to feel this way.'

By the time she finished her voice had risen alarmingly. But William only stared down at her. She had the sudden urge to wipe the smug, cocksure grin from his face. 'What do you find so amusing?'

'You. I think you grow more emotional each passing moment. By the time the child arrives you should prove a joy to be around.'

His sarcasm hurt her deeply. Sarah's rage disappeared under the weight of the pain. To her horror she felt her lower lip tremble. 'I am *not* emotional.'

William wiped a fingertip beneath her eye and held it up before her. 'Then what is this? Rain?'

When she turned to leave, he wrapped his arms around her waist and pulled her tightly against his chest. 'Sarah, stop this.'

She tried to remain stiff in his hold, but the warmth of his chest against her back and the safety offered by the strength of his arms were too much to ignore. She relaxed against him. 'What are you doing here?'

'I can leave if you want.' He started to loosen his hold from around her.

Sarah grabbed his forearms. 'No, don't.' When he tightened his embrace, she sighed. But she didn't know what to say, or to do. She longed to turn around and beg forgiveness, but feared he would only reject her once again. That would be too much to bear.

Sarah closed her eyes, giving herself time to tamp down the longing, and the need. Certain she controlled her emotions, she asked, 'Why did you come here, William?'

'A little matter of an annulment.'

'Oh.' Of course, why else *would* he have come?

Keeping one arm about her, he pulled a missive from his belt and handed it to her. With both arms holding her close and his chin resting on the top of her head, he explained, 'That is the petition for our annulment. King Henry never sent it to the Church.'

Her hands shook as she broke the wax seal and read the document. 'You could have sent it yourself.'

He brushed his cheek against her hair. 'I leave that choice to you, Sarah.'

Without a second thought, she tossed the document into the fire.

She felt his chest shake against her back and knew he chuckled to himself. Let him laugh. She didn't care.

This time when William released her, he took her hand and walked toward the hut. 'We need to talk.'

Her heart thudded, her pulse quickened as she followed. Sarah swallowed back the sudden gladness in her chest. Yet he'd not said anything that should create such an emotion.

Once inside the hut, William dropped down on to the bed with his back against the wall of the hut and his legs stretched out on the straw-filled mattress. 'It seems that we have two choices before us, and I need to determine which path I wish for us to follow.'

Sarah closed the door, then turned to face him. '*You* wish for *us* to follow?'

'It would be rather foolish of me to give you all of the choosing. You tossed the petition into the fire without asking my thoughts. So what if I disagreed with your future decisions?'

She was speechless. Not quite speechless, but the words on the end of her tongue weren't fit for public use. Her hands clenched into fists. She stared at him.

William appeared relaxed enough to fall asleep. His head was even tipped back, his eyes closed.

She rose and leaned over him, ready to berate him for his arrogance. And when he opened his eyes, shimmering golden flecks mocked her rage.

'Oh!' Sarah jerked upright. 'You...you...knave!'

Strong hands circled her waist and held her captive when she would fled. 'How can you still be such an easy mark, Sarah? Sit down.'

He moved over enough for her to sit beside him on the bed. 'I loathe you.'

'You need put a little more feeling into that statement. Otherwise, it rings false.'

She chose to ignore his comment, asking once again, 'Besides your need to send me into fits of madness, what did you wish to discuss?'

'Two things.'

'And those are?'

'First, I thought you might like to know that it seems Aryseeth's ship floundered and sank in the Channel.'

She couldn't say the news upset her. 'Did it have any help?'

'I don't know, but it seems one of Henry's men was able to rescue a few items.'

'Such as?'

'The charts to Sidatha's Palace.'

Sarah took a moment to let the satisfaction seep into her veins. 'Sometimes the Lord is good.'

'That He is.'

She wasn't foolish enough to believe that was the only thing he'd come to tell her. 'You said there were two reasons? What is the other one?'

'We do have two choices before us regarding our marriage and I want this settled now.'

'First you want an annulment, then you leave it up to me and now you think we should decide together?'

'No.' He shook his head. 'An annulment is no longer a viable option. Seems that option went up in flames.'

'William, I swear you will truly drive me to madness. What are the options then?'

'I have already spoken with King Henry and Queen Eleanor.'

She shuddered, wondering what he had told them.

'You have a place at court for as long as you wish— even if that means for ever.'

She had no desire to return to court. She would rather live in a ramshackle keep alongside her husband. But she wasn't telling him that. 'That is good to know, since I do not see myself living off the land in the woods somewhere.'

'You have another home, Sarah.'

Her heart soared with hope, but he hadn't asked her to live at Bronwyn as his wife. Perhaps he deserved a taste of his own trickery. Sarah narrowed her eyes, then jerked back as if he'd slapped her. 'I will never, never return to my father's keep. I would not subject any child of mine to that man's care and attention.'

'I wouldn't permit you to raise our child there, even if it was an option. But I was talking about Bronwyn.' He looked away from her, adding, 'However, it is interesting that Bronwyn didn't cross your mind first.'

'I would never think of imposing on your—hospitality.'

'How considerate of you.'

'My Lord Bronwyn, did you think I would throw

myself at your feet, begging you to let me make this my home for ever?'

'Since it is your home, no. But the thought does create an interesting vision.'

She sat up on the edge of the bed and glared at him. 'Do not make light of this, William. We are not talking about some jest bandied about the court.'

'Would you rather I shout at you? Or perhaps toss you over my shoulder and simply cart you back to the keep like some unfeeling barbarian come to claim his wayward wife?'

Sarah gasped. 'You wouldn't dare.'

'No?'

His deeper tone of voice, the glitter of gold in his eyes that she'd so missed, and the mere mention of claiming her made her hesitate a heartbeat too long. William moved past her to rise, and before Sarah could determine his intent, she dangled from his shoulder.

'William!'

Without a word, he hung on to her flailing legs, and strode towards the door.

'Put me down this instant! I was but teasing you about my father's keep.' She pounded his back with her fists.

He paused at the door. 'You thought this a good time for jesting?'

'I only thought to hand you back some of your own—' She closed her mouth when he grasped the door latch. 'You wouldn't.'

'I tire of you telling me what I would or wouldn't do.' The coolness of the evening breeze raced across her legs as he opened the door.

Certain he'd make good his threat, Sarah lowered her

voice. 'William, I am sorry. Please, don't humiliate me in this manner.'

He would never embarrass her intentionally. He'd known she wasn't serious about her father's keep, but her avoidance of answering his question cut him deeply.

William turned around and kicked the door shut. 'You have about two seconds to make up your mind.' He dropped her on to the mattress, then stood with his arms crossed at the foot of the bed. 'You can either return to Eleanor's court. Or you can stay here at Bronwyn where we will somehow devise a way to live together.'

She came up on her knees and faced him. 'Who do you think you are to treat me thusly?'

'I am your husband,' He reached out and freed the girdle about her hips. 'And I am waiting for an answer.'

Sarah smacked his hands away as he reached for the hem of her gown. 'What do you think you're doing?'

'Waiting for an answer.'

'I will not be bullied about.'

He headed for the door. 'So be it.'

She scrambled from the bed and raced towards him. 'William, wait.' Just before she could grab his arm to stop him from leaving, she tripped over her unbelted gown and landed at his feet.

William stared down at her. Certain she wasn't injured, he bit the inside of his mouth to keep from laughing. 'So, you *are* going to beg?'

To his amazement, she wrapped her arms around his legs. 'Stay, William. Please, stay.'

He reached down to help her from the floor, only to find his legs pulled out from beneath him. He hit the floor with a loud thud.

Sarah lunged atop of him. 'Seems we are both grovelling.' With her hands planted on his chest, she leaned forwards and stared down at him. 'What will you say if I decide to return to court?'

'Nothing. It is your choice. I ask only that you use discretion.' To think of Sarah using discretion was hard to imagine. But to think of her wanting to return to Eleanor's court was harder to bear.

'Discretion?' She sat up. 'I don't understand.'

'What is there not to understand? You would live at court, with people you know and are comfortable with. Since you are far too passionate to remain celibate, I only ask that you use discretion when taking a lover.'

'A lover?'

The confusion etched on her face was priceless. Lady Sarah of Bronwyn, formerly Remy, also known as the Queen's whore, had not an inkling of what he was saying. He obviously needed to explain in greater detail.

'Yes, Sarah, a lover. A man you take to your bed. A man you will spread your legs for, moaning and writhing in ecstasy.'

He knew the instant she understood. And fully expected her to raise her hand. So, it was easy to snatch it mid-air.

She jerked her arm free. 'You...you... Good God, William, what do you take me for?'

He grabbed her around the waist and flipped them over. William pinned her flailing hands to the floor. 'Will you cease? I am not accusing you of anything.' He leaned forwards and slid his tongue along the seam of her lips. When she shivered beneath his touch, he released one wrist and cupped her breast, his thumb teasing the peak. 'You are a passionate woman. If you return to court, you cannot think for a moment that you will spend the rest of your life without being kissed, touched, or loved by a man.'

She closed her eyes tightly. William saw the tell-tale sign of tears gathering in the corners, and pushed on. 'I am not cruel enough to demand that of you. I only ask that if, on the rare occasions, I am at court, you do not flaunt your lover before me.'

Her lips trembled, but she asked, 'And you?'

'I would be your husband in all ways, when we are together.' He stoked her neck and breathed against her ear. 'But I am not a saint, Sarah. I am as passionate as you.'

She fought to throw him off, crying, 'Go away. Leave me alone, William.'

He knew she was upset now. He was also certain that it would take very little to make her emotions ride towards anger. And when Sarah was angry, she spoke without thought. That was what he wanted—for her to share only what was on her mind, without the addition of words she thought he wanted to hear.

'No, Sarah. I will not leave you alone. Not now, not ever. Tell me how to make this marriage work.'

When she remained silent, he nearly shouted, 'Sarah, open your eyes and look at me.'

She finally opened her eyes and he nearly drowned in the liquid gaze. 'Sarah, Sarah, you claim to be able to read a person's emotions. Yet you, the Queen's spy, can't tell when your husband is begging you to want to stay?'

She narrowed her gaze and glared at him. 'You are begging me to stay by telling me how to be discreet while at court?'

'You started it. Did you not ask me what I would do if you decided to return to court?'

'Yes, but—'

'But what? You were only testing me?' He rose and pulled her to her feet. 'What did you expect me to do? Laugh and say it was fine, that it wouldn't bother me in the least?'

'Would it?'

He didn't answer. Instead, he wrapped a hand around her neck and forced her against him. 'You have now lost the chance to choose.' William lowered his lips to brush across hers. 'You are staying here, Sarah.'

She smiled in utter relief against his lips. 'I'm not certain I want to. Perhaps you should convince me.'

'Convince you? After all you've put me through I still need to convince you that I love you dearly?'

Sarah's breath caught in her throat. Her heart seemed to stop. 'What did you say?'

He grazed his lips against the side of her neck. 'You heard me.'

'No, I don't think I did.'

'I love you—dearly.'

She gasped softly. 'You do?'

'Yes. I do.'

Sarah threw his own words back at him, 'But love doesn't exist. It is selfish and makes one weak.'

William sighed loudly. 'I was wrong. Very wrong. I admit freely that I obviously don't know everything. I do, however, know that loving you isn't selfish. It still makes me want to give you everything. And it doesn't make me weak. This feeling in my heart and mind gives me strength to face whatever responsibilities I must.'

'Oh, William.' She rested her head against his chest. 'I don't know what to say. I never dreamed you would speak of love to me.'

'You could say you love me, too. Otherwise, I'm going to feel ill used.'

Sarah lifted her head to gaze up at him. 'I do love you, William. I have for a time. It was just hiding behind misplaced dreams.'

He hugged her tightly. 'See the things you put me through?'

'The things I've put you through?'

'Good God, woman, you hide the truth from me, you lie every time I turn around.'

She couldn't deny those charges. 'I promise never to lie again.'

He laughed. 'And I'm supposed to believe you?'

'Yes, William. If you care for me at all, you will believe me because I love you dearly.'

'Care for you at all?' With a growl, William dropped to one knee before her. He held both of her hands in his. 'Lady Sarah, you are the love of my life. My heart is yours. You are the mother of my child. You are everything I dared never dream of and more. Will you please stay at Bronwyn with me as my wife?'

Sarah hesitated half a heart beat. She'd wanted an honourable man. One who would care for her, protect her, give her children and a life worth living.

She stared down into the glimmering golden flecks and knew she'd gained more than she had ever desired.

'I love you so much it hurts at times, husband.' Sarah stroked his cheek. 'Wherever you are is home, William. I will gladly follow where you take me.'

He rose and gently gathered her into his arms. With a wickedly sinful smile on his face, he whispered, 'Right now, I am thinking that bed looks mighty inviting, my love.'

Epilogue

❦❦❦

Bronwyn Keep—June 1178

The mid-day sun streamed down on the keep. A light breeze fluttered the crops growing in the fields. The bustle of activity in the walled bailey paused as a boy raced headlong through the gates, across the grounds and into Bronwyn.

'Father!' The high-pitched voice echoed against the newly laid stone walls of the Great Hall to drift up the twisting stairwell. 'Mother!'

In the well-appointed bedchamber, William sighed. 'We will soon have company, my love.' He gathered his wife's still trembling body closer to whisper, 'You grow more insatiable with every passing year.'

Sarah's languid laugh floated across his ears like soft, inviting music. 'I am not the one who left the orchards to drag you from your chores and to our bed in the middle of the day.'

He shrugged. 'Perhaps not. But when I left here this morning, it was to the sight of you standing naked in the streaming sunlight, preening and stretching just to tease me. How else was I supposed to rid myself of that vision?'

'I did no such thing. Besides, you could have kept to the task at hand until this evening.'

'Woman, save your lies for someone who might believe them—if such a person still exists. Had I kept to the fields, I would have spent the next few days being punished for not recognising your open invitation.'

Sarah patted his cheek. 'You are sorely misused.' She hastily yanked the covers over them, adding, 'His Lordship approaches.'

No sooner had the words left her mouth when the chamber door banged against the frame. 'Father!'

William lowered his lips to Sarah's ear. 'We will continue this.' He then looked at their eldest son with mock disapproval. 'Is this how you enter a chamber with a closed door?'

The boy immediately left the room, closing the door behind him. Sarah's chest shook with silent laughter at the knock upon the door.

William called out, 'Enter.'

The blonde-haired lad solemnly approached the bed, but he couldn't hide the glee in his magnificent bright blue eyes. William wondered if the day would ever come when he didn't marvel at the perfection of the children Sarah had given him. He pulled her closer. 'Yes, what is it, Gunther?'

'They are nearly here.' His excitement burst free and he bounded on to the bed, his words spilling out in a rush. 'Uncles Guy and Hugh and their whole families are in the village. There's wagons and horses and guards and, oh, Father, can I go out to greet them?'

William ruffled the lad's hair. 'I would be grateful if you did.'

Sarah added, 'Take Simon and Eleanor with you.'

'Eleanor?' The boy's excitement fell from his face. 'She is just a baby.'

'Do as your mother tells you.' William softened his harsh tone. 'We will be along to relieve you of her soon. Now, go, see if Hugh remembered to bring the puppies with him.'

Gunther's distaste at dragging along his little sister disappeared at the mention of the dogs. He raced from the room, slamming the door closed behind him.

Sarah tossed the covers aside. 'They are a day early. I need to make certain all is ready.'

Before she could move away, he pulled her beneath him. 'In a moment. You need first beg forgiveness for misusing me so.'

'William—' Her words trailed off as she stared up at him. 'Oh, no, my lord, we have no time for more of that now. It will have to wait until later. We have not seen Hugh, Adrienna, Guy, Elizabeth and the children in over two years. Would you keep them waiting like strangers?'

'Of course not, but I have more pressing matters at hand.' He kissed the curve of her neck, chasing the shiver with his tongue. 'Have I told you yet today that I love you?'

She wound her arms around his neck and toyed with his overlong hair. 'You need a haircut.' At his soft growl, she said, 'I forget. Have you?'

'I love you, Lady Sarah, I love the children you have given me, and the life we have made together in this keep.'

'And we love you, William.' She kissed his chin, while tracing the length of his spine. She moved seductively beneath him. 'Maybe they will take their time.'

William swallowed a groan as his body responded to her movements. 'Have you chosen any names?'

'Names?' Sarah frowned. Understanding softened her face. 'I wasn't going to tell you until I was certain.'

'Trust me, Sarah, after three children, I know when another is on the way. It is the only time you are overly emotional and completely insatiable.'

'I am never emotional.'

'No, of course not, my love.' With her first pregnancy he'd learned just how emotional she could be. And he'd learned during her second pregnancy not to argue with her. As Gunther had once told him, it was easier simply to agree.

She stroked him, asking, 'And if I am insatiable as you claim, are you complaining?'

William laughed. 'Have I ever complained?'

'Not really.' Sarah ran her fingers through his hair. 'Have you ever regretted asking me to stay, William?'

He dropped a line of kisses from her shoulder, up to her ear, making her shiver with need. 'Regrets? No, Sarah, never. Why do you ask?'

'Sometimes I wonder if you wouldn't have been happier with someone less…emotional and…insatiable.'

'And I would have been bored to tears.' He rose up on his elbows and held her face between his warm hands. 'No regrets. Ever. If you even thought of leaving me, I would beg you to stay.'

Sarah rubbed her cheek against his hand. 'It would take little begging on your part, my love.'

'Good.' William brushed his lips against hers. 'Because I could not exist without my heart, Sarah.'

* * * * *

*Celebrate 60 years of pure reading pleasure
with Harlequin®!*

*Harlequin Presents® is proud to introduce its
gripping new miniseries,*
THE ROYAL HOUSE OF KAREDES.
*An exquisite coronation diamond, split as a symbol
of a warring royal family's feud, is missing! But
whoever reunites the diamond halves will rule all....*

*Welcome to eight brand-new titles that unfold to
reveal the stories of kings and queens, princes and
princesses torn apart by pride and power, but finally
reunited by love.*

*Step into the world of Karedes with
BILLIONAIRE PRINCE, PREGNANT MISTRESS
Available July 2009 from Harlequin Presents®.*

ALEXANDROS KAREDES, SNOW DUSTING the shoulders of his leather jacket and glittering like jewels in his dark hair, stood at the door. Maria felt the blood drain from her head.

"Good evening, Ms. Santos."

His voice was as she remembered it. Deep. Husky. Perfect English, but with the faintest hint of a Greek accent. And cold, as cold as it had been that awful morning she would never forget, when he'd accused her of horrible things, called her terrible names....

"Aren't you going to ask me in?"

She fought for composure. Last time they'd faced each other, they'd been on his turf. Now they were on hers. She was in command here, and that meant everything.

"There's a sign on the door downstairs," she said, her tone every bit as frigid as his. "It says, 'No soliciting or vagrants.'"

His lips drew back in a wolfish grin. "Very amusing."

"What do you want, Prince Alexandros?"

A tight smile eased across his mouth and it killed her that even now, knowing he was a vicious, arrogant man, she couldn't help but notice what a handsome mouth it was. Chiseled. Generous. Beautiful, like the rest of him, which made him living proof that beauty could, indeed, be only skin deep.

"Such formality, Maria. You were hardly so proper the last time we were together."

She knew his choice of words was deliberate. She felt her face heat; she couldn't help that but she damned well didn't have to let him lure her into a verbal sparring match.

"I'll ask you once more, your highness. What do you want?"

"Ask me in and I'll tell you."

"I have no intention of asking you in. Tell me why you're here or don't. It's your choice, just as it will be my choice to shut the door in your face."

He laughed. It infuriated her but she could hardly blame him. He was tall—six two, six three—and though he stood with one shoulder leaning against the door frame, hands tucked casually into the pockets of the jacket, his pose was deceptive. He was strong, with the leanly muscled body of a well-trained athlete.

She remembered his body with painful clarity. The feel of him under her hands. The power of him moving over her. The taste of him on her tongue.

Suddenly, he straightened, his laughter gone. "I have not come this distance to stand in your doorway," he said coldly, "and I am not going to leave until I am ready to do so. I suggest you stand aside and stop behaving like a petulant child."

A petulant child? Was that what he thought? This man who had spent hours making love to her and had then accused her of—of trading her body for profit?

Except it had not been love, it had been sex. And the sooner she got rid of him, the better.

She let go of the doorknob and stepped aside. "You have five minutes."

He strolled past her, bringing cold air and the scent

of the night with him. She swung toward him, arms folded. He reached past her, pushed the door closed, then folded his arms, too. She wanted to open the door again but she'd be damned if she was going to get into a who's-in-charge-here argument with him. She was in charge, and he would surely see a tussle over the ground rules as a sign of weakness.

Instead, she looked past him at the big clock above her work table.

"Ten seconds gone," she said briskly. "You're wasting time, your highness."

"What I have to say will take longer than five minutes."

"Then you'll just have to learn to economize. More than five minutes, I'll call the police."

Instantly, his hand was wrapped around her wrist. He tugged her toward him, his dark-chocolate eyes almost black with anger.

"You do that and I'll tell every tabloid shark I can contact about how Maria Santos tried to buy a five-hundred-thousand-dollar commission by seducing a prince." He smiled thinly. "They'll lap it up."

* * * * *

What will it take for this billionaire prince to realize he's falling in love with his mistress…?
Look for
BILLIONAIRE PRINCE, PREGNANT MISTRESS
by Sandra Marton
Available July 2009 from Harlequin Presents®.

We'll be spotlighting a different series every month
throughout 2009 to celebrate our 60th anniversary.

Look for Harlequin® Presents in July!

TWO CROWNS, TWO ISLANDS, ONE LEGACY
A royal family, torn apart by pride and its lust for
power, reunited by purity and passion

Step into the world of Karedes
beginning this July with

BILLIONAIRE PRINCE,
PREGNANT MISTRESS
by
Sandra Marton

Eight volumes to collect and treasure!

COMING NEXT MONTH FROM

HARLEQUIN®
HISTORICAL

Available June 30, 2009

- **THE DISGRACEFUL MR. RAVENHURST**
by **Louise Allen**
(Regency)
Dowdy cousin Elinor's family connections are extremely useful, but
Theo Ravenhurst is convinced her drab exterior disguises a passionate
nature. He'll give Elinor the adventure she's been yearning for—and
discover she has talents beyond his wildest imagination!
The latest tantalizing installment in Louise Allen's Those Scandalous
Ravenhursts *family miniseries!*

- **MOUNTAIN WILD**
by **Stacey Kayne**
(Western)
In the snow-dusted mountains of Wyoming, a blizzard brings a
blond-haired cowboy and a blue-eyed mountain woman close.... Two
isolated souls, Garret Daines and Maggie Slade share a common enemy.
The bond they forge to overcome the threat against them is unbreakable—
and when the storm is over, a connection lingers as wild as the mountains,
yet seductively tender....
A love worth fighting for

- **A WICKED LIAISON**
by **Christine Merrill**
(Regency)
Gentleman by day, Anthony de Portnay Smythe steals secrets for the
government by night. When Constance Townley finds a man in her
bedroom, her first instinct is to call for help. But the stranger gracefully
takes his leave—with a kiss for good measure! Constance knows it won't be
the last she sees of this intriguing rogue....
Conventional lady...uncommon thief!

- **THE CONQUEROR'S LADY**
by **Terri Brisbin**
(Medieval)
Giles Fitzhenry is a born warrior. The lady Fayth is a Saxon heiress, forced
to marry this Breton conqueror. Though she yearns to be rid of him, a deep
desire ignites each time she holds her new husband's piercing gaze.... Giles
has conquered all: title, lands and respect are his. But the ultimate battle is
for his new lady's love—and her utter surrender.
The warrior's unwilling wife...

HHCNMBPA0609